lily of the valley

OTHER BOOKS AND AUDIOBOOKS BY SARAH M. EDEN

The Lancaster Family

Seeking Persephone

Courting Miss Lancaster

Romancing Daphne

Loving Lieutenant Lancaster

*Christmas at Falstone Castle**
in *All Hearts Come Home for Christmas* anthology

Charming Artemis

Stand-Alones

Glimmer of Hope

An Unlikely Match

For Elise

*The Best-Laid Plans**

The Jonquil Brothers

The Kiss of a Stranger

Friends and Foes

Drops of Gold

As You Are

A Fine Gentleman

For Love or Honor

The Heart of a Vicar

Charming Artemis

The Gents

Forget Me Not

Lily of the Valley

*Novella

CHRONOLOGICAL ORDER OF ALL RELATED SARAH M. EDEN GEORGIAN- & REGENCY-ERA BOOKS

Forget Me Not
Lily of the Valley
Seeking Persephone
Courting Miss Lancaster
Glimmer of Hope
Romancing Daphne
The Kiss of a Stranger
Friends and Foes
Drops of Gold
For Elise
As You Are
A Fine Gentleman
For Love or Honor
Loving Lieutenant Lancaster
Christmas at Falstone Castle
The Heart of a Vicar
The Best-Laid Plans
Charming Artemis

Lily of the Valley

When gruff meets grace,
opposites . . . distract.

SARAH M. EDEN

Covenant Communications, Inc.

Cover image: © by Melea Nelson

Published by Covenant Communications, Inc.
American Fork, Utah

Printed in the United States of America
First Printing: April 2022

30 29 28 27 26 25 24 23 22   10 9 8 7 6 5 4 3 2 1

ISBN 978-1-52442-125-0

Praise for Sarah M. Eden

"Sarah M. Eden has created a heart-warming historical romance book. *Lily of the Valley* is a beautifully written story of love, grief, friendship, and dedication. Eden's character development is to be applauded. The reader will see each character standing in front of them in their mind as they read. Each Gent has a unique nickname given to them, which they absolutely live up to. I found it very difficult to put the book down. The story growth was perfectly laid out and exceptionally planned. The reader can envision themselves standing in the library of Livingsley Hall, searching through the vast volumes of books, as well as becoming involved in the nightly games the Gents and the Ridleys played after dining. I highly recommend *Lily of the Valley* by Sarah M. Eden. If you are looking for a heart-warming story of strength, love, and dedication, this is it!"

—Readers' Favorite five-star review

"Filled with witty banter, colorful characters, and tender moments, *Lily of the Valley* will plant itself in your heart!"

—*InD'tale Magazine*

"*Lily of the Valley* is a masterpiece. With her trademark wit and meticulous attention to historical details, Sarah M. Eden has written a touching story with a marvelous cast of characters whose fallibilities are offset by their refreshing sense of honor, comradery, and loyalty. There's no doubt that by the time readers reach end of this book, they will all wish that The Gents were truly part of their lives."

—Sian Bessey, *USA Today* best-selling author, INDIES award-winning author of the Georgian Gentlemen series

Praise for *Forget Me Not*

"Julia is an admirable heroine who resists the social convention of the Georgian era, determined to have a marriage built on mutual respect, and Lucas's sincere attempts to understand and please her will win the hearts of romance fans. Eden's light, sweet story is sure to delight."

—*Publishers Weekly*

"*Forget Me Not* is an optimistic, witty romance in which wedded bliss arrives on the coattails of memorable Gents."

—*Foreword Reviews*

"*Forget Me Not* is a cute romance. This relaxing read was wonderful . . . over tea in an imagined drawing room. This is a blossoming start to Eden's the Gents series, one I look forward to reading more of."

—Historical Novel Society

"*Forget Me Not* is everything I've come to eagerly anticipate from Sarah M. Eden! Lucas and Julia's story kicks off a new series sure to delight fans of Eden's Jonquil series (and if you haven't read that series yet, what are you waiting for?!) as well as win her brand-new readers. The banter is witty, the romance is charming, and the premise is immediately intriguing. Plus, I liked getting a sneak peek at the other Gents. I adored every page of this story. My only complaint? I finished it in a day. But I have plenty of practice happily rereading Eden's past books, so there's no doubt in my mind this one is destined for my reread pile too. Highly recommended!"

—Melissa Tagg, Carol Award–winning author of the Walker Family series and *Now and Then and Always*

"What a treat! Old friends and new ones abound in this delightful new series."

—Esther Hatch, INDIES Silver Medal Award winner, author of the Proper Scandals series

"What a delightful start to this new series! Eden's witty dialogue and charming gift of storytelling shine bright in this sweet story of love and trust."

—Sarah Ladd, ACFW Award winner, author of *The Light at Wyndcliff*

Chapter One

Eton College, Berkshire, England, 1772

Kester Barrington would enjoy Eton more if there were fewer students and fewer "opportunities" for socializing. People were fine in small doses, but nobody seemed to define *small* the way he did. And absolutely no one overestimated the definition quite like Lucas Jonquil, Stanley Cummings, and Digby Layton.

For two years, Kester had done his best to avoid them. But they always found him. They were a year ahead of him at Eton and, it seemed, always a step ahead as well.

This time, they approached as he sat reading on a low wall. He eyed them over his spectacles, exhausted already.

Lucas was the first to hop up on the wall and sit. Stanley sat on Kester's other side. Digby kept his feet on the ground, striking a dashing pose despite not having an audience who was likely to be impressed.

"We're going to propose a new society at Eton," Stanley said without preamble. "Tragically, these hulverheads wouldn't go along with my brilliant idea for a Land Pirate Society."

Digby hmphed. "I will not lower myself to dress like a highwayman, Stanley, no matter how adventurous you promise it will be."

"You have to admit, my adventures never disappoint."

Stanley was probably grinning devilishly.

Kester was choosing not to look at any of them. If they realized he was disinterested, they might go away. Of course, the strategy had never worked in the past.

Lucas took hold of the conversation, if one could call it that. They were speaking *at* Kester more than *with* him. "We mean to propose that a Travel

Society be started for those who wish to go wayfaring and adventure seeking around the globe."

"What could this possibly have to do with *me*?" Kester grumbled.

"Compared to you, we're a collection of bottleheads," Stanley said.

"While I am not questioning my intelligence or your dunderheadedness," Kester replied, "you did not answer my question."

With a laugh under his breath, Digby repeated, "Dunderheadedness."

"We're not *completely* bacon-brained," Lucas said. "But we all heard you knock a bit of the wind out of Finley's sails yesterday, making him look the fool he is by countering all his half-formed blusterings. That degree of cleverness would help us make our case for the Travel Society."

"But I don't wish to travel," Kester said. "More than anything, I want to be left in a quiet corner *alone* with my books." He emphasized the word *alone*.

"For being fifteen years old," Digby tossed back, "you sound eighty, my friend."

Kester shook his head. "I'm not actually your friend. Any of you."

Stanley slapped a hand on his shoulder. "Beg to differ, Kes. You have three friends here, whether you want us or not."

"Not," he muttered.

They all laughed. Stanley and Lucas hopped off the wall.

"Will you help us?" Lucas asked. "We'd appreciate it."

Kester took in a lungful of air, then pushed it all out in a whoosh. How was it he always, in the end, agreed to their schemes? It was not precisely an argument in favor of his intellect. He snapped his book shut. "I'll help with your proposal." He, too, jumped off the wall. "But that doesn't mean we're friends."

"Someday you'll admit it, Kes," Lucas said, grinning mischievously. "We're friends, and we're always going to be."

Brier Hill, Cumberland, fourteen years later

"I denounce every last one of you," Kes grumbled.

Lucas was unmoved. "You've been saying that since Eton."

"Not to me." Lord Aldric Benick never was one to be swayed by idle threats.

"If you'd known him then, he would have said it to you too." A hint of amusement always lingered somewhere in Lucas's expression. "And you would have ignored it just like the rest of us."

"I'm in earnest this time," Kes said. "After years of being dragged to social events rather than being permitted to return to my own home, I am putting my foot down."

Lucas's wife, Julia, passed by. "Stop being so grumpy, Kester."

"*Et tu*, Julia?"

"*Ego sum maxime sapiens*."

That she knew Latin did not surprise him, though it was very rare for a lady to possess such knowledge. Julia was remarkably intelligent. He had discovered, upon making her better acquaintance, that she was self-taught and ambitious in her studies.

So he answered her Latin declaration in French, saying that while she might be the wisest among them, that did not mean she was correct.

She replied, in stilted Italian, that he was being stubborn as well as grumpy.

"I am beginning to suspect there is nothing you don't know, Our Julia," Aldric said.

"I most certainly do not know why Kes objects so vehemently to attending what promises to be an absolute romp of a house party," she said.

"I do not romp," Kes answered.

"You also once insisted that you don't travel," Lucas said with a grin, "but you've done a tremendous lot of that."

"I've done a ridiculous amount of it *recently*. You and I"—he addressed Lucas—"returned from our Grand Tour only a year ago. Since then, we've had a house party here at Brier Hill and have journeyed to Portugal. I traveled to the homes of my brother and sister while you were having your own little house party with the Harrow set—"

That led to a silent exchange between Julia and Lucas—small smiles and expressions of remembered enjoyment.

Kes continued his recounting. "We have only just left London after a month of the social whirl. It is time and past I returned home." He needed to be back at Livingsley Hall. He needed a chance to breathe and rest before the next whirl of activity began.

"I have the perfect solution," Lucas said. "We will simply have our own house party at Livingsley Hall."

"That is not at all what I meant."

Julia, in a show of theatrics far more common to their friend Digby or even to Lucas, floated down onto the settee in a mock bout of the vapors. "Oh, dear me," she opined. "I had hoped to have one more bit of company, one last time with my friends before my confinement begins. I fear this heartbreak will render me too weak to go on."

Kes shot a quick assessing glance at Lucas. If Julia's health was fragile on account of her "interesting condition," he wanted to know. But Lucas gave a subtle shake of his head. Julia was, then, putting on a performance. And that, logic told him, meant all of this had been planned.

"You wish for the Gents' annual gathering to be held at Livingsley Hall this year?" he asked.

The Gents were a group of friends, the three who had forcibly adopted him at Eton and three others who had joined their ranks at Cambridge. They were friends still, despite having been out of school for many years. Stanley, killed in the war with the former colonies, was no longer among them, and his loss was felt acutely, by Kes especially.

"It *is* your turn to play host." Aldric hadn't joined in the dramatics around him, but neither did he appear the least confused by the performances.

"Why the push to attend this other house party, then?" Kes asked.

Lucas shrugged. "Aldric sorted the need for a less desirable option."

Ah. "You knew, given the choice, I would inevitably insist on Livingsley Hall."

Aldric dipped his head in acknowledgment of the rather brilliant bit of strategy. He was known among them as the General for a reason.

Kes fully meant to continue grumbling about this, but he knew it would make no difference. The Gents always gathered in the autumn, and he had only ever missed two: the one held while he and Lucas were on the Continent and one he'd chosen to forgo ten years earlier, a decision he'd regretted ever since. He'd known whatever respite he was afforded would have come to an end when the yearly festivities began. It seemed there was to be no intermission this time.

Holding their annual party at his estate meant he could go home, which was at least a bit more restful than being a guest elsewhere. And though it meant Livingsley Hall would not be as peaceful as he would have preferred, he likely could still find time to himself. At least a little.

"Do you promise it will be a quiet and uneventful few weeks?" he asked.

"Of course not." Lucas had embraced the mischievous adventurer role that Stanley had filled before his death. Lucas likely intended to make certain this gathering was as topsy-turvy as ever.

"I am going to regret this," Kes muttered.

Lucas laughed. "That's what friends are for."

Friends. They had insisted all those years ago that he would eventually admit they were friends. He didn't resent that they'd been proven correct—he was unspeakably grateful to have the Gents in his life—but they did tend to introduce chaos into his otherwise orderly existence.

A Gents house party . . .

One thing was absolutely certain: anarchy was about to descend on Livingsley Hall.

Chapter Two

Irthing Grange, Cumberland

VIOLET RIDLEY NEEDED TO MEET people. In the fortnight since her family had moved from Portsmouth to their new home in Cumberland, she'd seen no one but them, gone nowhere, done nothing. She was getting a little desperate.

"Why did we have to move so far away from the sea?" her young cousin Georgie asked. "Can't rich men like Uncle Ridley live in Portsmouth?"

Rich men like Uncle Ridley. Violet didn't know if she would ever grow accustomed to hearing her father described that way. They'd never been destitute. Indeed, they'd always lived in tremendous comfort. But his recent investments in iron had proven extremely lucrative. Enough so that he and Mother had decided to purchase a country estate and join the gentry. The estate they'd found was far, far inland.

"I miss the sea as well." Violet removed the sleeping cap from Georgie's hair. They hadn't yet found a governess for the girl, one who could tend to her hair in the mornings. Georgie's tightly coiled curls required effort, more so even than Violet's, whose hair was a similar shade of almost-black and very nearly as curly but was decidedly more cooperative than her cousin's.

"Livingsley Hall has a lake," Georgie said, sitting very patiently as Violet used her hand to carefully detangle those areas of Georgie's hair that had knotted a bit despite the cap. "Perhaps Mr. Barrington will let us visit his lake. That will be nearly like being at the seaside again."

Violet hoped their neighbor proved generous and personable and friendly. And she wouldn't complain if he also proved handsome. She had no designs on the gentleman—she'd never met him—but a handsome face was not a terrible thing in a neighbor.

"Mrs. Peters said Mr. Barrington is very scholarly. Do you think he has a big library?" Georgie flinched when one of her spring-like curls caught on another. She accepted Violet's apology before turning her head a bit to look at her. "Our library here doesn't have a lot of books."

"Not yet," Violet said. "But we will soon begin addressing that, won't we?"

Recognizing that the girl's enthusiasm was about to overcome her patience, Violet handed her a length of burgundy ribbon and motioned her to the mirror on the side table. Georgie slid off the bed and, eying her reflection, worked at wrapping the ribbon from the back of her neck, up behind her ears, and into a bow just behind her hairline to create a lovely mass of springy coils.

Georgie continued adjusting her hair and tucking uncooperative bits into place. "Do you think we will find a book about John Blanke for our library?"

"I do not think my father will rest until we do."

Georgie shook her head. "John Blanke is *Aunt* Ridley's ancestor."

"And your father's. And yet, mine is as proud to call John Blanke family as he could be if he were related by blood rather than marriage."

John Blanke had been a trumpeter in the court of Henry VII, having come from Africa to England nearly three hundred years ago. He was featured on the Westminster Tournament Roll, an honor not afforded many people. Mother's family had long held to the belief that they were descended from the musician, though they hadn't proof. Mother was quite an adept musician herself, and her brother had been as well. Violet found it the most reasonable thing in the world that they shared that gift with a long-deceased ancestor.

Georgie hopped onto the bed once more and sat with her legs crossed in front of her, her dress, fashionable but plain, as Georgie preferred her clothing, pooled in lumps around her. "And perhaps Mr. Barrington will let us explore his gardens. I saw them through a gap in the hedgerow."

"That would be lovely."

Violet was excessively fond of nature and being outdoors. Irthing Grange was not one of those grand estates that had been manicured to the point that Mother Nature herself would struggle to recognize what corner of the world she was viewing. There was still a wildness to it, a feeling of seeing the grounds as they originally were before a single person had ever set foot there. She loved that about this place, but she also adored what she'd seen of the grounds of Livingsley Hall. There were formal gardens as well as sections where wildflowers were left to grow in abundance. Old, stately trees grew near more newly planted ones. The hedgerows were tidily maintained but also contained a variety of vegetation. The lake—*oh heavens, the lake*—she had admired from the moment she'd first set eyes on it from a distance. How she hoped Georgie's wishes about their neighbor proved to be true. She could lose herself for hours at that lake.

"Mrs. Peters said that Mr. Barrington doesn't talk much with his neighbors," Georgie said. "Perhaps he's a grump, and we'll not ever be invited to see anything at his house. Perhaps he will convince our other neighbors not to let us see anything at their houses either."

The girl needed a bit of sunshine. Violet's family had long called Violet that. She had a knack for cheerfulness and encouragement even when those things didn't come easily. "I think Mrs. Peters would have heard if Mr. Barrington were cruel. That she hasn't is a *very* good sign."

Georgie nodded.

"And he cannot possibly be a terrible person and have claim on such a lovely lake. I refuse to believe otherwise."

A little smile tugged at Georgie's lips.

"And though he does have a hole in his hedgerow, I think we can still think well of him."

Georgie shook her head. "You are silly."

"That doesn't mean I am wrong."

"You always think everything will be wonderful." Georgie sighed, the sound more sorrowful than petulant. "Sometimes things are horrible."

Violet's heart ached for her cousin. Georgie had been orphaned not quite two years earlier. That loss understandably weighed on Georgie's heart. Violet wished she knew how to ease some of that sorrow.

The words of their Portsmouth vicar repeated in Violet's mind, as they always did when faced with sorrows and worries. "Be sunny or be silent." He'd implored his congregants to exude happiness and cheer, to lift by being buoyant. She'd already known she had a cheerful disposition; his admonition had convinced her to fully embrace that tendency. Even when the effort wore on her, even when it meant not talking about her own worries and struggles, she kept the commitment she'd made during that sermon.

"Life may not always go the way we expect it to, but there is always reason to be happy," she told her cousin. "We can and should always try to have hope."

"I hope"—Georgie closed her eyes and pressed her palms together—"Mr. Barrington will let us see his lake and his library and his gardens. And I *really* hope"—Georgie opened one eye and looked at Violet—"my favorite cousin will let me fuss with her arm."

It was a familiar request between the two of them. Anyone hearing it without understanding the context would think they had both gone utterly mad.

Two years earlier, an injury to Violet's left arm had turned to putrid infection, which had progressed steadily, quickly, and alarmingly. Amputation had been her only option.

"Do you solemnly vow to return it to me?"

Georgie shrugged. "What use would I have for your arm after I am finished fussing with it? I don't need *three* arms."

Violet laughed. She unbuttoned the bottom of her wrist-length sleeve. Current fashions favored sleeves that ended just below the elbow. That had proven problematic for her. So, she adhered to the longer sleeve and directed her dressmaker to make the left sleeve buttonable from wrist to elbow. With the sleeve fully open, she revealed her arm from just above the elbow. There, with all its buckles and straps was the secret few people beyond her family was aware of.

She wasn't ashamed of her prosthesis, but she'd discovered that other people were often odd about it. The endless questions and intrusive stares had grown a bit vexing. After a time, she'd concluded that she'd rather keep it tucked away and enjoy an extra portion of peace.

Violet unbuckled the straps holding it in place and slipped the prosthesis off. She gave it to Georgie, who slid from the bed and plopped herself into a chair in the corner of her bedchamber. They'd brought the chair from her parents' house after their passing. Georgie sat in it for hours at a time and took such comfort in it. She also enjoyed "fussing" with Violet's false arm. Anything that brought her a degree of comfort, Violet readily gave her.

The false arm had been expertly carved. It matched her right arm quite perfectly. The hand was the right size, the fingers tapered as they ought. With her gloves on and her long sleeves, few would guess that one arm was made of wood. When she added a long shawl or undersleeves with layers of lace or ruffles, the disguise was nearly impenetrable.

But the prosthesis was heavy and often uncomfortable. Even a tiny bit of dust inside the cuff caused sores and rawness. She could hold nothing with the unmoving hand and fingers. In reality, it served no purpose in its current state beyond offering her a more "normal" appearance.

And she wanted more than that.

She'd pondered for two years the possibility of creating a prosthesis in which the fingers could move or the wrist could bend. She'd sketched any number of ideas involving clockwork bits and marionette strings and anything she could think of. Her own long hours of "fussing" with her arm had not yet resulted in any ingenious ideas, though she did not intend to give up hope. She could not change the loss of her arm, but she could—she *would*—find a means of improving what she had in its place.

Mother stepped inside the bedchamber in the next moment. Violet had always thought her mother was the most beautiful lady she'd ever seen. Even in those years when money had been a bit leaner, she'd always looked quite elegant. She took care with her appearance but wasn't ever pompous. Silver strands had begun to show in her dark hair, something only the family saw since Mother never left home without her hair powdered. Her wide pannier gown flattered her figure and added to her inherent elegance. Violet recognized she was entirely biased, but she did not believe for a moment there was an equal to her mother even in the royal court.

"Why, Georgiana, you've finished setting this room to rights. It looks splendid." Mother always called Georgie by her formal name, which the girl didn't seem to mind, though she objected to it from anyone else.

Without looking up from her inspection of Violet's unchanging prosthesis, Georgie said, "Violet thinks Mr. Barrington might allow us to go see his lake."

With her innate grace, Mother sat on the other chair in the room. "Mrs. Peters has heard that Mr. Barrington has a group of fine friends visiting him just now: young gentlemen and a lady who is married to one of them. Amongst their ranks is a Frenchman who is believed to have connections to the French aristocracy, a future earl and countess, as well as the younger son of the Duke of Hartley. I knew Mr. Barrington was well connected, but I hadn't realized *how* well." Mother pressed her hand to her clavicle as she released a tight breath. "He may very well be ashamed of his new neighbors."

"Well, if he is, I feel sorry for him," Violet declared. "Some people object to those who come from trade and those who haven't two arms or haven't any lords or ladies in their families. But those who make such objections miss the opportunity to know some wonderful people."

"The fact that every one of those 'objections' applies to this family does make me a little nervous about starting anew here." Mother brushed her fingers over the brooch pinned to her lace-edged tucker. "I'd hate for us to discover ourselves entirely alone in our new corner of the world."

"I am convinced all will be well," Violet said.

"Forever the optimist." It was not spoken as an insult nor in dismissal. Indeed, Mother sounded as though she felt heartened and comforted.

Georgie, flicking at the buckles on Violet's prosthesis, offered her thoughts. "We should always try to have hope."

Mother looked to Violet, a laugh in her eyes. "That sounds like something you would say."

"I did say it. Clearly, my genius is finally being recognized."

"Put your genius to discovering how we are meant to go about making the acquaintance of our neighbors, and I will agree to recognize your intelligence as well," Mother said.

They hadn't yet sorted that bit out. Everything in the upper echelons of Society was governed by rules. Everyone born to that life seemed to know instinctively how to navigate those requirements, while everyone looking in from the outside was left to guess. The Ridley family had not made the acquaintance of any of the surrounding families, both on account of their home still being put to rights, it having been empty for some time before father purchased it, and also because they didn't know the rules surrounding such introductions.

How Violet hoped they'd sort it quickly; she was lonely.

Chapter Three

"I HATE TO THINK OF how lonely Julia must be with all of us away from the house." Lucas clicked his tongue.

Kes shook his head. "You've misspoken, my friend. The question is how *ecstatic* Julia must be."

"No," Aldric said, "that is how *you* would feel if left entirely alone."

He wasn't wrong.

The Gents were spending the late morning riding the back acres of the Livingsley Hall estate. It was a favorite pastime of theirs. Julia's relief at being afforded some time to herself had, no doubt, increased Lucas's enthusiasm for the jaunt. Though they'd had a difficult beginning, no one seeing the two of them together could possibly doubt that Lucas would do anything in the world for his wife.

While Niles and Henri were quieter than the other Gents, except for Kes, neither of them needed solitude the way Kes did. And they likely didn't feel the same guilt he did when they claimed it. The Gents were something of a miracle in his life. They'd saved him from a lifetime of loneliness and seen him through times of sorrow. They were like brothers to him. And yet, he often wished them to Hades.

What kind of a friend feels that way? What kind of a brother?

That day's ride was not bound to be a bruising one. Indeed, calling their current pace a sedate walk would have been overstating the enthusiasm of their undertaking. It did give them the opportunity to talk. Or, in Kes's case, listen.

"How fares Our Julia?" Henri asked Lucas. "She looked a little piqued this morning before we left."

"She is quite well most days. Now and then she feels poorly, like she did early on. I do try not to worry about her, but I can't help myself."

"I do not recommend it," Digby said as dramatically as he had during their days at Eton and Cambridge. "Worrying causes the most inconvenient wrinkles."

A quick glance showed that Digby was not the least bit wrinkled, in face or clothing. Even riding a horse, he looked ready to be presented at court.

They were a mismatched group, to be sure. And yet they were as close a group of friends as had likely ever existed.

"I do believe our next adventure should take us to France," Aldric said. "Portugal was a great lark, and for Stanley's sake, I'm glad we made the journey. But I fear if we don't allow Henri to travel home sometime soon, he will defect and we will never see him again."

"Where the heart is, the body must follow," Henri declared with his usual quiet elegance.

"Perhaps," Niles said, "your family could come to England to visit; then you would not need to abandon us to follow your heart."

Aldric gave a nod of approval. It was saying something when he looked pleased with another person's strategy. He wasn't stingy with praise. He simply had extremely high standards.

While Kes understood the intelligence of Niles's proposed approach, he also knew that a visit from Henri's family would necessitate another house party, another gathering, another commitment he could not in good conscience ignore.

"Is it true that Irthing Grange has been purchased?" Aldric asked.

They all looked to Kes.

He nodded. "By the Ridleys, a family from Portsmouth. Little is known of them beyond that Mr. Ridley was an iron merchant. They've called on no one."

"Not anyone?" Lucas asked.

Kes shook his head. "The prevailing theory, at least amongst those on my staff who have chosen to speculate, is that Irthing Grange, having sat empty for a time, has proven in need of repairs, and they are seeing to the work before beginning their foray into local society."

"But it is also possible"—the General's mind never did allow for only the simplest explanation—"having come up from trade, Mr. Ridley does not realize *he* is meant to initiate the connections. When I meet with men in the City, they do not always understand the particulars of Society's requirements. The rules that govern our interactions are as much a mystery to them as their financial calculations often are to us."

"Perhaps Mr. Ridley simply prefers to be left alone," Kes suggested.

At that, chuckles rippled through the group.

"'Prefers to be left alone.' A familiar refrain," Digby repeated in a theatrical tone of pondering. "Is it possible *you* have actually purchased Irthing Grange and don't realize it?"

"I do believe it is possible for more than one person to enjoy peace and quiet." Kes was growing so adept at slipping into the role of Grumpy Uncle that it happened almost without thinking.

"I have a suggestion," Lucas said, his tone the one that always portended some ill-advised adventure. "We ought to ride near Irthing Grange to see if we can't accidentally make the acquaintance of the elusive Ridley family."

The rest of the group agreed so readily that Kes hadn't even a moment to verbalize his objections, and he had plenty. So they rode in that direction. Irthing Grange bordered on Livingsley Hall, with a tall but not overly thick hedge separating the two estates.

As they approached the hedge, Lucas pulled his mount up short. He pointed in the direction of the distant house. "There's smoke."

Sure enough, smoke billowed above the roof but not from a chimney.

Without needing to consult, the entire group rode directly toward it. Aldric was the first one up the steps. Harried servants met his urgent knock.

"We saw smoke," Aldric said. "How can we help?"

The poor woman didn't seem to know how to answer. "Fire's in the family wing."

Aldric held up a hand to stop further frantic declarations. "Direct us there, and tell us how to procure buckets of water."

"Yes, sir."

They followed the woman, buckets handed to them as they rushed up the stairs. The air tasted of smoke as they turned down a second-story corridor. Though they coughed as the ashy air hit their lungs, they weren't rendered entirely unable to breathe. That was a good indication that fire was not a full conflagration.

At the front of the group, Aldric nearly ran into a bushy-browed, silver-haired man. "We have water."

The man pointed to the nearest chamber, then led the way. "In there."

The room proved to be a family bedchamber. Though there were flames, they were few and small and not at all out of control. Kester breathed a *figurative* sigh of relief. The air was too ashy for anything but tiny breaths.

He tossed his bucket of water onto a smoldering chair. Hands now free, he tugged off his cravat and tied it over his mouth and nose to create a barrier against the ashy air. The other Gents followed suit.

Aldric called out to servants carrying furniture out and pulling down drapery to return with more buckets of water.

"Snatch up the pulled-down drapes and beat out the embers popping up," Kes said to Lucas and Henri.

The silver-haired man stomped out a few hot spots.

"Are there flames elsewhere?" Aldric asked.

"Only in here." The man coughed deeply. "Smoke everywhere."

Kes turned to Niles and Digby, who were handing newly filled buckets of water from the servants to Aldric and the man. "Take buckets to the next room over. Douse anything that looks even a little warm."

They rushed out. Lucas and Henri were beating every bit of smoke, every glow with the heavy tapestry curtains.

"I've not had a chance to account for everyone." The man's raspy voice emerged quick and worried. "The nearest rooms are the most likely—"

"I'll look in them all." Kes spun on the instant and rushed out. He checked one chamber after another. Smoke hung in the air. Servants, along with Niles and Digby, tossed water anywhere it might be needed. People surged in and out of rooms. All was chaos and urgency.

Fires too often proved deadly.

Kes had looked in every room apart from three and had seen no one who appeared injured or in danger.

A young lady emerged from one of the rooms he'd not yet checked, a look of concern in her eyes. Her stunningly beautiful eyes. Breathtakingly beautiful. Her abundant coils of hair, their dark color obvious even under the light powdering, were mesmerizing. Lovely. She carried herself with confidence and assurance but also with grace and an air of welcoming.

Though she held a handkerchief over her mouth and her long shawl was marred with ash, her very appearance rendered him utterly unable to speak. He could hardly form a coherent thought, an odd experience for him.

The worry in her eyes finally pulled him to the present and the severity of the matter at hand.

"I cannot find my cousin. I've checked these rooms"—she motioned to the bedchambers behind her—"as well as the nursery, where her bedchamber is. I've not found her."

Good heavens. "I saw no children in any of these rooms." He indicated the ones he had checked.

That the girl was not in this wing increased the chances that she was safe. Still, he did not at all like the idea of a child alone somewhere in this house, likely terrified.

The lady coughed, keeping the handkerchief over her mouth and her shawl wrapped tightly around her.

Kes adjusted the cravat tied over his mouth as the taste of ash grew stronger. "Does your cousin have a favorite place in the house?"

She thought on that a moment, her brows pulling low. She truly did have beautiful eyes.

"The library," the lady said after a bit. She moved at a fast clip but one Kes kept pace with.

They left the family wing and took the stairs to the ground floor. He followed his guide inside a room with the easily identifiable bookcases of a library.

The lady lowered her handkerchief and called out into the room. "Georgie?"

Georgie? Kes was certain the cousin they were searching for had been identified as a little girl. Her full name, then, was likely Georgiana or Georgette or something of that nature. But if Georgie was what she was likely to respond to, he would do best to use it.

"Miss Georgie?" Kes said, stepping farther into the library. The air was clearer in here, but the smell of smoke lingered.

His companion searched behind chairs and under tables, keeping her shawl firmly in place. For a moment, Kes was distracted. She moved with unmistakable grace. The Gents liked to tease him about being uninterested in any woman who wasn't on the pages of a book, but he'd had his heart pricked before. He'd learned through difficult experience not to allow himself to tiptoe down that path. It led only to heartache. He would not allow that to happen again, no matter how beautiful his current companion was.

He made for the large desk on the far side of the room. He had spent enough of his childhood hiding from company in his family's library to know that the perfect place to tuck oneself out of sight was beneath a desk like this one. He moved around to the side where the chair would normally have been, though it was a bit away from its spot.

He hunched down. There, beneath the desk, curled into the open space, was a girl of most likely nine years, her mouth and eyes much like her cousin's, with the same springlike curls.

She looked up at him, worry evident in every inch of her face. "Don't be angry," she pleaded.

He maintained his hunched position. The gorgeous, as-yet-unnamed lady knelt next to him, facing the little one.

"No one is angry," the lady said. "I'm simply happy to have found you. This kind gentleman helped."

"How do you know he's kind?" Georgie asked in a tone of challenge.

"He has helped put out the fire and look for you. He seems kind. I am more than willing to rescind that evaluation if he proves otherwise."

"Are you going to prove otherwise?" Georgie demanded of him.

"I've no plans to."

The lady beside him smiled, the sight utterly dazzling. And quick as that, his mind emptied and his tongue tied once more. Curse his traitorous heart. It did not often override his more logical side, but when it did, it never failed to cause him grief in the end.

"Violet, you've got smoot on your favorite shawl," Georgie said.

Violet. He now had a name for the lady who'd left him decidedly bellows to mend, the breathless experience not one he was accustomed to.

"I'm afraid most everything we own is all but covered in smoot." Violet used the same endearingly imaginative word for soot and ash that her little cousin had.

"There was a lot of smoke," Georgie said. "Every room in the family wing was filled."

"I know, dearest. I can still taste the ash in my mouth."

So could Kes, and he hadn't been in the house as long as the resident family had.

"Is it safe to be inside?" Georgie asked.

"The tiny remaining embers were extinguished," Kes said. "The fire doesn't pose any ongoing danger."

"Will we be able to stay here?" the girl pressed.

"Likely not," Violet said. "But I do not think we will be required to be away long." She held out the hand not tucked under her shawl to her cousin, but her offer was not accepted. "We can be happy even if we are required to find a temporary new home. We can be happy anywhere."

"We just have to try to hope," the little girl said in that stilted style of speaking that indicated one was repeating something one had heard often.

"Precisely."

Georgie crawled out from underneath the desk, though she seemed more than a touch reluctant to do so.

Violet pulled her cousin into a one-armed embrace. "All will be well. You'll see."

"You always say that."

The house had sustained damage, both from the fire itself and from the smoke. Even the water used to douse the flames would have caused damage.

Violet and Georgie were correct in assuming they'd need to live elsewhere while things were set to rights at Irthing Grange.

They were new to the area and hadn't yet made friends or acquaintances. Where would they go? They likely had no close friends outside of Portsmouth, which was on the other side of England.

Kes was worn out from years spent without time or space of his own. He had visitors already. He had an unkept promise tearing at his conscience. But there was only one gentlemanly option available to him.

"Sir," Violet said, still holding young Georgie in her arms. "I fear I've neglected to ask your name. I am Violet Ridley, and this is my cousin Georgiana Watkins. To whom do we owe our thanks?"

"Mr. Kester Barrington of Livingsley Hall," he said. "I am your nearest neighbor, and as such, I wish to extend the invitation to you and your family to stay at the Hall while your home is set to rights."

And with that offer, Kester Barrington committed himself to adding more people to the already overly long list of guests and to what might otherwise have been a peaceful and restful sojourn at home.

Chapter Four

The Gents returned to Livingsley Hall several hours later, covered in ash, blackened cravats hanging loose below their chins. The fire at Irthing Grange had been fully extinguished. The house would remain standing, with no danger of collapse or further troubles, but the damage done to the family wing had led the Ridleys to accept Kes's offer of accommodation while repairs were made. The family was gathering a few things and would be arriving at Livingsley Hall shortly.

Kes and the Gents stepped inside the Hall, and Julia immediately accosted them. She looked them over, eyes pulled wide with alarm. "What's happened?"

"There was a fire at Irthing Grange," Aldric said.

She frantically searched their faces, and Kes didn't doubt all his friends knew precisely who she was looking for. The group parted and gave her a direct route to Lucas.

She rushed to him and pressed her hands to either side of his soot-smudged face.

Fondness filled his eyes. "All is well, sweetheart. No need to fret."

"Not fret? There was a fire. And you were in the midst of it."

He shrugged as if a fire were nothing at all. "It's out now."

"Lucas." She spoke firmly. "You were in danger. I've lost too many people in my life to take that lightly."

He looked immediately apologetic. "We are all well, and we were all careful. Well . . . careful *enough*."

Julia eyed them all. "No doubt the lot of you rushed in to assist without knowing whether the fire was tiny or large." It wasn't a complaint or a reprimand. Indeed, her voice held the oddest combination of approval, worry, and amusement.

"Not one of us would leave someone to suffer," Henri said.

"Though being heroic does leave one in such a state." Digby motioned to his deep-blue jacket and pantaloons now covered in unflattering patches of soot and smoke stains. He did a fine job of playing the role of mindless dandy, but he had not hesitated to rush in with the rest of them. His flair for fashion, unwavering adherence to social niceties, and deference to expectations did not override his generous and compassionate heart.

"I have every intention of offering you an embrace and a kiss," Lucas said to his wife, "but I would prefer to do so after I have cleaned up."

"I can easily clean up any soot you manage to transfer," Julia objected.

"I know that, but Kes has a favor to ask you. I will leave him to do the asking and you the subsequent preparation."

She turned to look fully at Kes. "A favor?"

"The Ridleys, who live at Irthing Grange, will be displaced for a time as a result of the fire. I've extended the hospitality of this house to them."

Her auburn brows arched. "You are to have even more houseguests?"

"So it would seem."

The Gents laughed as they departed for their various bedchambers to undertake their needed washings. None of them would actually wish Kes to be unhappy. They'd simply known each other so long and so well that a bit of good-natured raillery generally proved irresistible.

Julia moved a touch closer. "Are you equal to the chaos of hosting additional people?"

He held his hands up in a show of helplessness. "What else could be done? They are new to the area, without friends and acquaintances. The family wing of their home has been rendered temporarily uninhabitable. Livingsley Hall is the nearest neighboring estate, and I have room. The most logical conclusion is for them to be guests here."

"And you *always* come to the 'most logical conclusion,'" Julia said, eyes dancing.

"As do you, the only lady of my acquaintance who taught herself differential calculus."

"Then trust my intelligence when I explain my concern at your offer," she said. "The Gents like to prick at you over your preference for solitude and quiet. While I am not as dependent upon moments of isolation as you are, I appreciate your need more than they do. As you have rightly said, you could not refuse houseroom to your neighbors in need. But if having the Gents here while the Ridleys are proves too much for you to endure, you need only say the word. I will see to it that these rowdy gentlemen are sent on their way. And you know I can manage it."

Heaven help him, he was tempted to simply ask for an exodus right then and there. And yet, he would feel blasted guilty at having prematurely ended their annual tradition. Or they would simply reconvene elsewhere, without him, proving how comparatively unnecessary he actually was. He'd spent too many years trying to prevent them from realizing what he fully suspected to be true. He'd not risk it now.

"This is where the favor I'd hoped to ask comes into play," he said. "I haven't a wife or mother here to act as hostess. Would you be willing to take on that role when the Ridleys arrive and, in so doing, help me 'endure' an overflowing household?"

"Of course," she said. "Tell me a little about the soon-to-arrive guests."

"Mr. Ridley showed himself to be calm and methodical. I did not meet Mrs. Ridley. Their niece, who is nine years old, gave every indication of being wary of strangers. And their daughter, who is likely about your age, showed herself . . ." Everything that came to mind, he wasn't willing to speak out loud: to be beautiful, intriguing, impossible to stop thinking about.

"Ah." Julia's expression turned far too knowing for his peace of mind.

"None of your conjectures, Julia."

"I will say no more."

"But you will think it." He knew her too well to doubt that. But he did trust her not to press the matter. "Mr. Ridley came up from trade, which will be a source of objection from some, I am sure."

"Not from me," Julia said. "And I cannot imagine any of the Gents would reject a family because their origins were not exalted."

Kes hadn't any concerns on that score either. He couldn't guarantee the rest of the neighboring families would treat the Ridleys well. There would be plenty in Society who did not. People could be remarkably dismissive, especially those who had every reason not to be.

He coughed again, something he suspected they would all be doing for several days.

"Go change from your soot-covered clothes, Kes," Julia said. "And take a moment for yourself. You are about to embark on an exhausting few weeks."

Violet studied the tired faces of her family. After a fortnight of ceaseless effort to put their new house to rights, following it with a fire had dampened all their spirits. The house had been saved, though there was now new work to be done. The weight of unexpected setbacks could be heavy at times.

She'd wanted to rail against the frustration of it all, to bemoan their continuing struggles. *Be sunny or be silent.* She repeated that again and again until the urge to voice her aggravation dissipated.

In the carriage, making their way to Livingsley Hall, Violet sat with her arm around Georgie. Georgie was not falling to bits, but she did seem in need of a touch of encouragement, and that was Violet's talent.

Mother and Father had, as they had throughout her life, proven the surest foundation a person could hope for. They had known tragedy. Mother had lost her mother as a young girl. Father had been orphaned at the age of twelve. As mother's father had not remarried, she had, in many ways, taken on the role of mother to her younger brother. That brother, Georgie's father, had died two years earlier. Violet's injury that had ended with amputation had been a source of great worry to the family. Yet, through it all, her parents had been as steadfast as lighthouses in a gale.

Seeing them across the carriage, Father with his arm tucked around Mother, she with her hand in his, a wave of reassurance washed over Violet. Much had changed in their lives. Much would yet change. But her parents' devotion to each other was steadfast and dependable. Violet was often described as the sunshine in their family; her parents, however, were the lighthouse in the storm.

Violet had long dreamed of finding that same connection to another person and having a warm home and loving family of her own.

Being the daughter of an increasingly affluent merchant had put some limitations on her ability to find what her parents had. It wasn't unusual for people to feign interest in her because her father's money appealed to them. There were plenty who'd given the very real impression that they were excited at the prospect of a fortune but had no intention of caring for the person who came with it.

She'd worked hard to keep her spirits up. Their Portsmouth vicar's counsel to keep her peace if she couldn't offer rosy encouragement had saved her from being a burden, but it was often exhausting. She hoped this new start in Cumberland would offer her a bit of respite.

The carriage came to a stop at the front of Livingsley Hall. The brown stone edifice stood grand and imposing, framed by green hills in the distance, the crystal lake nearby, and ancient trees declaring their permanent place in the landscape. One wing ended in a rounded bay tower, the other in a squared corner with decorative gables. Rows of leaded-glass windows reflected the late-afternoon sun.

Georgie stared at the stately home. "It's so much larger than I imagined," she whispered.

Violet found she couldn't answer despite entirely agreeing. Mother sat with her palm pressed above her heart, looking out the carriage window without a word. Father's mouth pulled into a tight line, and his eyes drooped with worry. Livingsley Hall had been impressive through the hedgerow. Viewing it through the windows of the carriage, it was utterly intimidating.

"Mr. Barrington was very kind this morning," Violet reminded them. "We will, I am certain, be received sincerely into his grand and awe-inspiring home."

"I fully agree," Father said. He pulled in a breath that ended in a cough. "We no longer live on the dockside. Irthing Grange and the family who occupies it claim a place of some importance in this neighborhood. We needn't think of ourselves as below our company."

"Yes, but does our company agree?" Mother gave him a knowing look.

He raised her hand to his lips and pressed a kiss to her gloved wrist. "Only one way to discover, my dear."

"Between you and Violet, you'll have me believing in miracles," Mother said.

Be sunny, Violet thought.

They alighted. Violet made certain the brooch over her left shoulder was securely pinned, holding her shawl closed and in place, with the draping material laid over her left arm. The arrangement had been perfected months earlier as an effective way of keeping her arm from being too visible. Between the shawl, her ever-present gloves, and the ruffled and laced undersleeves worn longer than most to cover the majority of her unmoving hand, few people were likely to realize what they were actually seeing.

As the family approached, a decidedly proper and dignified butler opened the door. Without hesitation and without even a hint of displeasure, he said, "Mr. Barrington has suggested you be permitted to settle into your rooms without delay. When you are ready, he wishes you to join the other guests in the drawing room."

The thoughtful arrangements seemed to Violet a good sign. There were always rules governing the interactions of Society. Violet neither understood them all nor knew the entirety of them, but she was determined to learn. There would be no hope of finding friends and connections in their new life otherwise.

They were led into the entryway of the grand estate, and for a moment, Violet could hardly believe the sight that met her eyes. The polished parquet floor beneath their feet led to a tall stone lintel, beyond which stood the most gorgeous wooden staircase she'd ever seen. It made a quarter turn every ten steps, with thick, intricately carved newel posts at each turn.

Irthing Grange was lovely; Livingsley Hall was breathtaking.

A kind-eyed housekeeper ushered them up those magnificent stairs and to the guest wing. Violet peeked inside the nearest bedchambers. They were sumptuous yet still inviting. The one nearest Mother and Father was decorated in shades of red with dark wood trim. Yet the bed curtains were a thick, cream-colored fabric. The next room was decorated in a soft, buttery yellow, giving it a warm and inviting air.

The housekeeper, still standing among them, addressed Mother. "Mr. Barrington did not know if you would prefer that the young Miss Watkins reside in the nursery or in this corridor near you."

"Since our time here is to be relatively brief," Mother said, "it would be best for Georgiana to occupy a room here among us."

The housekeeper nodded her acknowledgment and repeated her insistence that anything and everything they needed would be seen to. She quickly curtsied and left them to sort the matter of which room would be used by which of them.

"I knew Livingsley Hall would be a welcoming place. I just knew it would be," Violet said. "This is our opportunity to come to know our nearest neighbor when we'd not managed the thing before. While I would not wish to repeat the chaos of this morning, we can at least move forward knowing some good will come of it. And through Mr. Barrington, we will meet others."

Father's mouth turned up. His eyebrows, bushy and unkempt as ever, arched softly. "Our ray of sunshine, as always."

"Would you rather I be a thundercloud?" she asked the question teasingly, but part of her did long to be thunderous at times or openly sad or disappointed or sometimes even a little pessimistic. Keeping so many thoughts and worries and feelings to oneself was tiring. And lonely.

He shook his head even as a silent laugh shook his chest. "I most certainly would not." Happy color touched his pale countenance. Father had once worked every day out of doors and had, according to Mother's memories of him, been tanned by the sun to nearly the color of the sand on Portsmouth beach. The past years had seen his days spent in his counting house, bent over ledgers and away from the sun.

"Your mother and I will occupy this room here," Father said, motioning to the crimson room. "You and Georgie choose the rooms you would prefer."

Livingsley Hall must have been a large estate indeed. She knew Mr. Barrington had a great many visitors just then, yet her family was afforded multiple empty rooms from which to choose. Georgie didn't hesitate to take the lovely yellow one directly beside Mother and Father's. Wanting the girl to feel as safe and secure as possible, Violet selected the bedchamber on the other side of hers, though she'd not yet looked at it.

She stepped inside and sighed immediately. The softest blue silk hung on the walls. The bed canopy was ruffled white. The white marble of the fireplace stood in beautiful contrast to the deep sapphire of the large rug. And adding to the appeal was the soul-warming vista beyond the tall windows, the lake and trees looking almost like a painting.

Violet could be more than happy in this room for the next few weeks; she could be at peace.

A half an hour later, Violet emerged dressed in her favorite *Robe a l'Anglaise* gown, with the skirts gathered in the back and tied up in luscious billows of fabric. She was secure in her knowledge that, while two years old, the lavish yellow gown remained fashionable, and though her lace undersleeves were decidedly longer than how other ladies wore theirs, they did not appear out of place in the ensemble. A silk shawl—a deep blue with strands of gold woven throughout—was pinned in the usual place, offering a complement of color.

Mother had helped her dress, as they hadn't yet secured a maid, and Violet had helped address what little damage the journey had done to Mother's hair. Georgie had also been made presentable. Father looked quite the part of comfortable country gentleman, with his wig and fashionably comfortable clothes. They were as prepared as they ever would be to meet their new neighbor and his important friends.

The family was shown to the drawing room on the ground floor, a spacious room with a rounded alcove boasting windows from floor to ceiling. Inside the elegantly furnished space was a collection of people quite clearly from the highest rung of Society's ladder.

Mr. Barrington stepped over to the family. Violet had last seen him with a neckcloth tied over his nose and mouth, covered in ash, in the midst of their efforts to locate Georgie and extinguish the stubborn remains of the small fire. He'd felt very human then. Seeing him now, dressed in fine silks, dark hair styled and lightly powdered, brown eyes studying them from behind his spectacles, she found him less relatable, less approachable.

The bow he offered to Father and Mother was perfectly executed and deferential but also noticeably stiff. "Welcome to Livingsley Hall, Mr. Ridley, Mrs. Ridley, Miss Ridley, Miss Watkins. Allow me to make the needed introductions."

Father acknowledged the offer, and they followed their host into the room.

"This is Lord Aldric Benick, younger son of the Duke of Hartley." He indicated a gentleman with dark, lightly powdered hair and eyes that seemed to study every detail of everything and everyone in the room. She would do best to keep her arm fully hidden from him.

Lord Aldric offered a bow. "A pleasure to make your acquaintance."

Mr. Barrington pushed forward without pausing long enough for a reply from Violet's parents. "This is Lord Jonquil and Lady Jonquil, heir to the Earl of Lampton and the Baron Farland, respectively."

Multiple titles held by that one couple. *Good heavens.*

"Mr. Henri Fortier of France." Mr. Barrington seemed determined to complete the introductions without delay. "Mr. Niles Greenberry of Cornwall. Mr. Digby Layton of Pledwick Manor in Yorkshire."

As Mr. Layton came forward to offer his bow, Violet's breath whooshed from her. He was, in a word, gorgeous. Every aspect of his appearance, from his ruby-silk jacket and dark-silver pantaloons to his perfectly coiffed and powdered hair, spoke of perfection. His piercing blue eyes and symmetrically handsome features were impossible to look away from. How anyone, male or female, managed not to stare at the gentleman was beyond her comprehension.

Lady Jonquil approached and saved Violet from enduring any embarrassment over her shock. "I'm so pleased your family has come to stay here for a time. As much as I adore these gentlemen, I have found that being the only lady among them is often exhausting."

"Do they have a tendency toward mischief?" Violet liked the idea.

"Heavens, yes." Lady Jonquil's tender gaze fell on Lord Jonquil, matching the one Mother so often bestowed on Father. The lady's hand rested lightly on her rounded middle.

"Are these gentleman particularly close friends?"

Lady Jonquil nodded. She blushed a little, something people with red in their hair did quite easily. Violet suspected she was a little shy, not overwhelmingly so but enough that she might need a bit of encouragement to think of Violet as a friend.

Violet motioned to a nearby sofa. Lady Jonquil followed with every indication of pleasure. Violet's new acquaintance dressed fashionably but without the truly wide panniers so many employed. Violet herself had abandoned the extreme silhouette two years earlier, finding it wreaked havoc on her use of her prosthesis, forever bumping against it and awkwardly jostling her arm. She would not feel out of place in terms of fashion with Lady Jonquil nearby.

Violet kept her left arm tucked as close to herself as she could, comforted that it was hidden beneath her silk shawl. She laid her right arm atop it, unhidden. Sometimes people, in the enthusiasm of a conversation, reached out and touched another person's arm. If her right was the visible one, it was more likely to be the one touched. Violet didn't particularly want to delve into the topic of her prosthesis. As Mother rightly pointed out, they had enough obstacles to overcome without introducing this one.

"I have never been to Portsmouth," Lady Jonquil said. "I would enjoy learning about it."

"And I am new to Cumberland," Violet returned. "I would be delighted to hear about this corner of the kingdom. In all honesty, I would be delighted to talk about anything and everything."

"Some of the ladies in London found my conversation a bit tedious," Lady Jonquil said in a tone of warning. "I discovered, to my cost, that mathematics and scientific pursuits and deep evaluations of history are not universally enjoyed."

"I think that sounds fascinating," Violet said.

"Truly?" Lady Jonquil must have been met with a great many disapproving looks and comments to sound as unconvinced as she was.

"Truly."

An expression of relief spread over her features. "I promise not to talk about *only* those things. And I would very much like to introduce you and your mother to the other ladies in the area."

"We would appreciate that."

Lady Jonquil visibly relaxed the longer they were in conversation. Violet liked the thought that she was already offering something beneficial to this lady with whom she would very much like to be friends.

"Will Mr. Barrington and his friends be annoyed at having extra guests?" Violet asked.

"They will not." Lady Jonquil smiled broadly. "Mr. Layton and my husband will be delighted to have a large audience for their antics. Lord Aldric will appreciate having more people with whom to converse. Mr. Fortier and Mr. Greenberry will enjoy quietly coming to know your family better."

"And what of Mr. Barrington himself?" Violet had been intrigued by him from the moment she'd first seen him, cravat tied over his nose and mouth, searching her house for anyone in need of rescue.

"I will confess, he might give the impression of being annoyed, but he won't actually be. He keeps very much to himself and sometimes struggles with the social niceties when he reaches the end of his endurance for interactions."

That didn't sound promising.

"In fact, his friends"—Lady Jonquil indicated the other gentlemen—"have given him the teasing moniker of Grumpy Uncle."

A laugh sputtered from Violet. "Grumpy Uncle?"

"His name among them is not entirely unearned," Lady Jonquil expounded. "And yet, it also is not entirely fitting. He is somehow precisely what they have called him and nothing like it."

"Do they all have nicknames?"

Lady Jonquil nodded. "Lord Aldric, after all, is known among them as the General because he is overbearing." She made the declaration with just enough humor to tell Violet it was a little exaggerated. "Henri Fortier—he's the tall Frenchman with a gaze that makes a person feel she ought to . . . repent of something—he is called Archbishop."

"Because of the unspoken call to repentance?"

Lady Jonquil nodded solemnly. "Niles Greenberry, whom you have probably already forgotten, is known as Puppy. He has a tendency to follow after them all, eager to be part of whatever mischief they're undertaking."

The General. Archbishop. Puppy. What a delightfully odd group they seemed.

"My husband is called the Jester because he is quick with a joke and always eager to lift spirits. Digby Layton, whom I *guarantee* you have not forgotten—"

"The gentleman so handsome it's more than a little overwhelming?"

Lady Jonquil nodded. "They call him the King, and he embraces that role wholeheartedly."

Violet found herself excited at the prospect of witnessing that. "Do they have a name for you?"

She pressed her palm to her ruffled neckline, her fingertips resting against the silver and blue-stone pendant she wore. "Our Julia."

"They have thoroughly adopted you, then."

"For which I am infinitely grateful." She raised an auburn eyebrow—Violet hadn't known many people with red hair, and while Lady Jonquil's leaned heavily toward brown, there was no mistaking the red in it—and in a voice of feigned offense said, "Though I cannot convince the lot of them to adopt my approach to hair powder."

"You do not wear hair powder."

A gleam entered Lady Jonquil's eyes. "Precisely."

This happy-hearted lady was warming to her, showing less hesitancy as the minutes passed. Violet was so pleased to be making her acquaintance. She lived nearby. She was kind and friendly. Perhaps she would prove the first friend Violet made in Cumberland.

"I have never cared for the way powder turns my hair an odd pink-hued, muddled mess," Lady Jonquil said. "I decided several years ago that if I didn't care for what powder did to my hair, I oughtn't consider myself under any obligation to conform to the fashion."

"Powdering dries my hair terribly," Violet said. "My lady's maid in Portsmouth was a genius at rescuing it. She put the most fragrant oils in and saved it from growing brittle. I wish she could have come here with us."

"Have you secured a new lady's maid?"

With an exaggerated sigh of relief, one that very nearly caused her to cough, she said, "That the state of my hair does not make my current lack of a lady's maid obvious sets my mind at ease."

"Your maid-less state will be kept a strict secret," Julia said, matching her feigned tone of seriousness.

"We've not secured my cousin Georgie a governess either. There's been so much to do since our arrival."

"And a fire in the midst of all of that was hardly the further complication you needed."

Violet let her gaze slide to her mother. She stood among the gentlemen, holding herself regally and competently. Father was at her side with his arm tucked about her waist. It was, perhaps, a little more affection than most Society couples showed, but there was nothing in it that made a person uncomfortable. Indeed, Mother had a knack for setting people at ease. Watching her in conversation with these new acquaintances, clearly making a good showing for herself and quickly becoming a favorite, as she always was, did Violet's heart good. She had told herself they'd only needed an opportunity to make the acquaintance of their neighbors to find their place among them. That opportunity had, at last, arrived.

Mr. Barrington sat apart from the others, in the windowed bay alcove, not participating in their conversations. He dressed with as much care as the others but without Mr. Layton's flair or Mr. Fortier's quiet elegance.

"Does our host always sit apart from the others as he is doing now?"

"Not always, but often. He will be gracious and accommodating and genteel while you are here, but he will most certainly also be maddeningly cantankerous at times."

"I have been called 'maddeningly cheerful' on more than one occasion."

A bit of concern touched Lady Jonquil's expression. "Do you anticipate his grumpiness dampening your spirits?"

"On the contrary, Lady Jonquil, I have every intention of raising his spirits long before he depresses mine."

Lady Jonquil turned to face her more directly. "Please, call me Julia."

"And I am Violet."

Julia watched her with curiosity. "You mean to meet Kes's gruffness with cheer?"

"More than that," Violet said with a laugh, "I intend to out-cheer his grumpiness."

"I look forward to watching that."

Violet held out her right hand for her new friend to shake. "Violet and Julia: partners in mischief."

Julia smiled broadly, not the least put off by Violet's tendency toward ridiculousness.

This was proving even better than Violet had hoped. So quickly, she had a friend and an ally. And a bit of a lighthearted lark to look forward to.

Chapter Five

Kes sat in his library, filling his lungs with air that smelled of old books and his ears with the blessed sound of silence. There was, at last, space enough to think and breathe.

"You've friends here, whether you want us or not." Stanley's declaration often returned to Kes's mind.

His heart lightened a little at the memory. Regret hung heavy over every recollection of Stanley. He had created the Gents. For years, he was the thread uniting all of them. He'd pulled them into this lifelong friendship. He'd given them this gift but hadn't lived long enough to truly enjoy it himself.

How readily Kes had insisted all those years ago that he did not, in fact, wish for Stanley's friendship. What he wouldn't give now to have a moment of it back.

Another memory dropped into his mind, a moment from another time and place. They were at Cambridge. Stanley, Lucas, and Niles were finishing their time there. Digby, Aldric, and Henri were remaining but had attached themselves to a different college than Kes. For so long, he'd insisted he was one of them against his will, but he'd been nearly consumed with fear as they'd all left him behind in one way or another. He would be forgotten as their lives took them elsewhere.

Stanley had plopped down next to him in the sitting room of the flat they'd all lived in. The other Gents had been away.

"What deep thoughts are you pondering today?" Stanley had asked, that look of eager amusement he always wore firmly in place.

He'd not wanted to admit his worries over being abandoned. "I was contemplating how blessedly quiet it will be after the three of you leave behind the hallowed halls of Cambridge."

Stanley laughed. "You'll miss us. Admit it."

"I admit nothing."

"I don't believe a word of it, Grumpy Uncle. I predict you'll spend every term break rushing to join us wherever we might be."

He'd liked the idea but couldn't let himself believe it would happen. The General, the King, and Archbishop, whose course of study was taking longer than the other three, would still finish their time at Cambridge before Kes did. Who was to guarantee they would even tell him where they were, that they would remember he wasn't with them?

"I know how to get you to London." Stanley arched a single light-copper eyebrow, even as his smile turned impish. "That, my friend, is where the Royal Society meets. Lecture after lecture. Rooms filled with intellectuals spilling their academic discoveries and ideas into each other's ears. You'd be in heaven."

Kes perked up, intrigued. He was, of course, quite familiar with the Royal Society. He'd read their membership lists with awe and more than a little envy. To spend even an afternoon among them would be the highlight of his academic life. "They're far more exclusive than you likely realize," he told his friend.

And Stanley, in true Stanley form, had replied without hesitation, without even a drop of insincerity, "And you, my friend, are far more impressive than you likely realize."

That one compliment, that one quiet moment, had carried Kes through so many difficulties, so many doubts. And through two denied applications for membership in the Royal Society.

Acceptance into the revered scientific society was far more likely if one had the backing of someone already a member. While Kes knew a few gentlemen from his Cambridge years who were among their ranks, he didn't want to gain entry if he hadn't done anything to truly warrant it. He wanted to be accepted on his merits, not merely his connections.

Someday. Someday, he'd be one of them. He swore he would. If he could manage to accomplish something scientifically worthwhile. And he needed to manage it whilst playing host to, or traveling with, or joining the London whirlwind alongside the very friends who had, just as he'd predicted all those years ago, enjoyed a great many larks after departing Cambridge that he had not been part of, nor had he seemed particularly missed.

Stanley had been the one to send Kes an invitation to the first Gents gathering held after that departure. He'd also been the one to invite Kes to the second, a year later. By the third, Stanley had been in the colonies, fighting, Kes had left

Cambridge, and he'd resolutely included himself in absolutely everything the Gents did.

A quick knock at the door pulled his attention in that direction.

The butler stepped inside, a package in his hands, roughly the size and shape of a few books stacked atop each other. "This has arrived for you, Mr. Barrington. From your brother."

Everett didn't often send him parcels.

Kes accepted the package with great curiosity. "How long ago did this arrive?"

"Mere moments, sir."

A mystery, to be certain. "Thank you, Gladwin."

"Of course, Mr. Barrington." The butler slipped out once more.

The parcel was wrapped in burlap and tied with twine. All sides felt solid and even, not at all how they would if it were indeed a small stack of books. The corners felt sharp. Something odd formed a lump on one long edge. And it was heavy. What in heaven's name had Everett sent him?

And why had he sent it now? Kes already had more claiming his time than he could address. To add a mystery to that felt more like a burden in that moment than an intriguing prospect.

And in the very next moment, Henri stepped into the library. "Might I claim a bit of your time, Kester?"

Another pull. Another distraction. Still, Henri didn't often ask favors. Ignoring his request was out of the question.

"*Oui*." Kes motioned his friend to the chairs on either side of the fireplace.

They sat, Kes leaving his brother's parcel on his desk.

Henri spoke first. "Knowing the Ridleys purchased Irthing Grange, I am curious if homes come available in this area often."

"Somewhat often," Kes said. "I've seen more estates in this corner of the kingdom that are free of entails than I have in most other places."

Henri nodded slowly, forehead creased and eyes a bit narrowed.

"Do you know someone wishing to purchase an estate?" Kes asked.

The poor man, as naturally pale as Digby managed to render himself through the current fashion for face powder, tended to blush easily. "I'm nearly thirty years old. I think perhaps it is time I had a place to live." He punctuated the declaration with a very Continental shrug.

"You do have your rented rooms in London."

Kes had suspected Henri was asking on his own behalf yet was still a bit caught off guard. Henri had left all his family in France when he'd come to England to study at Cambridge. He'd some income from his older brother's estate but no permanent roof over his head. None of the Gents had expected that to change.

"I am appreciative of having a place to live in London," Henri said, "but I—I've been dependent on others' charity for more than a decade, and—I—"

Recognizing his friend's struggle to be honest without sounding ungrateful, Kes pushed forward. "Country homes do come available, but they also come dear."

Henri nodded in humble understanding. "I suspect my funds will stretch only to something the size of a country vicarage. But if it were mine, I would treasure it no matter the size."

Few people were as genuinely humble and undemanding as Henri. Yet he was also far from naive.

"I've a man of business in Carlisle," Kes said. "He'd likely know of properties available or know someone who might know. It's not a quick jaunt, but a journey there would allow me to make introductions."

"Would you be willing?" Henri asked.

Another task pulling him from the quiet of home and the his desire to spend time on his projects and studies. And yet, how could he refuse? From the time he'd helped the first three Gents form the Travel Society at Eton, his place among them had been one of usefulness. Some of his heaviest regrets had grown out of the rare moments when he'd not helped them when he ought. "Of course I will travel there with you."

Miss Ridley and Miss Georgie stepped into the library. Kes jumped to his feet, the movement likely looking as frantically awkward as it felt. His heart's reaction to her had not calmed since their first encounter. It pounded and raced and generally demanded precedence over his much more logical mind. Was there to be no end to the sources of disquiet in his life?

"We have come to ransack your library, Mr. Barrington," Miss Ridley said, laughter lurking beneath her very somber tone. "And we aren't even ashamed."

"You are welcome to any book that strikes your fancy." Kes spoke quickly and efficiently, generally the best approach to interactions.

Miss Ridley nudged her little cousin toward the shelves. "Have a look, love."

But Miss Georgie didn't move. She watched Kes, lips turned down and eyes narrowed. "He doesn't want me to." She spoke to her cousin but still watched him.

"I do not make insincere offers," Kes said. He sometimes extended hospitality when he'd rather have solitude or agreed to adventures when he preferred to rest, but he was not one to go back on his word. "I have over two thousand books in this room, and they are all at your disposal."

She folded her arms and pursed her lips.

"I am in earnest." He motioned to the shelves. "Ransack to your heart's content."

Henri moved to where Miss Georgie stood defiant and, apparently, unconvinced. "I am too old a friend of Mr. Barrington's for him to object to me borrowing a book. May I snatch one on your behalf?"

She studied him. The girl was either stubborn or distrustful. Perhaps both. She seemed quite the opposite of her cousin in that regard.

"You are French," Miss Georgie said.

Henri offered a bow. "*Oui.* Does my being French present you with concerns?"

Miss Georgie shook her head. Her curls did not truly bounce with the movement, though the edges of her hair ribbon fluttered. "There were French people in Portsmouth. They talked like you."

"That is the flavor of *our* language seasoning our use of *yours*. When I first arrived on England's shores, I seasoned my words so strongly I could hardly be understood."

A flicker of a confidence touched Miss Georgie's face. "I can understand you."

"I suspect you are remarkably clever." Henri always spoke softly, whether to children or adults. And his sincere care for people was apparent to all who interacted with him. "Allow me to help you find a book. As Monsieur Barrington said, there are thousands in this library, so you have ample from which to choose."

She agreed with a nod, and the two of them moved to the nearest wall of volumes. In his generosity toward Miss Georgie, Henri abandoned Kes in the very moment he was faced with a lady who utterly undermined his equilibrium.

He looked to her once more, hoping to discover his mind had resumed control. She wore a dress of soft yellow that added a warm glow to her complexion. Her long sleeves and ruffled cuffs peeked out from beneath yet another shawl pinned as before at her left shoulder. Only the gloved fingertips of her left hand were visible behind the scalloped edge. A white-crepe tucker softened the angles of her squared neckline. Her unpowdered coils of hair shone like polished slate. She was a vision. His heart reminded him quite swiftly of its growing tendency to misbehave when she was near.

Retreat seemed the best solution.

Kes moved to the tall diamond-paned window. It afforded a frosted view of the grounds, not the sort one stood about admiring. This window was not made for gazing but for lighting the space without causing the many books inside to fade from harsh sunlight. Still, he could think of no better place in the room to plant himself.

In the end, it did not matter; Miss Ridley joined him there. "Thank you for allowing her to peruse your library. She is excessively fond of reading."

"I do not know that I have anything of particular interest to a nine-year-old."

Miss Ridley waved that off with one gloved hand. "She will enjoy simply looking at and through them. Though, there is something she would enjoy even more."

Kes looked at her only long enough to ascertain that she was indeed expecting him to inquire further. Her eyes danced with excitement. Excitement. While talking with *him*? That was far too improbable. It was much more likely that she was laughing at him. He was too tired, too wary, too in need of peace to knowingly undermine it in yet another way.

He set his gaze on the unhelpful window. "What else is your cousin in need of?"

"She has admired your lake from afar these past weeks. Would you allow her to explore it while she's here?"

"She may explore the grounds whenever she chooses, and not merely while your family is staying at Livingsley Hall."

"How considerate of you, sir. What a pleasure it is that we will all see each other so often."

He glanced once more in her direction. Again, her eyes gave the undeniable impression that she was deeply pleased, even eager.

"Do you mean to come by often?" While he wasn't entirely unhappy at the possibility, he could not argue that the prospect was a bit overwhelming. He only ever had time and space to himself when he was at Livingsley Hall and the Gents were not. Was he to lose that very rare bit of peace?

"I mean to be an extremely attentive neighbor," she said. "You will, I daresay, find yourself wondering how you filled your days before the Ridley family came to Irthing Grange."

Panic rose in his chest. "You mean to 'fill my days' with visits?"

"As often as possible."

His mouth dropped open a bit even as his mind spun frantically at the possibility. "You—You mean to . . . often?"

She pressed her clasped hands to her chest. "I could call every day if you'd like."

Merciful heavens. He looked to Henri, hoping Archbishop could call down some sort of miracle. The Gents' resident saint was still assisting Miss Georgie but was clearly listening to Kes's last hope of peace evaporate. The infuriating Frenchman didn't bother hiding his amusement.

Every day. What could he possibly say? He wouldn't injure her feelings, and neither would he be rude. But . . . *every day*?

He looked back to her again, desperately trying to formulate a means of changing her mind.

Her obvious attempts at holding back a smile—or more likely still, a laugh—were not entirely succeeding.

"You are jesting?" His spectacles had slipped down his nose a bit, so he pushed them back into place.

"I cannot guarantee that Georgie and I won't explore your lake every day," Miss Ridley said. "We are both terribly fond of the out of doors, but I will not intrude upon your peace as often as that."

"But you still mean to intrude upon my peace somewhat often?"

She raised a shoulder in a coquettish shrug that was made almost theatrical by the laughter in her eyes. "Of course, Mr. Barrington. What are neighbors for?"

She flitted away. Something in the display felt precisely like that . . . a display. He didn't think she was being disingenuous or dishonest, and though he had wondered a little at first, he did not now believe she was having a laugh at his expense. Her jesting felt a great deal like the manner in which the Gents teased him. And though they were often exhausting, he very much liked their teasing. He often *needed* it. And now Miss Ridley was offering him that same desideratum.

A little laugh bubbled inside. With that one moment, that one brief conversation, he knew that despite his insistence otherwise, he'd added her to the list of people he wanted to matter to.

Chapter Six

VIOLET DIDN'T ALLOW ANY OF her uncertainty to show in her face. Julia had arranged for their nearest neighbors to call at Livingsley Hall. She had already undergone whatever steps were required for people of this class to visit one another and, therefore, was in a position to make the introductions needed. The *ladies* would be calling, and thus, Mother and Violet were the only members of their family in the drawing room.

Mother sat with regal bearing, looking as resplendent as the Queen herself. She'd dressed in a silver gown with an embroidered stomacher, with a thick black ribbon woven through her powdered hair. Everything about her spoke of elegance.

Julia's more subdued fashion sense suited her quite perfectly. She looked entirely at ease and confident in herself despite the fact that she was a little shy. Either her bashfulness did not undermine her social acumen, or she was as adept at masking her worries as Violet had learned to be.

Violet pushed from her expression any indication of concern or uncertainty. She knew how to appear perfectly pleased in any situation. She needed a word or two of encouragement in that moment, but she knew none would be forthcoming. When a person never expressed worries or struggles, one never received reassurances. Sometimes being sunny was quite a lonely role to fill.

"Thank you for arranging this, Lady Jonquil," Mother said. "We have wished to make the acquaintance of our neighbors but, thus far, haven't been able to."

"This will smooth the way," Julia said, "but for them to call at your home, your husband must call on their husbands."

Understanding dawned on Mother's face and likely was obvious on Violet's face as well.

Mr. Gladwin, the butler, appeared in the doorway. "Lady Collington, Mrs. Overton, Miss Overton, Mrs. Handley."

Mother rose. Violet did as well. Julia took a moment longer to get to her feet but not for lack of trying. In the next instant, four ladies, one likely Violet's age, one near Mother's, and the other two somewhere in between, stepped inside.

"Lady Jonquil, what a pleasure to see you," the taller of the ladies said. She wore her high-piled hair heavily powdered. Her clothing was all that was opulent and ostentatious. She looked as if she were on her way to a ball rather than calling on a neighbor.

The other ladies were dressed on a level with Julia. Violet could see that her mother's clothing and her own were plainer than what these ladies wore. Father had money enough; they simply hadn't yet had the opportunity to study the fashions adhered to by those in their new station in life.

"Lady Collington," Julia said in response to the lady who had greeted her. "I'm pleased you could come."

"I know my duty to the neighborhood." Lady Collington sat in a chair and motioned for the others to do so as well, quite as if *she* were hostess for the afternoon rather than Julia.

No one else sat.

Violet looked to her friend, wondering if this breach of etiquette required a response. Julia didn't say anything, but her stiff posture communicated clearly that Lady Collington had made a miscalculation.

Julia eyed the newest arrival sitting quite at her leisure before turning slowly to the other ladies. "Allow me to make introductions," she said to those ladies still standing. Nods of acceptance were universal. "Mrs. Ridley, Miss Ridley"—she then looked back to the other women—"this is Mrs. Overton and Miss Overton, of Denton House." Curtsies were exchanged. "And Mrs. Handley," Julia said, indicating the lady of whom she spoke, "of Boltonsfield Manor."

Again, they undertook the expected responses.

Then, turning slowly toward the lady who still remained seated, Julia said, "Lady Collington, of Hoppleforth, might I make known to you Mrs. Ridley and Miss Ridley, of Irthing Grange."

Lady Collington went through the motions, but there was a coldness to her. She had treated Julia with superiority, but when she looked at Violet and her mother, that changed. There was an edge to the haughtiness, making her gaze more piercing than arrogant.

"Please, ladies, be seated." Julia motioned to the empty chairs and sofa.

"Thank you, Lady Jonquil," Mrs. Overton said, her eyes darting for the briefest of moments to Lady Collington.

"We heard Irthing Grange had been purchased," Mrs. Handley said, "but we hadn't yet met your family."

"My deepest apologies if we have offered any offense in our delay," Mother said. "The house was empty for some time and was in need of great attention. And then two days ago, we had a fire. We have been temporarily displaced."

"Mr. Barrington does not often have guests beyond his particular friends." Lady Collington's assessing gaze swept over Mother and Violet in turn. "How fortunate for you that he made an exception."

"We are deeply grateful to him." Mother had the uncanny ability to remain calm and unruffled no matter the provocation.

On more than one occasion in Portsmouth, criticisms and dismissals had been tossed at them without the slightest attempt at subtlety. Those who, like Lady Collington, veiled their contempt and disapproval behind feigned manners were particularly frustrating. The dismissal was there. The disapproval. The superiority. But it was interwoven with just enough civility of manner that were any objection to be made, the offending individual would simply deny it, would insist the slights were imagined. Mother had long ago taught Violet that however unfair, however unpleasant, she would do best to keep her head up and press on.

"Have you been given house room at many other *fine* houses?" Lady Collington asked with the slightest curl of her lip. The emphasis on *fine* told its own story.

"The finest houses will always be pleased to receive the Ridleys," Julia said.

Miss Overton slipped from her chair to the one beside Violet. "You will forgive my impertinence," she said, "but I suspect you and I are near in age."

Violet nodded. "I suspect the same. And Lady Jonquil is as well, obviously."

"And with you living at Irthing Grange," Miss Overton said, "Lady Jonquil will likely visit more often. That would be a pleasant thing for the families here."

It was not exactly a declaration of joy at Violet herself living in the neighborhood, but neither was it a dismissal. Violet would accept the small victories where she could get them.

"Most of the families in the area have younger children," Mrs. Handley said. "I myself have a dear little boy: Jonas. He is four years old and quite handsome. A more intelligent little boy was likely never known. I suspect Mr. Barrington will be quite impressed with him when he is grown. Mr. Barrington is known for having a quick intellect and a clever mind."

"Your Jonas must be very clever," Julia said.

"He is a dear boy, though I say so myself." Mrs. Handley spoke extremely fondly. "And he is quite devoted to his mother. Jonas is the very best of boys. You will find him quite the most wonderful child you have ever known."

"He sounds remarkable," Mother said. How she managed to make the observation without the slightest bit of amusement or annoyance, Violet didn't know. She herself had to bite her lips to prevent any comment.

Mother turned to Lady Collington. "How far from Irthing Grange is Hoppleforth?"

"Anyone from this area knows of Hoppleforth. It is quite a remarkable estate. I daresay the finest hereabouts."

"It outshines Livingsley Hall, does it?" Violet asked.

Lady Collington sputtered a little. Miss Overton hid her mouth behind her hand. Violet suspected she had hit upon a point of regular neighborhood discussion. Livingsley Hall was remarkably grand, even someone with little experience in such things could see that. It seemed Hoppleforth was not, in fact, this estate's rival for grandeur, no matter Lady Collington's remark otherwise.

"Hoppleforth may not be so large as Livingsley Hall, nor boast quite so many rooms and fine vistas, neither does it have its own lake," Lady Collington said, her tone overly sweet to the point of being biting. "It *is* larger than Irthing Grange though. And the grounds are better maintained."

"I like the grounds at Irthing Grange," Violet said, remembering to keep her demeanor pleasant. "They are warm and inviting without being inelegant. There is something beautiful about the wildness of them."

"Well, no matter how quickly one might acquire wealth, it does take more time to acquire taste," Lady Collington said. She turned with slightly pursed lips to Julia, apparently expecting to be joined in her insulting assessment.

"Alas," Julia said, eying the lady with the slightest bit of pity, "for some, good taste never comes." On that declaration, made offhand and breezy but hitting its mark with precision, Julia turned to Mrs. Overton. "I do hope your husband intends to call soon. I suspect the gentlemen would like to introduce him to Mr. Ridley."

"I suspect he will," Mrs. Overton said. "My husband's friendship with your father-in-law has endeared your husband to him."

Julia turned her attention to Mrs. Handley. She was managing this rather disparate group with tremendous skill. "And should your husband return from London whilst we are all still here, I hope he will do the same."

"I daresay he will. And if not, Mr. Ridley can call on him." She looked to Mother. "And I assure you, when he does, he will be received."

There was something odd in the promise Mrs. Handley added to her invitation, but Violet couldn't immediately identify what. She pondered it as the ladies continued to talk. She didn't need long to sort it out. Father's visit was the only one that had been deemed in need of a specific reassurance of welcome.

"There really aren't many people our age in the area," Miss Overton said. "This may be a lonely corner of the country for you."

"Portsmouth was sometimes not lonely enough," Violet answered.

"I've not been to Portsmouth, though I have visited Plymouth. Are the two similar?"

The two, of course, had similarities, but anyone from either city was keenly aware of the differences. She did not suspect Miss Overton truly wanted a detailed description, simply to know if her limited experience had any bearing. "They are both bustling port cities. Much about them is similar."

Miss Overton looked instantly pleased. "Have you been to London?"

"Sadly, no. We have spoken of going in the spring."

"Oh, that is when you must go. All of Society will be there. There are so many more people there than here."

Violet felt a kinship with the lady in that moment. "Are there really so few in the area?"

Miss Overton nodded with emphasis. Lowering her voice, she said, "And unfortunately, one of them is Lady Collington."

Her tone was so wry that Violet actually laughed out loud. That brought the other ladies' eyes to them. Julia looked utterly pleased. Mrs. Overton seemed to feel the same. Mrs. Handley's mannerism indicated nothing so much as indifference. Lady Collington looked downright annoyed. When meeting new people, Violet had learned to assess quickly which ones might prove friendly and which were best given a wide berth. The Overtons were on the first list, Lady Collington firmly on the second. Mrs. Handley remained a mystery.

"As I was saying," Mrs. Handley said to the ladies, apparently having been interrupted, "my Jonas—"

"Mrs. Dalforth," the butler interrupted and announced from the doorway. He stepped aside to allow yet another lady to enter. She, like Mrs. Handley, was older than Violet but not of Mother's generation. Lady Collington fell into that category also.

Julia greeted Mrs. Dalforth more warmly than she had the other arrivals. It seemed Julia was either better acquainted with the newcomer or was simply grateful for her arrival. Introductions were made, and Mrs. Dalforth sat among them.

"I'm so pleased to meet you," she said to Mother and Violet. "Irthing Grange has been empty for so long. It is a fine thing for the area that it is finally occupied."

"We couldn't be happier here," Mother said. Her calm and flawless manners always made her an instant favorite. It seemed she was managing precisely that with most of the women present.

"You will forgive me for acknowledging that I have been listening to gossip," Mrs. Dalforth said, "but it is my understanding you have a niece or cousin living with you."

"My niece," Mother said. "Her late father was my brother, and as she was sadly orphaned, she's now our ward and makes her home with us."

"Oh, the poor dear." Mrs. Dalforth adjusted so she faced Mother directly. "It is a difficult thing to lose a parent at any age, but it is especially painful for a child."

Mother acknowledged that with a nod and a few quickly offered words.

"I am hopeful she is the same age as my children, or very nearly," Mrs. Dalforth said. "My sons, William and Charles, are ten and six, and my daughter, Phoebe, is eight."

Mother perked up. "Georgiana is nine years old and, I fear, has been terribly lonely without other children about."

"The Dalforth children are well behaved and kind," Julia said. "And Georgiana has shown herself to be bright and personable. I suspect they will be the best of friends before long."

That launched Mrs. Handley into a long, drawn-out explanation of why "dear Jonas" was the *very* best of children.

In the midst of it, Miss Overton leaned a bit closer to Violet once more and said, "Lady Collington has a son as well. His name is Hubert, and he is six years old. And while I suspect your cousin cannot avoid interacting with him, it might be wise for any interactions between them to occur under your parents' supervision."

Violet nodded her understanding. "Is he cruel to the other children?"

"He can be. But I worry that since his mother has already decided to disapprove of your family and her husband, Sir Randolph, is certain to do likewise, their son will almost certainly follow suit."

It was all too familiar to Violet. But she pushed aside the frustration and worry. "She will have the company of William, Charles, and Phoebe, and they seem perfect companions."

"And though Mrs. Dalforth is, I would wager, nearly ten years our senior, her company is quite enjoyable as well," Miss Overton said.

Violet met Julia's eye for the briefest of moments. She received a nod of recognition, one she didn't struggle to interpret. Julia had arranged for this afternoon so that Violet could meet her neighbors and gain an understanding of them. She and Mother would now know how to navigate the principal homes and families in the area, something they would have struggled to do on their own.

Chapter Seven

"Why have you not powdered your hair?" Mother hadn't begun their walk through the Livingsley Hall garden with that question, but she hadn't waited long.

"Powdering is beginning to lose fashion amongst the younger set."

Mother turned her head ever so slowly, bestowing on Violet a look of mingled warning and disapproval but one offered in complete jest. "The 'younger' set?"

"The less-experienced set?" Violet tried.

Mother's nostrils flared, and her brows reached ever higher.

Violet kept her enjoyment tucked away. These exchanges were far funnier when they both managed to maintain the facade of being quite somber. "Less-wise?"

A tiny shake of Mother's head.

"Foolish. The *foolish* set."

"Much better." Mother pursed her lips. "And what does the foolish set have against the idea of hair powder?"

"It is the growing opinion that if a person does not care for the look or impact of powdering, then she is free to forgo it." That was the impression Violet had received from Julia. "I do not care at all for the state in which powdering leaves my hair."

Mother's pretended show of regal censure slipped on the instant. "Especially without the benefit of Lavinia's ability to salvage even the worst of hair disasters."

"I do wish she could have come with us," Violet said. "I wouldn't for the world have pulled her from her family, but I do miss her, and not merely because my hair is suffering without her."

Violet slipped her prosthetic arm through Mother's arm. They had needed time to perfect this arrangement, and it still felt a little awkward. If she could manage the seemingly impossible and design a prosthesis with moveable fingers, she could rest her false arm more naturally on her mother's arm. It was a small thing, but those small things piled atop each other.

"You did powder your hair before the ladies visited yesterday," Mother said.

"I thought it best to begin our acquaintance with as few controversies as possible."

"Wise," Mother said with a nod.

They walked beneath a canopy made entirely of carefully grown and cultivated trees so closely interwoven that the branches appeared to be an actual roof above their heads. The gardens at Livingsley Hall were not as carefree as those at Irthing Grange, but they were surprising in the best of ways.

"Mrs. Overton said the nearest city of any size is Carlisle. We might find someone there who could, to some small degree, fill Lavinia's shoes. Perhaps even a promising governess."

"How far away is Carlisle?" Violet asked.

"From what I gathered, we would need to stay overnight," Mother answered. "But the entire trip and our efforts there could be accomplished in two days."

Violet liked that idea very much indeed. A bit of a journey and a change of scenery. She did enjoy being at home and having the stability of that to return to, but she also enjoyed seeing bits of the world. It helped keep her spirits up, which, in turn, helped her maintain her sunny disposition. As home was not currently available to her, undertaking a journey would prove more than welcome.

"Mr. Fortier is coming this way." Mother spoke a bit under her breath.

Violet easily spotted him on the path ahead. He was the most pleasing combination of humble and elegant she'd ever known in a gentleman, but somehow, the contradiction didn't feel inconsistent at all.

"He was wonderfully kind to Georgie the other day," Violet said. "He helped her find books and listened to her speak of her interests."

"I've been impressed with what I've seen of him." There was no mistaking the conspiratorial look Mother gave her.

"Are you scheming?"

Mother shook her head. "Only pondering."

"Pondering if you remember any words in French?" Violet pretended to be genuinely asking.

"Nonsense, dear." Mother turned all-too-innocent eyes on her. "You and Mr. Fortier both speak English. That will work as well as anything."

"As well *for what*?"

"I leave that to you, Violet." She patted Violet's left arm.

"Best pat the other one, Mother, so I can't ignore it."

They both laughed. For the first six months after Violet's amputation, they'd not been able to find humor in any of it. There'd been a tremendous number of tears and untold frustrations. Violet had eventually found her way again, but these moments when they laughed together brought a surge of gratitude for how far they had all come.

Violet adjusted her lace undersleeves to lay over her left hand more fully. With her arm threaded through Mother's, her shawl was not providing its usual disguise.

Mr. Fortier reached them in the next moment. He bowed quite properly. "A pleasure to cross paths with you, Mrs. Ridley, Miss Ridley."

"It is our pleasure as well." Mother returned the greeting with a curtsy.

Violet offered one as well, the effort slipping her arm from her mother's.

"I must offer my gratitude for your kindness to Georgiana in the library," Mother said.

"I was more than recompensed by the delight of her company. The *petite fillette* is very bright and personable."

"Not everyone is patient with precocious children," Violet said.

His smile, though small, was unmistakably amiable. Everything about him was quiet but not in a shy way. He seemed to be a person who thought a great deal, pondered, wondered, listened.

"Are you fond of children?" Mother asked Mr. Fortier as he walked alongside them.

"I am. I have a niece in France. She is two years old, and I have seen her only once, shortly after she was born, but I fully adore her. I could not help but hope, as I spoke with your niece, that little Adéle grows to be as precocious as Miss Georgie."

"Does Mr. Barrington share your appreciation for somewhat impertinent children?" Violet asked.

"He was not displeased with her presence."

Violet studied him. He'd made the declaration so matter-of-factly. "He seemed a bit vexed."

"He often does," Mr. Fortier said. "But he is not."

"And that is why you call him Grumpy Uncle." She glanced in Mother's direction, unsure if she'd heard the Gents' monikers for each other. But Mother had hung back, leaving more than a small gap between herself and Violet and Mr. Fortier.

"Who told you about Grumpy Uncle?" Mr. Fortier asked.

"Julia."

"She quickly learned all our secrets." He did not seem upset by that turn of events.

"Do you ever attempt to tease him from his grumpiness?" She was quite determined to do so herself after all.

"I haven't a knack for that, I fear. But Lord Jonquil and Stanley Cummings—another friend, who passed away a few years ago—were better at it than anyone. They could even convince him to participate in a great deal of mischief and merrymaking." Mr. Fortier's expression turned more thoughtful. "He's not been the same since Stanley died."

"Lord Jonquil or Mr. Barrington?"

"Both, truly. Both of them. All of us."

So much grief lay in those words. "You must have loved Stanley very much."

"We are all like brothers to each other. Stanley was no different."

Violet didn't overly care for the idea of continuing to tease Mr. Barrington if his grumpiness was, in fact, grief. "Does anyone still try to tease your Grumpy Uncle from his doldrums?"

"We do, and we are sometimes successful. None of us dislikes that he's reserved. But we do miss the lighter-hearted version of who he used to be."

"And you would not object if someone were to make efforts to bring lightness to him?"

"Not at all." Mr. Fortier shook his head. "We would consider ourselves forever indebted to any person who managed it."

That decided her. She would not give up her scheme. Grumpy Uncle would smile and laugh, and his heart would be lightened before she departed Livingsley Hall. She was determined that he would.

Chapter Eight

One hour.

Kes had one hour in which to take time for himself before his duties as host claimed his attention once more. But what to begin with?

He was tempted to simply sit in silence for sixty minutes to try to regain the energy to be social. His goal of earning membership in the Royal Society couldn't be realized without discovering, explaining, or inventing something of significance. And he still hadn't found even a moment to discover what his brother had sent him. Two days had passed. Inexcusable. What if Everett was awaiting a response?

That made his decision for him. Disappointing people never sat easily on his mind.

He returned to his library and the large, stately desk inside. On the shelves directly beside it, the burlap-wrapped parcel remained where Kes had placed it shortly after receiving it.

Still baffled by its shape and weight, he placed the package on his desk. The twine didn't easily untie; Everett never did anything halfway. In the end, Kes used a penknife and cut the twine away. The burlap unwrapped easily after that, and he peeled it back to reveal something he had not been expecting.

It was a small, metal strongbox. It would easily fit on a lap and could be carried without too much difficulty. The surface was plain and unornamental. He'd never seen one quite like it. These tended to be quite large and quite ornate. Why would Everett send him this?

A folded, sealed bit of parchment had been tied to the top, his name written across it. Kes cut it free. The wax seal on the back was his family's crest. He broke it and unfolded the thick paper.

Kester,

This arrived from the Admiralty. It has been stored with a great many unclaimed items from various naval ships. Nothing identifiable was found with it, and the key is sadly missing. An enterprising undersecretary took rubbings of the sides in search of clues and found, barely visible on the bottom, the inscription "K. Barrington."

When you sort out what it is, please send word. Rosabel and I are overwhelmed with curiosity.

Yours, etc.,
Everett

The Admiralty? Kes had never in his life been onboard a naval ship. And he had never owned a strongbox like this one. Why would his name be etched into a strongbox found aboard one?

Kes turned it over carefully—he didn't know what was inside after all—and looked for the inscription that had sent the box to him. It was so covered in scratches he was amazed anyone had found a single letter among them, let alone an entire name. Kes couldn't find the inscription referred to.

He set the strongbox on the desk once more. Its keyhole was on the lid, directly in the center. But the letter said there was no key.

How was he to open a strongbox without a key? It couldn't be pried open; it was held closed in multiple places by a complicated system of bars and levers turned by a substantial metal purpose-made key.

Everett hadn't sent him a task. He'd sent him a mystery. And yet another distraction.

The desk he sat at contained several journals' worth of ideas and sketches. They were his best chance for acceptance into the Royal Society. He ought to be focusing on that in what little time he had to himself.

His eyes wandered to the tallboy on the side of the room. Atop it, several small miniatures were set out. One of his parents when they were young and newly married. His brother who had died in childhood. A miniature of Everett and their sister, Bellamy, as well as a small painting of the family home in Norfolk. Why was it his eyes were always drawn to the people he'd lost?

He forcibly pulled his attention back to his desk and the strongbox sitting there. Solving logical mysteries was easier than dissecting his unending grief.

Easier and far less painful.

He tucked the strongbox under his right arm, using his other arm to help hold it up, and left the library in search of Aldric. If anyone could help solve this mystery, the General could.

The first of the Gents he crossed paths with, though, was Lucas.

Lucas eyed the strongbox with obvious curiosity. "Planning to unseal a will tonight?"

"Hoping to solve a mystery."

Aldric and Niles stepped into the corridor in the next instant. Lucas waved them over.

"This arrived from my brother," Kes said. "The Admiralty sent it to him."

"What connection does Everett have to the Navy?" Niles asked.

"None."

"Then why did they send him that?" Aldric motioned to the strongbox.

"Because it has my name etched on it."

That earned him looks of shocked confusion that likely matched the one he'd worn upon reading Everett's letter.

From a few paces away, a royal edict reached them. "We ought not stand about in corridors like confused felines."

"His Majesty does not approve," Lucas said under his breath.

"His Majesty is also not wrong," Aldric said. "To the drawing room, Gents."

One did not ignore a directive from the General. They made their way to his chosen destination, Lucas quickly explaining things to Digby as he joined them and then again to Henri, whom they snatched up along the way.

The six of them settled into the drawing room. Time yet remained before they needed to dress for the evening meal.

Kes set the box on his lap. "This was found in storage amongst things unclaimed from the country's naval fleet. It was, apparently, left behind by someone. The information I received did not indicate how long it had been waiting to be identified. A rubbing done of the sides of the box showed that, amongst the many scratches, was the inscription 'K. Barrington.' As I've never owned a box like this and have never been aboard a naval ship, I cannot imagine why my name is on it."

"Perhaps it belongs to a different K. Barrington," Niles suggested.

That had occurred to him. "The solving of this mystery appears to have been handed over entirely to me."

"I will assume there was no key provided," Aldric said, reaching for the box. "Otherwise, you'd have opened it already."

Kester handed the box to him. “No key.”

The Gents gathered around their General, asking an endless chain of questions none of them had answers to. They could find no breaks in the seal of the lid, no obvious weaknesses in the box.

“Without a key,” Aldric said, “I don’t know how we’ll open it.”

“We? This is to be a group effort?” Kes asked.

“Of course,” Lucas said. “If there’s one thing the Gents cannot resist, it’s a mystery.”

“I believe you mean ‘an opportunity to be nosey.’” Kes did his best to look and sound grumpy despite the smile tugging at his lips. He sighed and shook his head. “It is a very good thing I endure you all.”

“Endure?” Digby tsked. “You *enjoy* us.”

“In small doses, Your Majesty.”

They laughed off his grumpiness, as always. He wasn’t entirely joking though. He did need some time to himself. But he would far rather live with exhaustion than with even more regret.

Chapter Nine

VIOLET HAD, ON ANY NUMBER of occasions, spent an evening with neighbors and friends, indulging in parlor games. She was deeply pleased to discover that the Gents fancied such things as well. She sat among them and her parents a week into her sojourn at Livingsley Hall as preparations were made for what promised to be a rousing game of the three kingdoms. Lord Jonquil had at first suggested hide-and-seek, but that had been laughingly dismissed in favor of this more clever contest.

Guessing games were among her favorites, but this was one she hadn't played often. The aim was for one participant to guess a word the others chose but to which he or she was not privy. The one doing the guessing was permitted a maximum of six questions in which to discover the chosen word.

Mr. Fortier had been selected to slip out of the room first. Those remaining inside had decided upon *fleur de lis* as the word he was meant to guess. Violet exchanged an amused glance with her mother and father; they enjoyed games of intellect as much as she did.

Their resident Frenchman returned to the room, his demeanor as serene and content as ever. "Has a selection been made?"

"One has," Lord Aldric answered.

Mr. Fortier stood among them all. His eyes glided over each person but stopped on her. He posed his first question, the one that always began each guesser's attempt. "To which kingdom does the thing thought of belong?"

The answer was not as simple as it might seem on the surface. *Fleur de lis* was, in fact, a flower, placing it in the vegetable kingdom. It was also a symbol used throughout France in carvings and manuscripts and jewelry and such, placing it in the mineral kingdom. Animal was the only one she could eliminate. Since the symbol was itself based on the flower, she chose to identify *that* as its primary definition.

"I assert," she said, "that the item belongs to the vegetable kingdom."

He studied her a moment. Had he sorted that there was more to her answer than seemed on the surface? That was, after all, a common difficulty in this game.

"*Merci*," he said after a moment, then turned to Mother. "Madame Ridley," he offered a little bow, "would you assert that the thing thought of, which belongs to the vegetable kingdom, is valued more for its usefulness or its aesthetic appeal?"

Mother set one gloved hand atop the other, her posture and presence as polished and sophisticated as ever while she pondered the question. "While the thing may have some useful purposes, its aesthetic appeal is its more defining characteristic."

"*Merci beacoup*." Without hesitation, Mr. Fortier turned his attention to Lord Jonquil. "You, my lord, are unquestionably the most versed of the Gents in the area of flowers, which are, of those things belonging to the vegetable kingdom, decidedly favored for their aesthetic appeal."

Lord Jonquil only smiled ever more broadly, neither denying nor objecting to the assertion of his area of expertise.

"Is the item thought of a particularly well-known variety of flower?" Mr. Fortier asked.

"It is both a flower and quite well known," Lord Jonquil said.

"*Merci*." Mr. Fortier turned to Julia. "Does this flower grow in the walled garden at Brier Hill?"

"*Oui. Il pousse dans le jardin.*"

Violet didn't speak French beyond the occasional word. She did recognize *oui* as "yes."

Mr. Fortier did not turn to another player. The rules of the game allowed him to ask questions of whomever he wished whether or not he'd asked a question of that participant already. "Might one accurately say that speaking your answer in French might have some significance to the item chosen?"

"One might," she replied.

"Only one question remaining," Lord Aldric warned.

With a pleased expression entirely devoid of arrogance or conceit, Mr. Fortier said, "I am not in need of another. I guess the thing thought of is *la fleur de lis*."

The room erupted in laughter and applause and congratulations for a game well played.

Father leaned a bit closer to Violet. "I like Mr. Fortier. He is intelligent and seems an altruistic gentleman."

Her parents had begun pressing the possibility of her developing tender feelings for Mr. Fortier. She'd been tempted to tell them directly that she'd nothing but the earliest inklings of friendship for the gentleman and to insist that was terribly unlikely to change. But contradicting her parents and dashing what hopes they might harbor was hardly in keeping with her designation as the family's source of encouragement and positivity. A less direct, if frustratingly less effective, approach was decidedly best.

"Mother likes Mr. Fortier as well," Violet said to her father. "Best show *yourself* intelligent and altruistic. You may have competition."

The teasing was received precisely as she knew it would be. Father laughed and squeezed Mother's hand, which he'd been holding throughout the game.

Violet knew her parents were intrigued by Mr. Fortier, and not necessarily on their own behalf. They were not eager to see her married off as some parents were with their daughters who'd passed twenty, as she had, but she knew they did have hopes for her, hopes that paralleled her own.

And her parents were not wrong in their assessment of Mr. Fortier. She had enjoyed her interactions with him and anticipated with pleasure any future ones. But she felt that way about all the Gents. They were showing themselves wonderful companions, precisely the sort of friends she'd long dreamed of being embraced by.

If she could find a means of seeing herself accepted by them, as Julia had been, she would be delighted beyond words. Maintaining her facade of constant cheer would not be terribly challenging among them nor as tiring as it often was. They were themselves a ray of hopeful sunshine.

The night proved an utter lark. They all took their turn at guessing. Some were successful; some were not. Laughter was abundant. Intelligence was evident. Mother and Father were never made to feel unwanted despite being of a different generation and having come up from the merchant class. It gave Violet hope. And she had seldom enjoyed herself so much during an evening.

She reentered the sapphire-draped drawing room to take her second turn at guessing. The moment alone in the corridor had allowed her to double-check that her shawl and undersleeves still hid her arm well. She was able to return fully confident that she would need to make no explanations.

Mr. Barrington had grown a touch less enthusiastic during the last couple of rounds of play. Mr. Fortier had said teasing him from his irritability had proven efficacious in the past.

Violet took up the effort in that moment. To Mr. Barrington, she posed the opening question. "To which kingdom does the thing thought of belong?"

"Mineral." His response, while short, was not delivered in a terse tone.

"Does this thing of mineral construction possess great monetary value?"

"Not great monetary value."

Which meant it had value that was not necessarily monetary. "Of what variety is its value?"

He seemed pleased that she had sorted so quickly the significance of what he hadn't said. "It is of pragmatic value."

It was not his approval of her cleverness that captured her in that moment. It was his eyes. They'd come alive in a beautiful, heart-warming way. How had she not noticed before how lovely his eyes were? Perhaps it was his spectacles. Perhaps she'd not been paying attention.

"That is three questions, dear," Father warned.

Violet pulled herself together again. "Never fear. I will be triumphant."

She grinned at Mr. Barrington. He sat in stoic patience. The gentleman gave the impression of being displeased and grumpy at continuing his evening with them all, but she suspected that wasn't entirely true. His eyes, in fact, were still dancing.

"Is anyone in this room currently utilizing this pragmatically valuable thing belonging to the mineral kingdom?" she asked.

"Indeed." He dipped his head, then had to adjust his spectacles because they'd slipped a bit down his nose.

She suspected he was offering her another subtle clue: that he was the one utilizing the item. Clothing was made of fibers derived from the vegetable or animal kingdom and, as such, were classified in that area. Jewelry, such as his cravat pin, did belong to the mineral kingdom but was not particularly pragmatic. Buttons, pocket watches, watch chains, shoe buckles, all were made of minerals and were useful, but she suspected he would not have hinted that he was specifically the utilizer of the item in question if all the others in the room were in possession of it as well.

Something unique to him. Not made of animal or plant products. Pragmatic.

In the next moment, she knew. He'd given her more of a clue than she'd realized. "I guess the item is spectacles."

Her success was made apparent by the applause in the room. Some in the group had proven themselves quite adept at hiding their excitement when they'd correctly solved a riddle. She didn't bother. One ought not be ashamed of enthusiasm.

A smile pulled at the corners of Mr. Barrington's mouth. His smile was lovely. She'd simply meant to tease the Gent's Grumpy Uncle from his crabbiness. Mercy, she had not expected to discover her neighbor was, in fact, quite handsome.

"I propose we fill the miles to Carlisle by playing the three kingdoms and holding ourselves to difficult-to-guess items," Lord Aldric said. "I daresay it will make the journey pass faster."

"Is a trip to Carlisle in the planning?" Father perked up at the name of the city he, Mother, and Violet were in need of visiting.

"Mr. Fortier, Mr. Barrington, and I mean to travel there tomorrow, in fact," Lord Aldric said. "As the journey requires nearly a full day in each direction, we will not return until two days later. Lord and Lady Jonquil, Mr. Layton, and Mr. Newberry will remain at Livingsley Hall."

"Would we ruin your plans if our family made the trip at the same time?" Father asked. "We've been looking to travel to Carlisle and would enjoy doing so with company."

Lord Aldric and Mr. Fortier looked to Mr. Barrington. He was the host of the gathering after all.

"The more, the merrier." Mr. Barrington didn't seem insincere, yet neither could one honestly say he seemed enthusiastic.

Julia stepped up to the silk-upholstered sofa as Violet's parents delved into a discussion of the logistics of the suddenly planned excursion. "Are you utterly weary of the lot of us?" she asked.

Violet rose. "Not even the tiniest bit. I could pass every night precisely like this one."

"The Gents are a lively bunch," Julia said, almost in a tone of warning. "Even the most social of people require some time away from them."

They began a slow circuit of the room. Violet was careful to keep her right side the one nearest her new friend.

"Is that why you aren't making the journey to Carlisle?" Violet asked.

"We do not have business to see to there, and carriage rides have become a bit uncomfortable." Julia set her hand on her clearly pregnant belly. "I intend to avoid them whenever possible. And I won't complain about having Kester's library all to myself. He has an impressive collection of volumes."

Julia had said that studying and learning were passions of hers. In the time Violet had been at Livingsley Hall, she had discovered how very true that was. More often than not, Violet found her friend in a quiet corner with a book or bent over a sheet of parchment, making frantic notes on something she was learning. It was admirable, even if Violet didn't entirely relate to it.

Mr. Barrington rose from his seat and moved to a chair in the rounded alcove, taking up a book on a side table. He didn't seem unhappy being in company with his friends, but he didn't remain among them. It was little wonder no one could manage to permanently lift his spirits; he retreated too often.

"I really do wish you were coming to Carlisle," Violet said. "I suspect we could make quite a lark of it."

Julia slipped her arm through Violet's. Thank the heavens she'd positioned herself as she had. "I *am* fond of larks."

"As fond as your husband?"

Julia shook her head. "No one is as fond of larks as he is, and I suspect no one has as much energy for undertaking them as he does."

"Mr. Fortier said he and another friend of theirs, Stanley, were quite adept at teasing Grumpy Uncle from his low spirits."

Julia's countenance grew a bit heavier, and she didn't immediately answer.

"Have I said something wrong?"

"Stanley was my brother. Sometimes reminders of him strike more forcefully than I expect them to."

Her heart immediately ached for the lady. "Georgie's parents died two years ago. Sometimes mentions of them cause her such grief. At other times, she herself speaks of them with lightness and joy. I haven't sorted any pattern to it."

"I've discovered there is no logic to grief."

Mother had once described Violet's emotional struggles after her amputation as grief. That had also proven impossible to predict. She still, at times, found herself angry or sad over the change, though she'd grown far more accustomed to it over the past two years. Grief did indeed defy logic. "Have you discovered any secret to helping someone who is enduring it?"

"We had a little boy stay with us earlier this year who is himself mourning a devastating loss." Julia hooked a finger around the silver and blue-stone pendant she wore, a look of pondering pulling at her features. "Those things that helped him the most were actually quite simple. We showed him he was loved and safe with us. And we made certain he had ample opportunities for enjoyable pastimes."

"Distractions?"

"In some ways, yes but mostly moments when he felt unspoken permission to be happy."

Permission to be happy. Sometimes, Violet wished she had permission to be sad. *Be sunny or be silent.* There was no room in that for outward expressions of mourning, especially when she was helping a little girl navigate her own grief.

"Georgie might enjoy coming along on the jaunt to Carlisle," Violet thought out loud.

"She very well might. If, however, it is decided she will remain here, Lucas and I will happily look after her. We adore her already."

They sat on an obliging sofa.

"Do promise me," Julia said, her eyes dancing with mischief, "that you will continue your mission to nudge our grumpy friend a bit from his gloominess. You made headway tonight. I cannot wait to see what progress you make going forward."

"I think he enjoyed the three kingdoms."

"He seemed to especially appreciate how quickly you sorted his clues," Julia said. "He is quite intelligent and enjoys discovering other people who are as well."

He had seemed to enjoy the final turn, which the two of them had played exclusively. And, heavens, those eyes of his. She'd not been prepared for that. She was only just beginning to come to know him, to discover if there could be friendship between herself and her nearest neighbor. As unjustified as her parents' nudges toward Mr. Fortier were, her little heart palpitations over Mr. Barrington's lovely eyes were even more so.

She hoped she yet proved adept at bringing some lightness to their resident Grumpy Uncle and that they did prove friends in the end. That was plenty enough to be working toward on such a brief acquaintance.

Chapter Ten

The Dappled Chicken was not the only inn found in Carlisle, but it was the best of them and, therefore, where Kes had brought those who'd made the journey. He'd not intended to spend the morning of their second day wandering through the inn's side garden, but Henri and Aldric had found him unnecessary to their efforts, leaving him at loose ends.

Aldric was the strategist amongst them, yes, but Kes was the loyal assistant in any and all difficulties, the source of reason in their adventures and undertakings. Being useful was what he had to offer. He hadn't the first idea what to do with himself when the Gents were nearby but quite specifically didn't need him to be.

It was little wonder he hadn't a place in the Royal Society yet. A man who found *himself* confusing was hardly an intellectual giant.

Fate meant to add weight to that argument, it seemed. His wanderings in the garden brought him face-to-face with Miss Ridley and Miss Georgie. The bright smile on Miss Ridley's face sent his heart skipping a bit, as it always did. The passage of several days with her as a guest at his house and again here at this inn had not lessened her impact on him or the pull he felt to know her better.

"Mr. Barrington," she greeted in her usual cheerful tone. "We are well met. I didn't realize you meant to pass the morning here."

He dipped his head. "Are you enjoying your morning?"

"Violet always enjoys time spent in nature," Miss Georgie said. "She would live in a hedgerow like a sparrow if Aunt Ridley would allow it."

Miss Ridley laughed. "Are you saying I am bird-witted?"

Kes had always appreciated a clever turn of phrase. "Perhaps," he said, "she is accusing you of being flighty."

That earned him a laugh from his companions. He was not accustomed to being the one who made people laugh. It wasn't an unpleasant experience.

"I want to look for the chipmunk again," Miss Georgie said to her cousin. "I won't wander far."

"Go on, then. Stay to the garden path."

Miss Georgie skipped off, looking pleased as anything. It was a change in the girl from what Kes had seen before. She did not seem as weighed down or wary. Perhaps the out of doors was good for her spirits. He found himself pleased that he'd given her full permission to access the lake at Livingsley Hall. It would mean a greater chance of having his solitude there interrupted, but that would be worth sacrificing if it brought happiness to a child.

He motioned for Miss Ridley to resume her walk along the garden path. He kept pace beside her. As always, a shawl was pinned about her shoulders, falling in elegant waves over her arms.

"Did Mr. Fortier decide not to begin his search for an estate today?" Miss Ridley asked.

"He and Lord Aldric are, in fact, doing precisely that as we speak. It proved a *two*-person undertaking."

She studied him. "You must be disappointed to have come this far only to be left out of the errand you traveled here to complete."

Miss Ridley had sorted his feelings on the matter very quickly, but she likely didn't realize it wasn't merely a matter of not completing things he set his mind to. "I do like to be of use. But they are more than capable of undertaking the task without me. I don't have any concerns about this journey proving a wasted effort."

"Do you always measure success in such utilitarian terms?" She didn't sound disapproving, only curious.

"Mine is a mathematical and logical mind more than a fanciful one. I struggle to define anything by metrics that are not easily measurable."

"That must be exhausting."

He'd not ever evaluated the impact of his need to quantify things, of his need to say with certainty if a choice was right or wrong or an action of his useful or not. But she was correct. It was, in many ways, utterly exhausting.

"Your parents indicated they meant to see to business today," he said. "Have they gone about that and left you to the tending of your cousin?"

"They have, though I don't truly mind. Georgie is rather fun company, and this garden is lovely." There was hesitation in her answer.

"Did you have business *you* had hoped to undertake?"

She moved with a light fluidness, a testament to her happy disposition. "I was told you were perceptive. That is proving true."

As compliments went, it was small, but he found it radiating as warmth in his chest.

"I had wanted to walk to the high street," she said. "I meant to discover what shops Carlisle boasts. It is to be my nearest city of any size from this time forward but is not a quickly undertaken journey."

The garden was not a large one. They'd completed nearly half a circuit. It was a pleasant spot despite its diminutive size. The trees provided ample shade. The shrubbery gave interest to the late-autumn landscape. The breeze brought to him the light and increasingly familiar scent of her floral perfume. It ruffled the tasseled edge of her ever-present shawl.

"Was there anything in particular you were hoping to find?" Kes asked. "I could at least tell you if your search would have been in vain."

"A clockmaker's shop," she said, "which likely seems an odd destination to you."

He offered her a look of reassurance. "I can hardly declare that odd when I, too, had hoped to visit that shop while in Carlisle."

Her eyes brightened further. "You had?"

He nodded. Strongboxes' locking mechanisms often utilized clockwork. It seemed a good place to start. "If you think Miss Georgie wouldn't mind an excursion that doesn't include searching out chipmunks, we could pay a call at the clockmaker's shop while your parents are seeing to their business."

"You would accompany us?" She sounded genuinely pleased at the possibility.

Little did she realize she was offering him the chance to be useful. He needed that. "I would accompany you with pleasure."

Her smile turned to a grin. Did she ever look or sound anything other than happy? If she did, he hadn't seen it.

"Your declaration surprises me a little," she said.

"It surprised *me* a little as well."

Her left arm rested across her middle, tucked beneath her shawl, while her right lay atop the fringed fabric and the arm beneath. In some people, the posture would have looked defensive or unhappy. She made it seem far more like a joyous hug. "I intend to operate under the assumption that I am such lovely company that you cannot help but be pleased at the prospect of time spent with me, however out of character."

His smile came quickly in that moment. He was not an unhappy person, but shows of pleasure that arose without warning, without effort, without any embarrassment were a bit of a rare thing for him.

"Georgie," Miss Ridley called out to her cousin. "We are going to visit the high street."

The girl rushed over, the same excitement that marked her hunt for the chipmunk evident on her face now. "Truly?"

Miss Ridley nodded. "Mr. Barrington has offered to accompany us."

Miss Georgie eyed him with great focus. "Is there a bookshop on the high street?"

"There is," Kes said. "Though it is not so large as the shops found in London."

"Is it terribly far?" Miss Georgie asked.

Kes shook his head. "It is an easy walk from here."

She nodded firmly. "We will go there first."

He looked to Miss Ridley. "I see who is truly in charge of this venture."

"Georgie is *always* in charge," Miss Ridley said. "Always."

"Lead the way, Miss Georgie."

"I can't, sir. I don't know where we are going."

He bent a little to speak more directly to her. "I suspect, Miss Georgie, you are more intelligent than the rest of us."

"My Uncle Ridley says that I am quite clever. And Mr. Fortier said that too."

"They are clearly very perceptive." He straightened once more and offered his free arm to Miss Ridley. She watched him with a far more serious mien than she usually wore. "Is something amiss?"

"Everything is just lovely, Mr. Barrington. Just lovely."

Why, then, did she look as if she, who never stopped smiling, was trying to avoid growing emotional? As confusing as he was to himself, Miss Ridley was proving even more so.

Mr. Barrington's offer to accompany them to the high street had been as welcome as it had been surprising. But it was his kindness to Georgie that touched Violet the most. Mr. Fortier had insisted that his friend wasn't as standoffish as he sometimes seemed and that he had not been upset by Georgie's presence in his library a few days earlier. Because the Frenchman had shown himself unlikely to lie about such things, Violet had believed him on the surface but had harbored some doubts. She was pleased to have so many of those uncertainties put to rest now.

They had left word at the inn of their destination should Mother and Father return before they did, then the happy group had made the short journey to the high street, with Mr. Barrington guiding the way amidst a friendly and inconsequential discussion among them all. Georgie asked questions about things they saw, and Mr. Barrington answered with patience.

He had told Violet he didn't mind that he'd been left out of Mr. Fortier and Lord Aldric's efforts that day, but she hadn't been entirely convinced. He seemed to be grateful to have joined this new venture, yet she didn't doubt he liked to be alone more than he liked to be in company. She had told Julia that Mr. Barrington was a mystery. That was proving more and more true.

They slipped into the bookshop. It was a small space, but one filled near to bursting with various volumes. Books came dear, so Violet knew they might not be able to purchase everything that caught Georgie's eye, but there was no harm in looking. Should they find something within their means, it could be added to the library at Irthing Grange.

Georgie wandered from bookcase to bookcase, her eyes wide with excitement. She didn't even bother taking any volumes down or examining them more closely. She took delight in the simple pleasure of being surrounded by books.

Mr. Barrington remained at Violet's side, watching her cousin with every indication of enjoyment. "I liked books at her age. My brother and sister tormented me endlessly over it."

"Did they?"

He nodded. "They used to insist it was an oddity in me and that they could not imagine spending days on end with someone so dull as to lose himself between the covers of a book."

"Children might not appreciate that preference, but surely they have come to see the value in it now that they're older."

"My sister is married to a barrister, and his occupation keeps him forever tied to books. I have had the great joy of pointing out to her that she has needed to figuratively eat her words." Mr. Barrington tossed out one of his rare but dazzling smiles. Heavens, the sight of it did the oddest things to her heart.

"I never had a brother or sister," Violet said, looking away lest she never manage a sensible thought again. "Georgie is the closest I have."

The girl came skipping back over to them. To Mr. Barrington, she said, "Does this shop have any books about John Blanke?"

"I cannot say with certainty. We can ask the proprietor, as he is more likely to know. Have you a keen interest in John Blanke?"

Georgie nodded emphatically. "He is our ancestor, through my father and Violet's mother. We're certain of it."

He looked to Violet, though whether for confirmation or explanation, she wasn't sure.

"We cannot prove the connection, but it has long been taken as truth."

"Does anyone in your family share his musical abilities?" Mr. Barrington asked.

John Blanke was not an entirely unknown figure in English history, a famed musician from Africa who had joined the royal court two centuries earlier. Yet, many people with whom she had shared this connection of which her family was quite proud had responded to her revelation with empty, glassy-eyed stares.

Not Mr. Barrington. He had known of John Blanke without having to be told.

"My mother is quite musical, as was Georgie's father. And from all my mother tells me of her mother, she was a remarkably talented musician also."

"I haven't personally a talent for music, but I do appreciate it," Mr. Barrington said. "Lord Jonquil's mother has a beautiful singing voice. I've always envied her it."

He waved over the shop proprietor.

"How may I be of assistance?" the man asked.

Mr. Barrington looked to Georgie. Many gentlemen of rank and station would never defer to a child, but Mr. Barrington did so without hesitation.

Georgie, who did not generally lack in boldness, took up the opportunity. "Have you any books about John Blanke, trumpeter to His Majesty Henry VII?" She spoke with such pride in their family's most famous name.

"None exclusively about him," the man said. "But he might be mentioned in a couple of books we have on the topic of Henry VII's reign."

Georgie pouted. "I'm not interested in reading about a stodgy old king."

Violet bit back a laugh at the shop owner's expression of shock. Few in England would refer to any of their monarchs as a "stodgy old king," at least not out loud in public whilst in conversation with strangers. But as Henry VII was long dead, there was no risk of being tried for treason.

"I haven't any books about John Blanke," the shop proprietor said.

Georgie's pout turned to a quiet sort of sadness. Though the girl did her utmost to tuck it away, Violet could see she was deeply disappointed.

"Do not lose hope, Miss Georgie," Mr. Barrington said. "I can send letters to a few bookshops in London. Perhaps one of them might have a book that is to your liking."

"Violet said there might not be any written about only him." Georgie turned pleading eyes to their neighbor. "It makes John Blanke seem unimportant, but he isn't. My father told me John Blanke was important."

Violet hadn't realized the reason Georgie's heart was so set on a book dedicated to John Blanke. For her father's sake, she wanted to solidify that connection.

"Your father was absolutely correct," Mr. Barrington said. "John Blanke was important, and you have every reason to be proud of your connection to him."

The tiniest shimmer of tears glistened in Georgie's eyes. "What if there aren't any books about him?"

"I don't mean to give up, Miss Georgie Watkins," Mr. Barrington said. "I even know of bookshops on the Continent. I'll write to them if need be."

Georgie smiled a little. "No one there will know who he is. He lived only in England and Africa."

"Then perhaps we should write to bookshops in Africa."

Her smile turned to a small laugh. "I think you're teasing me."

Mr. Barrington hooked an eyebrow upward. "I *never* tease about books."

Georgie's spirits were well and truly lifted. Once again, Grumpy Uncle showed himself to be deeply considerate. It was little wonder Lord Jonquil and Julia's brother Stanley had made such an effort to tease him into happier moods. It was a shame how often his good heart was overshadowed by his tendency to grow aloof.

They remained a little while longer at the bookshop, casually perusing what was there but all of them knowing they would likely not buy anything on this visit. After a time, they stepped out, Georgie and Violet each slipping an arm through one of Mr. Barrington's, with Georgie positioning herself so that Violet could use her right arm without having to explain the necessity.

"Our next stop is the clockmaker's," Mr. Barrington said to Georgie. "It will likely not be the most interesting shop for you, but I feel I can trust you will behave despite your boredom."

"I know how to behave." Georgie sounded a little offended by the insinuation that she might not.

Mr. Barrington did not ruffle up at the somewhat sharp response but simply nodded and led them to their next destination.

Violet was grateful to have been afforded this opportunity. Ladies hadn't as much freedom as gentlemen. She couldn't make the visit entirely alone, and she hadn't a lady's maid to accompany her. Without Mr. Barrington's generosity, she'd have been out of options. But with him there, how was she to go about obtaining what she needed without having to explain her secret efforts at designing for herself a new prosthesis?

They stepped inside, and Georgie promptly sat herself on a chair and began visually inspecting the many clocks in the shop from her perch. That would keep her occupied for a time but not indefinitely.

"I know you had hoped to come peruse the shop," Violet said to Mr. Barrington. "Please feel free to do so without worrying that I will feel abandoned. We needn't be in each other's pockets."

"If I did not know any better," he said, "I would think you were getting rid of me."

"Perhaps I am," she said with an overdone look of perfect seriousness.

A little hint of amusement entered his brown eyes. He bowed, then slipped his spectacles back into place, a mannerism she suspected he didn't realize he employed as often as he did but one she found rather endearing. He wandered away a pace, and she had room enough to begin her own perusal.

People generally looked in at clockmakers' shops in order to purchase timepieces or have them repaired rather than to obtain individual parts. But she hoped it wasn't entirely impossible to do so.

This shop was run by a man and woman who, based on their interactions, were husband and wife. The woman gave the impression of being pleasant and approachable. As Violet did not wish to draw attention to her purchases, discovering not only the location of the shop but also that one of the proprietors seemed a friendly sort was a stroke of luck.

"Do you sell clockwork parts?" Violet asked. "I realize it is likely not a common request, but someone in my household, who is a bit eccentric and admittedly odd, takes great pleasure in tinkering with such things. I would very much like to obtain a few bits and baubles that this person might fiddle with." What she didn't say was that she herself was the eccentric oddity looking for bits and baubles to experiment with.

"We do, in fact," the woman said with a knowing look, one that didn't say, "I know you're speaking of yourself," but rather, "We all have one or two in our families who are odd."

Violet was quickly brought around to a wall containing a bank of drawers with labels identifying the contents, everything from gears and watch cases to winding keys and clock hands.

"Which things would prove most useful to someone who enjoys designing moveable mechanical . . . things?" Violet attempted to get a point across without giving away too much.

"It is difficult to say when one doesn't know what is being made," the woman said.

"I wish I had more information to give you."

The proprietress didn't press. "A variety of the most useful things'd be best, I'd wager. You can most certainly return if your relative gains a better idea of what is being made and what is needed."

"I will."

She was forthwith supplied with a variety of gears in a multitude of sizes, winding keys, springs, rods, and wires. The bits were wrapped in paper and tied with twine. She hadn't the slightest idea if what she had would be useful, but at least she had a beginning. All she needed now was a place at Livingsley Hall where she could begin her efforts. Once they returned to Irthing Grange, she could manage it in her bedchamber, but she didn't want to wait that long. She was letting herself dream, and dreams were fragile things.

Mr. Barrington met her at the door of the shop, his own twine-tied bundle in hand. It looked like hers: too small and flat to be a clock, too large for a pocket watch. Had he also purchased gears and such? He had not been near the drawers of parts while she had been.

"Did you find what you were looking for?" he asked, indicating her parcel.

"I did," she said. "Did you?"

"I hope so."

That was not the answer she'd been expecting. And yet, it was the most accurate answer she could have given as well.

"What were you looking for?" she asked.

His expression quickly took on more than a hint of his Grumpy Uncle demeanor: not unfriendly but more closed off than it had been before. "A few odds and ends." He motioned for Georgie to stand and walk with them out of the shop. And he didn't speak any further of his purchase.

Curious.

Chapter Eleven

THEY ALL GATHERED FOR THEIR evening meal that night in the inn's private dining room. The day had been busy for all of them, though they'd been undertaking different endeavors. Mother and Father had gone in search of a lady's maid and a governess. They'd even entertained hopes of finding *two* lady's maids, one for Violet and one for Mother. Unfortunately, they had returned disappointed on all counts. Seated next to her at the table, they continued to discuss in low tones their ongoing difficulties in that area.

"Perhaps we would do best to travel farther afield," Father said. "Were we in Portsmouth, we could find someone without much difficulty. But these country cities rely far more heavily on hiring fairs than do the larger port cities. There's a possibility we won't be able to hire new staff until the next one is held."

"That could be months." Mother sounded increasingly discouraged. The styles of the day were not easily achieved. And though Violet did her best, she knew she was not as skilled or swift as her mother needed her to be. Even before her amputation, Violet hadn't possessed a particular knack for arranging hair. She was a little better at the cosmetics required of formal gatherings, but hair and powdering was not a skill she claimed. Mother did a fine job of making Violet presentable, but it mattered more to her mother.

"I'm not certain what we can do about a governess," Father said. "Georgie needs one and not merely to have someone to look after her. Her mind is active and curious. She'll quickly go mad if unable to learn new things and have someone to guide those pursuits."

Another legitimate worry. Violet was doing her best in that area also, but she knew her cousin needed more.

Violet was not being excluded from the discussion, so she didn't feel out of line entering it. "Perhaps we might ask Mr. Barrington or one of the other gentlemen if they know of a best approach to filling the vacancies." Violet was careful to keep her outward aspect hopeful and as free of doubt as she could manage, keeping her own concerns to herself. "Lady Jonquil would likely also have some thoughts for us."

"I hate to impose upon them further," Mother said. "I fear we have proven a burden already, and Mr. Barrington does not give the impression of being overly pleased."

That anxiety, Violet could easily address. "I'm told by Lady Jonquil and Mr. Fortier that Mr. Barrington, though quiet with a tendency to keep to himself, doesn't dislike company nor does he begrudge people's presence in his home. He is simply a little uncomfortable when interacting."

"That does seem to match what I've observed of him," Father said. "Still, we must be careful not to push him beyond what he is willing to endure. If we are to be neighbors for years to come, we'd best begin on a good footing."

"Indeed," Mother said.

Violet looked over the group. She didn't think any of them begrudged the presence of the Ridley family.

Mr. Barrington sat a bit apart from everyone else. He was bent over a paper, writing something. His friends didn't seem concerned by his distance. For her part, Violet was intrigued. He was, in so many ways, a contradiction.

"Were you able to find anything promising in your search?" Father asked Mr. Fortier.

"Alas, no." The French flavor of his words added a certain poetic quality to them. "There were three properties in this area available, but none proved suited to my needs."

"A shame," Mother said. "Both for your own wishes and for the area. All those living hereabouts would benefit from having you amongst us."

Mr. Fortier reddened a little. "I thank you for that, *madame*."

"Why is it you are not looking for an estate in France?" Father asked. "You must miss it."

"*Oui.* I miss my family there. I miss Paris and our country home. I long for a hot bowl of ratatouille on cold days." His voice had turned nostalgic. "But England is home to me now. I would not wish to live anywhere else. I should like a bit of it to call my own."

"We'll find something," Lord Aldric said. "I haven't any doubt."

"Niles has family in Cornwall," Mr. Fortier said. "They might be able to inform him of anything available there."

That launched them into a discussion of other people they knew. While the names they mentioned were at times unfamiliar to her, others were so well known to the entire kingdom that she was shocked to realize her new acquaintances were on friendly terms with such exalted individuals. She had been received warmly among them and sometimes forgot how different her origins were. These gentlemen belonged to the highest rung of Society. Her family had only just lifted themselves out of the realm of merchants.

But she would not allow herself to worry about that. She certainly wouldn't express it. She was not meant to add to anyone else's worries no matter that it sometimes multiplied her own.

Georgie was curled up in a ball on a small settee at the side of the room. She had fallen asleep almost immediately after taking her evening meal. A walk about the grounds surrounding the inn, a jaunt up to the high streets, and looking in various shops, all on the heels of the long journey the day before. It was a wonder she'd stayed awake long enough to eat.

Violet's gaze, however, did not remain on her small cousin for long. It slipped again to Mr. Barrington. It did that a lot. *Quite* a lot.

"May I ask, Mr. Ridley," Mr. Fortier said, "how you came to hear of Irthing Grange being available?"

"I can share with you what I learned and experienced in our estate search," Father offered.

"I would be greatly indebted to you, *monsieur*."

Lord Aldric, Father, and Mr. Fortier discussed estates and planning and men of business. The two gentlemen spoke to the elevated merchant like an equal. She appreciated that about this group. She appreciated that about Livingsley Hall. They weren't made to feel like interlopers. She suspected Mr. Barrington would prefer they return home sooner rather than later, but he never treated them like a burden. Perhaps that was why she felt eager to lift his spirits. He showed others thoughtful consideration, and he ought to experience kindnesses in return.

As Mother was drawn into the discussion of homes and estates, Violet found an opportunity to slip away from the table. She moved as quickly and unobtrusively as she could to where Mr. Barrington sat. He was nearer the fire than the rest of them and was so engrossed in his work that he didn't notice her approach. She sat in an empty chair across from him and quickly adjusted her shawl. Ought she to address him or leave him to work uninterrupted?

She hadn't yet decided when he spoke without looking up at her. "Were your parents able to find a lady's maid and a governess?"

"No, they weren't."

"I'm sorry to hear that. I'm certain that must be a frustration for you." His tone was both quietly conversational and sincerely empathetic despite his not even looking up. How he managed to be contradictory even in the way he spoke, she didn't know. Still, he was entirely correct: the prospect of needing to wait months longer to fill those positions was frustrating.

"We'll sort it all, I'm certain of it," she said. "All will be well. I have no worries on that score."

"No worries at all?" He looked at her, confused, and, if she didn't miss her mark, a little intrigued by the mystery.

How the tables had turned.

She assumed a breezy expression, as if she hadn't a care in the world, something she'd long ago perfected. "Not any worries at all."

For just a moment, his eyes narrowed. Whatever worried him seemed to quickly be resolved. His attention returned to his work.

"May I ask what has you so engrossed this evening?" she asked.

"A little project I thought of while we were on our excursion this afternoon."

"Truly?" She leaned a little bit forward, hoping to get a glance at it.

"Your cousin was discouraged to have not found a book about John Blanke, and I was sorry for that. I hated seeing her so disappointed. I know she enjoys being out of doors and seems to particularly like lakes."

"We both do."

He nodded. "With your family newly arrived in the area, I suspect you do not know where most of the neighboring lakes are."

She moved her spindle-back chair closer to him, close enough that she could see what he was working on. He didn't object, so she didn't think it inappropriate to look. It appeared to be a map, one he had drawn while sitting there.

"This is Irthing Grange." He pointed to a shape on the paper which matched the outline of her home. "This is Livingsley Hall." He indicated a shape like his house. "And this is the lake on my estate," he said while indicating what was clearly the lake. "I've marked on here the lakes in the surrounding area that are not particular to any estate and, therefore, do not require any permission to access. I've also included paths for walking in nature and where to find particularly pleasant vistas."

She moved her eyes from the map to his face. "You did all this while sitting here?"

He shrugged as if it were absolutely nothing. "It may bring Georgie a bit of joy while she is searching for her book."

"She needs joy more than most children," Violet said. "She has known too much sorrow."

"I lost both my parents when I was only a handful of years older than she is. When I met the first of the Gents, I was still deeply mourning. They gave me reasons to be happy. Children who are grieving ought to be looked after."

"She grieves so deeply."

He nodded. His gaze shifted to the fire. "I recognized it in her eyes. I saw it in my own reflection often enough."

With her right hand, Violet reached out and squeezed his silk-covered arm. "Thank you for this," she said. "And your kindness to her today. Thank you for thinking of her."

He set his other hand atop hers, a gentle and friendly touch. Her thoughts calmed in ways they didn't often. She had found a friend in him. She was meant to be the sunshine in every cloud, the unceasing ray of hope and cheer, but sometimes, she needed someone else to bear a burden, to reach out to her with an offering of encouragement. That she'd found that in the one they called Grumpy Uncle was both surprising and delightful.

He was uncomfortable in company, preferred quiet and solitude. He was also generous and compassionate. He did not hesitate to offer empathy to a grieving child.

"As your family's nearest neighbor," he said, "I hope I am able to continue offering Miss Georgie opportunities for happiness."

"I am infinitely grateful that *you* are our nearest neighbor and not Lady Collington." Violet assumed a feigned expression of solemnity. "Though I do have it on good authority that Hoppleforth is so grand, it makes Livingsley Hall look like a chicken coop."

A brilliant smile lit his face. But it didn't stop there. He laughed, the sound almost musical.

"Wait until you meet her husband," Mr. Barrington said, still grinning. "They are a match made in . . . well, not exactly in heaven, but they are as perfectly suited as two people can be."

"How nice for them." Violet tried to sound sober, knowing it would add humor to the observation, but his smile was undoing her far too much for anything but an answering smile of her own and an inward sigh.

She enjoyed his company more with every conversation, every interaction, every moment together. She'd hoped to find a friend in this corner of the kingdom. That she'd discovered one in her nearest neighbor was a delightful turn of events, one she didn't have to *pretend* to be happy about.

Chapter Twelve

On the first morning back at Livingsley Hall, Kes rose early, before any of his guests and before his duties as host would demand his attention, ate his breakfast in hurried silence, left the house without a backward glance, and made his way to the outbuilding where he worked on his inventions. The building was just as he had left it months earlier. He'd had so many distractions, so many travels, that he hadn't been inside in ages. The space was dusty and a bit damp—a seemingly contradictory situation all too familiar in England—but, overall, the space had weathered his absence well.

He set the mysterious strongbox on the large worktable inside, then pulled from the pocket of his wool coat the bundle he'd purchased at the clockmaker's shop and set it on the table beside the box. He opened the windows. Doing so would let the cold in, but it would also let the stale air out and make the space more amenable to what he needed. The day was overcast, as it nearly always was in Cumberland. A light breeze rustled the trees outside. The lake shimmered in shades of silver and gray. Framed as it was by the window, the view would make a fine backdrop to the morning's endeavors.

He turned from the window to face the space. There was ample room to work, though the outbuilding was not overly large. It was smaller than most of the guest bedchambers at Livingsley Hall but not by much. He had room enough for a worktable, several smaller tables on the room's edge, a tall bank of drawers, and shelves on nearly every wall. He'd spent a great deal of time in this place when he'd first inherited the estate, chasing his seemingly impossible dream of membership in the Royal Society.

Stanley hadn't thought it was impossible. He'd encouraged him and believed in him. He'd helped Kes work through his grief after his parents had died. But Kes didn't seem able to find any degree of peace with Stanley's passing. Ignoring that pain was getting harder all the time.

Kes took a slow, deep breath. He hadn't come to his sanctuary to think about Stanley. He'd come to put away the things he'd purchased in Carlisle and to try his hand once more at opening the mysterious metal box.

A quick tug on the twine untied the bundle of clock parts. He peeled back the paper. Gears and winding mechanisms and rods and wires and any number of other odds and ends sat inside. He'd needed to replenish his supply. Miss Ridley's wish to look in at the clockmaker's shop had been a fortunate coincidence.

Kes began sorting the bits and pieces, piling them according to their uses and sizes. It was not the most exciting part of his experiments, but there was something satisfying about undertaking a task that was easily completed, something with absolutely no emotional complications.

Stanley had been the first to discover Kes's workshop, which was then a small outbuilding at the Barrington family estate and had christened it the Cabin of Cleverness. That had always made Kes laugh. Stanley managed that even in difficult moments. But he never made a fellow feel laughed *at*. And somehow, Stanley made everything seem like an adventure.

Kes had often been annoyed with him during their Eton days, but he'd give almost anything to have even one of those "annoying" moments back. Lucas and Stanley had forcibly pulled him into their group of friends and, in so doing, had changed his life for the better.

There was no one in the world like Stanley Cummings. The grief of his death continually tore at Kes's heart. Nothing had been the same since he'd died. Nothing.

There he was again, thinking of the people he wasn't with. He pushed his thoughts to where the Gents meant to go next, where Henri would eventually find his own estate, what activity they ought to choose that evening. And yet he knew that long before the evening was over, he'd be ready for it to be finished. Was it possible for a person to be equally in need of company *and* isolation?

He pulled a few jars from shelves and began dropping the sorted items into them. After a Gents adventure had taken them to Scotland several years earlier, Kes had passed through a small village on the border between Northumberland and Cumberland, where he'd made the acquaintance of an apothecary. They still corresponded, and from time to time, the man sent Kes apothecary jars for organizing his supplies. The distraction of organizing was proving helpful in this moment.

Then into the silence of his workspace came a knock. Not just any knock but the particular rhythm Lucas, Stanley, he, and Digby had adopted as their own back at Eton.

Anytime he heard it, for just a moment, his mind would insist it was Stanley at the door. Then he'd remember that wasn't possible. It felt like losing him all over again every time. Over time, the pain had proven less sharp, but it never became less real.

The door opened just enough for Lucas to peek his head inside.

"I spotted you heading this way. I thought I'd see what your latest project is."

"And if I told you my project was avoiding you?" Kes muttered.

Lucas stepped inside. "I would say you need a new project." He snatched the strongbox off the table and examined it closely. "Have you sorted out anything new about this oddity?"

"Not yet. I still haven't managed to find where my name is scratched on it."

Lucas looked at all the tools and supplies spread out around the room. "Would any of these things help?" He tended to bounce a bit in place. The man had more energy than anyone Kes had ever known. He always seemed ready to burst out of his own skin. His eyes would sweep over a space, seeming to search for the next opportunity for excitement.

"If there is anything that can open the box, it's likely in here somewhere." Kes continued sorting his gears and springs and such into jars. "Or in the tiny sitting room on the ground floor of the Hall."

"Tools in a sitting room." Lucas shook his head. "I've debated since you first started keeping them there whether you'd simply run out of space in here or were getting disorganized in your old age."

"I'm younger than you are," Kes reminded him.

"That doesn't sound right." Lucas set the box down, giving Kes an overdone look of confusion. "Have you examined your sums on that?"

"Julia agrees with my mathematics," Kes said.

Lucas shrugged. "Then, you must be correct. You are, in fact, an infant."

"An infant with an unopenable strongbox." Kes tossed him a large winding key from the pile of clockwork mechanisms he was sorting. "Make yourself useful and see if this does anything."

"It's a strongbox, not a clock." Lucas tossed it back to him. "A chisel would probably be a better option."

"Tried it," Kes said.

"Prybar?"

"Too thick."

"Throwing it against a wall?"

Kes put his jar of small gears back on the shelf, setting the medium-sized-gears jar next to it.

"Stanley would have had dozens of suggestions for you," Lucas said. "And most of them would have been—"

"Intentionally preposterous." Stanley had *often* done precisely that when "helping" Kes with his inventions. "Yet, mixed in amongst the ridiculous would be suggestions that were absolutely genius."

"He was the greatest, wasn't he?" Lucas grinned broadly.

Lucas and Stanley had been friends literally their entire lives, born on neighboring estates within months of each other. Yet, Lucas managed to talk about Stanley with more equanimity than Kes ever did.

"It's a shame Henri wasn't able to find an estate in the area." Lucas pulled a needle file from a drawer. "He feels his lack of a home acutely."

"I suspect that feeling is made more poignant by his being away from his homeland as well," Kes said. "He has felt like a guest in this country every bit as much as a guest in the homes where he's been given space. Having a bit of this kingdom to call his own would give him a greater sense of connection."

Lucas worked at getting the file point into the tiny gap between the strongbox and its lid. "I can understand why Aldric has taken up the search so enthusiastically. He himself hasn't the flexibility to obtain his own house and, being a younger son, has no claim on any of the Hartley holdings. It's inexcusable that the duke is so miserly with Aldric's portion."

"And heaven knows what Niles is going to do," Kes added. "His family couldn't give him greater income even if they tried." Though Niles had never said as much, they all suspected his family intended an arranged marriage for him, one that would add money to the family coffers. That reckoning, they wagered, would come sooner rather than later.

Again and again, Kes wished he could go back to those days at school when life had been so much simpler.

"The Ridleys have proven a grand addition to the household." Lucas kept at his efforts. "Julia and I absolutely love little Georgie. Smart as a whip, and she has nearly as much energy as I do."

"*Nearly* being the operative word. No one has *entirely* as much."

Lucas laughed. "Miss Ridley has made herself such a fast friend of my Julia. I cannot say how grateful I am for that." Lucas turned the box and tried prying off the lid from a different spot. "Though neither Julia nor I can sort out what is the matter with her left arm. She hardly uses it, and it is always tucked up beside her under her shawl."

Kes had noticed that himself. "My best guess is an injury that either has not yet healed or has left her nervous and protective of her arm."

Lucas nodded. "Perhaps we should have Henri investigate. The Ridleys are particularly intent on a closer connection with him."

"What do you mean?" Kes set the last of his jars back in place.

Mischievousness spread over Lucas's face. "Digby and I strongly suspect Mrs. Ridley and her husband have decided Henri would make an excellent son-in-law."

Though Lucas had offered the observation with more than a hint of joviality, the idea landed as a sharp weight in Kes's chest. *Son-in-law.* A suitor for Miss Ridley.

Why did the idea strike him with such force? Henri was a fine and admirable gentleman, with income to comfortably support a family and an eagerness to secure an estate of his own. Still, Kes didn't like the idea. At all.

Lucas dropped his eyes to the strongbox once more. The lid hadn't budged in the slightest. "Digby thought that would get a response from you."

"Why would he say that?"

"That you are partial to your beautiful neighbor has not escaped our notice. But we couldn't be certain *how* partial."

"Not partial." But he could hear that his objections lacked weight. "She is intriguing and personable. She has shown herself to be clever, which I have always appreciated in another person. It would be rather ridiculous of me to insist that she wasn't exceptionally beautiful. But your inferences beyond that are—"

"Apparently painfully accurate."

Kes pretended to be entirely focused on fitting his new rods into the keyhole in the top of the strongbox. He hoped something would work as a replacement key.

Lucas didn't drop the topic so easily. "You're not one for taking note of a lady, no matter how lovely she might be."

"Untrue."

"You're not one for *showing* that you've taken note of a lady," Lucas corrected. "That we've seen your enthusiasm this time speaks volumes."

"Even if what you are hypothesizing were true, and I'm not saying that it is, the Ridleys are far more impressed with Henri than with me. Best focus your efforts there."

"He is not interested." Lucas made the declaration so matter-of-factly that Kes felt certain he was not guessing. "You, on the other hand . . ."

"Do not make me the Gents' latest project." He tossed aside the rods, none of them having done a thing.

"As the one who was the Gents' *previous* project," Lucas said, "I say your time has come, Grumpy Uncle."

"Very funny, Jester."

"Tell yourself I'm jesting if you'd like," Lucas said. "But we've already discussed it. Plans are already underway."

"The lot of you couldn't have spent your time conspiring to get this box open instead?"

"Oh, make no mistake. We are doing both." Lucas wriggled his eyebrows. Though the expression was clearly meant to be entertaining, Kes knew his friend was in earnest.

Heaven help him.

Chapter Thirteen

Kes knew the Gents far too well to not be nervous upon joining them in the drawing room after dinner that night. Their mischief-making rarely got wholly out of hand, but it happened often enough that he didn't dare leave them entirely to their own devices. He had far too often proven their voice of reason when odd fancies pulled at their interest. This time, however, he was to be the *focus* of their potential misadventures rather than merely the calming influence.

Mr. and Mrs. Ridley had declared themselves still weary from the journey to Carlisle. Georgie didn't join the group for their post-dinner gatherings, having already gone to bed for the night by then, so the absence of all the Ridleys other than Miss Ridley meant Kes hadn't a buffer between himself and the schemes his friends were likely concocting.

When Lucas addressed the group, he looked far too conspiratorial for Kes's peace of mind. "I believe this evening calls for a particularly exciting game."

"Not hide-and-seek," Aldric tossed back, earning grins from all the Gents and a theatrically hangdog expression from Lucas.

Their jester, however, rallied quickly and continued his announcement. "Though some among us have recently had the excitement of a journey, the rest are wasting away from boredom."

"Only the unimaginative ever die of boredom," Digby declared with his usual air of feigned superiority.

Niles, true to character, listened with quiet eagerness.

Henri looked to Julia. "Have you heard what he is about to propose? I must worry when Lucas has 'ideas.'"

She smiled, as she always did when they were ruffling each other's feathers. "I do know what he means to propose, and I think it a grand idea."

A chorus of approval and relief followed that reassurance, inspiring an answering headshake of pretended annoyance from Lucas. "Why have you no faith in me? Surely the years have taught you—"

"That you are troublemaker," Kes said.

"I am doing this for you," he said in the same tone of pretended offense.

"Heaven help us all," Kes muttered.

"What have you planned, Lucas?" Aldric asked. He often had to serve as the group's voice of reason.

"A lively game of move all!" Lucas declared, his eyes dancing in that way they did when anticipating something adventurous and likely far less calm than it ought to be.

"I'm not familiar with that game," Miss Ridley said. "Is it difficult to learn?"

"Not at all," Julia said. "We will play here in the open part of the room, with a number of chairs placed at intervals, one chair fewer than there are participants. The person given charge of instructing the group will declare, 'Move all!' Everyone will then be required to find a seat as quickly as possible. As there are fewer chairs than people, someone will be left without one, and that person will be eliminated. Another chair will be removed, and the undertaking repeats."

Miss Ridley nodded her understanding. "Eventually, there is but one chair and one winner."

"Precisely," Julia said. "And to make the game both fair and exciting, should a person jump up out of his or her seat before 'move all' is called or physically prevent another from obtaining a seat or sit in the chair he or she just arose from, that person is required to undertake a forfeit of the leader's choosing."

Miss Ridley didn't often look uncomfortable, but she did a little in that moment. She wrapped her arms more tightly around herself, only the right one at all visible among the folds of her shawl.

Kes didn't like the idea of her worrying or unhappy while in his home. "This group is fond of picking at one another, but I assure you no one would permit forfeits that were humiliating or inappropriate. Should something be chosen that you are not comfortable with, you need only say so. Something new will be chosen."

She did look a bit relieved at that, but her nervousness remained. "And it is decidedly against the rules to *physically* stop a person?" She appeared genuinely concerned by the possibility.

Henri, true to his compassionate nature, moved to sit in the chair beside hers. "Would it ease your distress if we all, here and now, vowed to strictly abide by that rule?"

She nodded firmly, with conviction and, if Kes didn't miss his mark, a little embarrassment.

"We enjoy larks and teasing one another," Aldric said. "But I assure you, Miss Ridley, we never intentionally inflict unhappiness. Further, we do not hesitate to call one another to account if necessary. If that aspect of this scheme causes you concern, we will, each of us, commit to strict observance of that rule."

"You will not consider me to have ruined your enjoyment of the evening?"

"Rendering someone unhappy is not enjoyable," Kes said. "No decent person could feel otherwise."

She turned away from Henri and cast her eyes instead on Kes. She looked at him with gratitude and appreciation. But more than that, there was confidence in her expression. She believed him and the assurances he offered. He was a reliable and trustworthy person, and someone showing faith in him was not unusual. Yet, seeing it *from her* meant something more. Though he had no intention of telling the Gents that.

"We will choose a different game if you would rather," Julia said to Miss Ridley.

She looked far less concerned than she had moments earlier. "I think the game will be enjoyable. It is nice to get a bit of exercise. The rain began falling so early this afternoon that we've been cooped up inside for a good half of the day."

Though Kes knew Miss Ridley and her cousin were fond of the outdoors and he had no objection to nature himself, he took great delight in being "cooped up inside."

The arrangements were quickly seen to. Furniture was moved to clear a larger space. Individual chairs were placed at distant intervals from one another. The Gents had played this game on multiple occasions, and it could, at times, get rowdy. But Kes knew his friends were trustworthy and kind and, having seen Miss Ridley's very real concern, would keep their exuberance safely within bounds.

Lucas placed himself directly beside Kes. He leaned a bit closer and, voice lowered, said, "Here is your opportunity to show Miss Ridley that in addition to being quite scholarly, you can also be a tremendous amount of fun."

"Is this the Gents' latest plan?"

"The beginnings of it, anyway. We had a meeting, you see. Just as the lot of you had one when I was attempting to win over my Julia. I must say, planning is far more enjoyable than being the one planned about."

"I suppose there's no way for me to avoid the group's efforts?"

Lucas shrugged. "You could always toss us all out."

"I would if not for the strongbox. One of you hulverheads might stumble on the means of opening it."

Aldric declared, "Move all!" and the room descended into the expected chaos. People rushed to chairs, some managing to claim them, others not. More than one participant attempted to claim the same chair, sending them off in search of another. In the end, Julia was left without a place to sit.

Instead of being disappointed, she offered a laugh and a curtsy and said, "Thank the heavens. While I do enjoy this game, it became immediately clear that undertaking it while in anticipation of a new arrival rendered it less enjoyable than it has been in the past."

That brought a quick halt to the game as everyone present, Lucas especially, worried over her. Had she exerted too much? Was she in pain? Discomfort? Ought the local midwife be sent for?

She brushed away all their worries. She also, however, insisted that she sit out the remainder of the evening.

"Would it cause great difficulty with the game if Julia were the one to call 'move all'?" Miss Ridley asked.

"Not at all," Aldric said.

Miss Ridley addressed Julia directly. "That would allow you to participate while not causing you further distress."

"Excellent suggestion." Julia sat on the settee that had been pushed to the side to make room.

Lucas fussed over her, seeing to it that her legs were stretched out in front of her and she was leaning comfortably against the arm of the settee. He flicked a blanket over her legs and inquired earnestly if she needed anything. Once she was situated, the game resumed.

The group was as enthusiastic as ever, while still being careful not to bump Miss Ridley, as she was particularly concerned about that. They scrambled for chairs and laughed good-naturedly when eliminated.

Miss Ridley laughed along with everyone and joined in the friendly banter. She really was a good sport, something Kes appreciated. And she had trusted them when they'd promised to be careful with her. She did keep her arms tucked up in front of her, likely protecting herself from the jostling she feared would happen accidentally.

Thinking back, he was certain she often kept her arms that way: folded across her middle, one atop the other, usually more than half hidden beneath her shawl. And she always wore gloves. Julia sometimes left hers off, but Miss

Ridley *never* did. Why was that? And why did he find the growing mystery of her so enjoyably intriguing?

They'd been undertaking their game of move all for the better part of an hour. Aldric had won all but one game. The one he had lost, Niles had won, which had been a shock to everyone. Niles was good at games and physically quite agile, but he tended to get so wrapped up in the enjoyment of an undertaking that he forgot to be competitive. To best Aldric, of all people, was an accomplishment indeed.

The current contenders had been narrowed down to Aldric, Lucas, Kes, and Miss Ridley. The three remaining chairs were not at all near each other. Henri stood ready to move one of them the moment Julia declared, "Move all!"

The remaining participants eyed each other with jesting looks of rivalry. Miss Ridley laughed once more. Kes adored the sound of it. He dearly hoped she would laugh throughout the evening. He generally grew weary of company by this point in the night, but he didn't wish for this evening to be over too quickly.

"Move all!" Julia called out.

The players jumped to their feet and began rushing about, each attempting to claim one of the few remaining chairs. Aldric managed to make the transfer from his seat to the nearest one with little effort, but as Miss Ridley had been aiming for the same one, she was forced to change directions quickly.

One of her feet slipped out from under her. The other buckled with the sudden change of momentum. She flung one arm out in an attempt to balance herself, but when that failed and she kept the other arm tucked closely against her, she hit the floor with enough force that the sound of it echoed the room into silence.

Kes was at her side in an instant. "Are you hurt?"

With her right hand, she rubbed at her ankle peeking out from beneath her gown. "I turned my ankle."

"Is it broken?"

She shook her head. "Nothing so serious as that."

He studied her features, looking for signs of greater distress than she was indicating. She was never anything but buoyant and cheerful. He didn't know her well enough to know if she would hide an injury behind a smile.

She met his eye and looked immediately apologetic. "I've ruined the game, haven't I?"

"Not a soul in this room is more concerned about the game than about you."

"You speak on behalf of them, do you?" Amusement filled her question.

"I am speaking in warning to them." He didn't bother looking at the others. Miss Ridley was his primary concern, and he knew they wouldn't be unempathetic. "Do you think you can walk?"

"With help, I believe I could."

Henri stepped forward. Kes quickly offered his hand to Miss Ridley. She set her right hand in his and carefully rose to her feet. He kept that hand in his and set his other arm around her waist, allowing her to lean more heavily against him and take weight off her injured foot.

"Come sit here, Violet," Julia said. "You can put your foot on the ottoman."

Kes saw her situated there and cocooned in Julia's compassionate care. He slipped over to the chest in the far corner where he kept light throws for a cold day. He pulled one out and returned to where Miss Ridley sat.

Careful of her foot resting on the ottoman, he laid the blanket over her legs, pulling it upward so it would pool around her and offer warmth; her shawl played that same role for her arms and shoulders.

"Is there anything else you need?" Kes asked. "A cool cloth? Powders?"

Under his breath, Lucas quietly added, "A declaration of undying devotion?"

"Perhaps you would feel better, Miss Ridley, if Lucas made himself a guest at Hoppleforth."

"Lady Collington would be the death of him," Miss Ridley said.

"Only if we are very, very fortunate," Kes replied.

Miss Ridley's smile blossomed fully. If Kes were one to blush, he most certainly would have in that moment. There was something too pleasantly satisfying about bringing her joy. He could happily spend hours doing precisely that.

Julia was watching the two of them, her expression growing more contemplative. A sudden look of understanding pulled at her features.

Kes did the only thing that made sense. He left the room as quickly as his feet would take him.

Chapter Fourteen

Violet was in a predicament. The ankle she had turned the night before was not severely injured but was sore and tender enough to require her to use a cane, at least for the day. As her prosthesis did not permit her to grasp a cane, she had to use it in her right hand, which, while suitable for aiding her pained foot, complicated other things. She usually kept her false arm near to her with her shawl draped over it when in company so no one would reach for it without warning or notice that it didn't move like it ought. Though she liked the people at Livingsley Hall, she wasn't yet ready to share with them this part of herself.

Still, the difficulty with the cane encouraged her to proceed with her reimagining of her prosthesis. Surely there was a means of increasing its efficacy. There had to be. She was not content to simply sit back and hope to stumble on it. Hers was not the most mechanical of minds, but what she lacked in experience and understanding, she felt she more than made up for in sheer determination.

Holding her packet of clock parts against her with her prosthesis and grasping her cane with her right hand, she hobbled about the ground floor, looking for a quiet and private space in which to work. Her efforts were best undertaken with no one the wiser.

The elegantly appointed west sitting room was not an option; she'd be sure to be found out there. Mother was in the drawing room playing the harpsichord. The house boasted a ballroom that the guests seldom wandered into, but there was just enough risk of discovery that she didn't care to undertake her efforts there.

In her search, she found a small room she'd not seen before. It was almost too small to be considered a room, but it was clearly not a wardrobe or a cupboard.

On the far wall was a narrow window large enough to let a little bit of light in but not so large that the room would be visible from the outside. Both sidewalls were paneled with light wood and not a single painting or other decoration. In the middle of the space was a round table with a single chair pushed up to it. That was all the room held. It was nearabout all it *could* hold.

Violet sat in the chair. She rested her cane against the edge of the table and placed her small package of clock parts on the tabletop. She had looked through the bits and pieces already, but this was her first opportunity to spread them out and discover how they fit together.

She'd had two years to think about what she wished to change about her prosthesis. Most people would probably assume that, more than anything, she wished to be rid of it, but though she considered herself an optimist and something of a dreamer, she chose not to dwell on the impossible when she could wish for truly wonderful things that were actually within reach. If she spent all her time focusing on what could never be, she would never learn to find joy in what was.

That had proven an important difference, an important shift in mindset after her amputation. She still sometimes mourned the change and sometimes thought about what it would be like if it hadn't happened at all, but she wasn't consumed by it any longer. Grief had begun to give way to an unexpected hope. Loss had turned into a new beginning. She had learned to navigate in a world not designed for those whose limbs were different from what was expected. She had learned to value herself beyond the physical. She'd adapted and adjusted and emerged still herself, still hopeful about life and the future. And she had discovered an unexpected drive to find solutions to the difficulties she faced.

If she could sort a means of not only bending the fingers of her prosthesis but also locking them in place, there was no telling what she might be able to do. She could hold things, perhaps even pick them up. She might be able to hold a cane in her left hand should she need one again in the future.

She moved the bits and pieces about on the table, wanting to look at them and better understand their relative sizes. The larger gears fit together with smaller ones; smaller ones fit together with those of the same size. There were a great many combinations.

She'd been given two tightly coiled springs. While she wasn't entirely certain how they might be used in her efforts to open and close the fingers of her prosthesis, she knew they were significant in clocks.

What she needed was a means of assembling these bits together so she could watch them as they functioned. She wasn't certain how to do that without attaching them to her prosthesis. Fingers that bent would require hinges, and the only way to put hinges in her current hand was to cut it. That terrified her. She had only one prosthesis. If she ruined it . . .

Experimenting was one thing, but permanently altering something that was, to a large degree, working was another thing altogether.

Still, she didn't intend to give up. Doing so was not in her nature.

She held up the winding key she had been given. It was small and fit between her thumb and forefinger. She set the key against her still-gloved prosthesis, trying to obtain a better idea of its relative size. It would protrude a bit once stuck into the arm, especially if there were gears and wires and other things attached as well. Anything protruding from it, she'd discovered before the carpenter had managed to sand it entirely smooth, snagged on things and bumped into things and proved inconvenient in other ways.

What was she to do about that? The key was crucial, as it was what turned the spring that turned the gears. If she were to use clockwork in her design, the key had to be there, but if it stuck out, she'd have a terrible time figuring out what to do with it. She'd also purchased a winding crank, but it would protrude even more than a mere key. And what of the many gears and springs? How easily would it all catch on things?

Of course, she would continue to wear her gloves, which would offer some buffer between the mechanisms and her clothing—or other people's clothing, heaven forbid—but what if the gloves became caught and prevented the gears from turning and simply rendered everything useless?

She leaned back a bit in her chair, eyeing the parts in front of her. If only she had the ability to test the mechanisms rather than simply guess how they would work. It would be far better to know now if she was moving in entirely the wrong direction than to let herself get deep into this before realizing it was never going to work to begin with.

Before he had begun investing, Papa had worked on the docks. She wasn't ashamed of his work—then or now—no matter Lady Collington's apparent opinion on the matter. But she did, in that moment, vaguely wish Father had been a clockmaker.

Without warning, the door to the small room opened.

Quick as lightning, Violet tucked her left arm beneath the table. It was, of course, gloved and covered with the edges of her shawl—she needn't have hidden it away—but she had grown so accustomed to doing so, she hardly thought about it anymore. She would have jumped to her feet, but she didn't trust her still tender ankle. And there was not time to hide the items she'd placed on the tabletop.

Mr. Barrington stepped inside. He looked every bit as surprised to find her there as she was to be found. "Why, Miss Ridley. What are you doing in here?"

How could she explain without revealing her efforts and the reason behind them? "I was looking for a quiet place. This seemed the likeliest."

He adjusted his spectacles. "Most people don't realize this room is here."

"Most people aren't as clever as I am." She shrugged a shoulder in a feigned show of self-aggrandizement.

With a hint of a smile, he said, "I suspect that is entirely true."

"I am not, however, clever enough to sort out why it is Lucas always suggests a game of hide-and-seek in the evenings."

"That is an easy quandary to resolve. He and Julia always hide together in some place difficult to discover. He enjoys having her very exclusive company."

That fit the affectionate tenderness Lucas so regularly displayed for his wife.

"Have you any other great mysteries I can solve?" Mr. Barrington asked.

"I do, in fact. I haven't the first idea what purpose this room is meant to serve. It's too small for most uses I can think of."

"I believe previous owners used it for storing coats and such when holding balls." He indicated the tabletop with a slight twitch of his head. "But you seem to have found another use for it."

This was a private space she had commandeered without permission in order to undertake an effort she had hoped to keep to herself. There really was no way of explaining at least a little of what she was doing to her friend. The space did, after all, belong to him. "I obtained these at the clockmaker's shop," she said. "You obtained something similar, I recall."

Mr. Barrington nodded, the movement a little awkward. "I did obtain a few things there, yes." He came closer and looked at the pieces on the table. "What is it you are working on?"

That was the question she had worried he would ask. She assumed her most nonchalant tone. "I've a curiosity about how these things work together."

Rather than disapproval, she saw a keen interest. "I have a similar curiosity."

"Truly?"

He nodded. "I've always liked learning new things. The Gents have teased me mercilessly about it over the years."

She assumed her most stern demeanor. "Do you need me to pummel them? Because I would be willing."

He laughed, the sound entirely natural and easy. Her grumpy neighbor was proving a very congenial friend. He'd shown himself to be a thoughtful person again and again, with Georgie at the bookshop, with Violet herself the night before when she'd turned her ankle, with the map he'd drawn for them.

"I'm struggling to learn more of these." She motioned with her right hand to the gears on the table. "They don't actually function when simply laid on the table like this."

He crossed to the wall and pulled open a door, one made of the very paneling that covered both walls. Behind it appeared to be a small cupboard. Did all the panels hide cupboards?

From within, he removed a board no larger than the cover of a book, with small holes at regular intervals. He also removed a brown-glass jar filled with pegs of varying sizes. After closing the hidden door once more, he brought the items back to where she sat.

"The pegs can be placed in the holes at whatever distance is needed to accommodate the gears and parts you're working with. You should be able to interlock them and manually turn the parts to see how they work together."

It was ingenious and absolutely perfect for what she needed. "Did you get this at the clockmaker's shop?"

He shook his head. "I made it. As I said, I, too, have an interest in understanding clockwork and how it functions. Having something like this has proven crucial."

"Could I borrow it sometime?" she asked.

"You can use it right now if you'd like."

She pulled back the immediate acceptance that jumped to her lips. A complication had occurred to her. "You were coming in here to fetch this, weren't you? So you could work with the things *you* brought back from Carlisle?"

"I was." He carefully moved the items on the table and set the board there. "If you'll permit me to obtain another chair and join you, I'd be happy to combine our efforts since we both are exploring the idea of clockwork."

"Are you looking to build a clock?" she asked.

His gaze narrowed a little on her. "Are you?"

"Does it matter *what* I'm attempting to do?"

Far from offended, he answered with his usual tone of logic and consideration. "We'll work together more efficiently and effectively if we're both aiming for the same thing and know what that thing is."

He didn't realize what he was asking. Telling him what she was trying to make meant telling him why. That was not something she'd shared with many people and not with anyone since moving to Cumberland.

Mr. Barrington was intelligent, which would be helpful in this endeavor. He also had an interest in clockwork, which was particularly convenient. More important still, he was considerate and had shown himself to be dependable.

Could she trust him with this? Dare she share such an enormous secret with such a new friend? Her efforts would be more fruitful if she did. But it was a risk.

She met his eye, looking for any indication that she ought not follow through with what she was considering. There was nothing but reassurance there, perhaps a hint of curiosity. Everything about him in that moment, combined with the warm memory of his kindness the night before and his sweetness toward Georgie, reassured her.

She took a breath. Then another.

"Mr. Barrington, can you keep a secret?"

Chapter Fifteen

Can you keep a secret?

With that one question, Kes was sent back years to Stanley's final year at Eton.

"Can you keep a secret?" Stanley had asked.

Kes had assured him he could. His friend had confided in him something he'd told no one else: he'd fallen top over tail for someone but knew nothing would come of it. He'd needed to share that burden but hadn't been entirely confident Lucas could resist taunting him about it or that Digby wouldn't accidentally let it slip. Stanley had trusted Kes. That had meant a lot. It still did.

"You are not the first to ask me if I can be entrusted with a secret," Kes told Miss Ridley. "I assure you, those who have confided in me have found their confidence well placed."

"And I can assure you, the secret isn't anything scandalous or illegal or immoral or anything of that nature, but it *is* rather personal. Still, it has to do with this"—she motioned to the supplies on the table—"so telling you would likely help our efforts."

He could see she was still nervous about whatever it was she wanted to tell him. That she was pushing forward despite that uncertainty told him her efforts in this room were not as casual as she'd made them seem.

"Allow me to bring in another chair," he said. "Then, take the time you need and tell me however much you feel comfortable sharing."

"If I don't change my mind by the time you return," she said with an air of lighthearted warning.

A few minutes later, he was seated at the small table beside her. He faced her and waited for whatever she felt she needed and ought to say.

"I've gathered these things"—she indicated the clockwork—"to improve something. To fix it, after a manner. Not that it is entirely unusable as it is, but I think it could be enhanced."

He might now actually understand *less* about the situation than he had before.

She took another slow breath, likely rallying her courage.

"A very good friend of mine," he said, "told me a great many things in confidence over the years. I've never revealed them to anyone. Not a single thing he asked me not to. I never would. I can promise you that same fierce protection of whatever it is you wish to tell me now. I swear to it."

That seemed to help. With a focused and decisive look, she squared her shoulders. But she didn't speak.

She flipped back the edge of her shawl and rested her left arm on the tabletop. She undid the button at the bottom of her left sleeve, then the button just above that one, and the button above that. The ruffles of her undersleeve hung in a cascade from her arm.

She tugged at her glove, pulling it loose from her fingers. Slowly, her arm was uncovered, and he knew, without needing to be told, the secret she'd been keeping: her lower left arm was prosthetic.

"It was injured two years ago," she said, "and took to infection."

Putridity claimed far too many limbs and lives.

"The arm is beautifully made, and with my glove on and my overly long undersleeves and the distraction of my shawl, few people notice anything odd about it."

He nodded. "Whoever carved it is clearly talented. The shape and proportions are perfect."

The worry that had pulled at her features softened into relieved appreciation. "The carpenter in Portsmouth was considered the best. And I'm grateful for his work."

"But now you're ready for something more?"

She ran her fingers over the wooden ones. "I can't help but think how helpful it would be if the fingers could bend. I could hold things, pick things up."

"They would have to be locked into position," he said.

She nodded, watching him with growing eagerness. "And they would need to be hinged. I could move them with my other hand if need be, but I do wonder if there is a means of bending them with these." She indicated the clock parts.

Ah.

She watched him with almost painful uncertainty. Miss Ridley very seldomly looked anything but cheerful. "I've no experience with clock mechanisms. I'm not certain it is the right approach."

"I have a little experience with clockwork, though not anything quite like this."

Her brow pulled low. "Do you think it can be done?"

"Absolutely."

Rather than appearing bolstered by his declaration, her expression crumbled a little. Tears filled her eyes.

Had he insulted her? Said something amiss? "I am sorry. What did I do wrong?"

"Nothing." But her voice shook.

There was no denying that she was emotional. She had shown herself to be ceaselessly cheerful and happy. Even while enduring the pain of her injury the night before, her spirits had never truly dampened. Whatever he had said wrong, it must have been significant.

"Do you need a glass of water? Or a handkerchief, perhaps?" He was entirely baffled.

She smiled a little tremulously. "I am not on the verge of falling to pieces, I promise."

He inched his chair closer to hers. "I cannot be at ease while you are in distress. The thought that I caused you any degree of unhappiness . . ."

She set her right hand atop his, the simple touch both comforting and thrilling. "I'm simply so relieved. So few people know about this." She lifted her prosthetic arm. "No one beyond my family or those who knew me when it happened. Amputations are not as rare in Portsmouth as I suspect they are here. Accidents occur on docks all the time. Those with missing limbs are considered fortunate; once infection sets in, most people don't survive. But coming here, tiptoeing into the world of the privileged class, I've been terrified of what people would think, what they would say."

He threaded his fingers through hers. "I wish I could with any confidence tell you those fears were unfounded, but I know Society for the fickle monster it too often is."

"As do I," she said. "And the Ridley family offers them ample opportunities for monstrously mistreating us. We come from trade. We have a home and estate now, but we've recently purchased it rather than inheriting it. That meets with the disapproval of many people. I am nearly twenty-two and not only unmarried but also have no prospects, which is a shocking thing for a lady. Georgie is an orphan, which, in the eyes of the upper class, labels her a 'poor relation.' Add to all that, this"—she lifted her left arm once more—"and I worry that no amount of effort will ever see me truly accepted."

"For some people, that will likely prove true."

She released a slow, deep breath. "But it doesn't seem to have earned me your disapproval."

"Not in the least," he said. "And I would wager everything I have that you'll find the same with the Gents and Our Julia. I cannot say that we are perfect—far from it—but I do think you can trust the goodness of these gentlemen and this lady."

"I have thought of telling Julia. But I would hate to lose her friendship." Miss Ridley's worried gaze dropped to the tabletop. "She wouldn't reject me over this though. I truly don't think she would."

"Julia is remarkable, though it took Lucas far too long to fully understand that," Kes said. "Truth be told, it is taking Julia some time to realize that about herself."

"She undervalues herself?"

He nodded. "Criminally so, but the Gents, Lucas especially, think the world of her."

"Do you intend to tell the Gents about my arm?" A little bit of uncertainty entered her voice again.

"I said when we began this discussion that I can be depended on. You told me this in confidence, and I will honor that for as long as you wish me to."

"You are a good man," she said. "For a Grumpy Uncle, that is."

He couldn't hold back a smile at that. She lightened his heart with hardly an effort. "What changes would you like to make to your prosthesis?"

She pulled her hand from his and gestured expressively as she explained the hopes she had and the difficulties she had already realized. She had already tucked her left hand against herself under her shawl. Kes suspected she did so more out of habit than embarrassment.

"If I used gears and rods and such, the bits and pieces would have to protrude from the wood of my arm," she said. "It would be difficult to prevent my clothes or my gloves from snagging on it. The pegboard will allow me to see just how bad that's likely to get, but I suspect I already know."

He nodded, having come to the same conclusion. "What if we were to carve grooves and trenches into the arm itself so that the added parts could sit below the surface instead of protruding out of it?"

She ran the index finger of her right hand along the edge of her wooden arm, bits of it visible beneath her shawl. "If we knew in what configuration the bits and pieces were held together, we could create pockets for them. That would give some degree of protection."

"May I touch your prosthesis?"

"If it won't cause you distress, I could take it off and you could observe it more fully."

It was a level of trust he didn't feel he had earned. He swore he would show himself worthy of the faith she was showing in him. "It is not my comfort but yours that must receive the most consideration in this matter."

"One of Georgie's favorite things is to hold the arm and study it. It doesn't bother me to take it off. In fact, when I am with my family and we are expecting no visitors, I often remove it."

She undid a few more buttons on her sleeve, opening it nearly to her shoulder. She stopped and looked at him once more. "It has only just occurred to me that it may be considered unseemly to reveal my upper arm like this. The merchant class is not the uncivilized lot we are often assumed to be, but we're not always as stringent about these things. I've found myself caught off guard now and then with what is expected and accepted amongst my new associates."

"It would not be acceptable to undertake such a thing in a ballroom or at the dining table, but I do not think you need to worry over the propriety of it just now."

Miss Ridley was a happy person, but Kes was beginning to recognize that her eyes often held an undercurrent of worry. How well she usually hid it. She undid the final button, and her sleeve opened widely. He watched with interest as she unfastened a series of buckles on leather straps that attached to a leather cuff at the top of the wooden arm. Her arm had been amputated just below the elbow. That was why she was not concerned about having an articulated elbow as part of her prosthesis. She retained her physical one.

She slipped it from her arm, the leather straps hanging off, and handed it over to him.

The Gents often teased Kes for his unquenchable curiosity. There were few topics on which he would not be interested to learn more. He found the world and the people in it endlessly intriguing, though he generally liked to observe the people from a distance.

"This is heavier than I expected," he said, testing the weight of it in his hand.

"I've grown more accustomed to that the past two years, but it is actually heavier than my right arm." She rubbed a little at the end of her arm where the prosthesis had been. "There are days when my elbow just aches from holding it up and moving it about."

He turned it over, observing it from different angles, looking at how it was pieced together. "Does it cause pain other than in your elbow?"

"Sometimes. It can rub wrong, and the skin grows raw. Sometimes I get sores under and around the cuff. There is even, at times, pain in—" She stopped.

He looked to her, unsure what she'd meant to say but hadn't.

"I think that's probably enough complaining." Her light tone sounded a little forced. "I have plenty of reasons to be pleased with what I have."

"But if our changes to the prosthesis can address pain you are having—"

"It can't fix this particular pain."

His eyes narrowed a bit. "Why do you not think so?"

"The pain isn't real. It *is*, but it's not." She shook her head, her brow pulling down sharply. "I'm not certain how to explain it. I feel pain in the part of my arm that isn't there anymore, particularly in the hand. I realize that likely makes no sense at all. It was frightening when it first started happening. Now it's mostly baffling. I don't know why or what causes it, but it happens. Less often than it used to, but it does happen. I can't imagine a change to the false arm will eliminate pain in the . . . ghostly arm, for lack of a better way to describe it."

Pain one couldn't address wore on a person, whether that pain was physical or mental or emotional. This pain—pain she struggled to even explain—must be exhausting.

"I wish I understood more," he said.

"I'm *determined* to understand more, particularly about prosthetics." She straightened her posture once more. "It is the one aspect of this I have some ability to control."

Kes returned his attention to the arm she had been using. "This is not overly complicated. The leather is riveted to the wood, which is all one piece and carved to match your other arm in size and shape."

"Yes. It is visually pleasing but not overly useful. You will think it terribly vain of me, but I would like the new version to be *both*."

"There is nothing vain about that." He looked to her. "You remember our game of three kingdoms? When Henri was attempting to guess *fleur de lis* and he asked if the plant in question was more utilitarian or more beautiful and that was a difficult question to answer because beauty is, in part, the function of the flower?"

"I do remember."

"I think it's far too easy to assume something has to be one or the other when it is a marvelous thing to create something that is unabashedly both."

"I think that should be our goal," she said.

Our goal. He liked that quite a lot.

"It would require you to spend time with me, and I know you generally prefer to be alone," she said. "And I suspect you have things of your own you'd like to be working on."

"I am excited to be working on this, I promise you. And it will allow me to learn more of clockwork, which I have an interest in anyway."

"If only either of us already knew more about it," she said. "We would be miles ahead of where we are."

"If you don't have any objections, I'd like to write to an apothecary I know who has a clockmaker father. I will not identify you; I will simply give a basic explanation and ask if he has any ideas to share."

"I would appreciate it. Thank you, Mr. Barrington."

"We are partners in inventing." He hesitated, finding himself caught on the words he meant to say next. But she'd trusted him, and they'd interacted so easily. They were friends, he hadn't a doubt. That gave him confidence where she was concerned. "I would not be opposed to being called Kester. Or Kes; the Gents call me that."

"I thought they called you Grumpy Uncle," she said with a laugh.

"They reserve that for when they are annoyed with me."

"While we are inventing, I believe I will call you Kester. And I hope you'll call me Violet."

"It would be an honor."

She held her right hand out to him. He took it, and rather than shake it as he might have if she were a gentleman, he raised it to his lips and kissed it.

His heart firmly in the clouds, he said, "My very real honor."

Chapter Sixteen

Kes brought his still unopened strongbox into the room on the ground floor where he sometimes worked on his projects. He had some tools in there that weren't duplicated in the Cabin of Cleverness. Perhaps one of those would finally get the box open.

He pulled open a couple different paneling doors and removed a few tools he thought might prove useful. He had only just set them on the table when the door to the room opened. He wasn't certain who he'd been expecting, but seeing Violet step inside proved the very best answer.

"I saw you coming this way," she said. "I thought you might be working on a project." She sounded genuinely intrigued. The Gents treated his interest in inventions and such with varying degrees of interest and amusement. She actually seemed excited.

"My current project is not my usual kind."

He held a chair for her, then set her cane carefully against the side of the table. She was walking much better, but her ankle was clearly still a bit tender.

"I prefer inventing or improving things," Kes continued, "but at the moment, I'm trying to solve a puzzle."

"I like puzzles."

"So do I."

Sitting in a secluded room, talking to an unmarried lady to whom he was not related was not entirely proper. Their last visit to this very room had involved her unbuttoning the entirety of one sleeve. What an odd connection they had. Odd but very enjoyable.

Violet turned her attention to the tabletop and the box and tools set there. Her sleeve was fully buttoned under her long sleeves and lace undersleeves, and she wore yet another shawl pinned in a way that draped it over her arms. Now that he knew her left arm was prosthetic, he could see that she didn't move it often or gesture with it. Her approach, though, was remarkably effective. One was unlikely to sort out the reason for any noticeable oddity in her use of that arm, assuming one was observant enough to have noticed.

"Is that a strongbox?" She nodded toward it. "My father had one very much like it in his office in Portsmouth."

"He didn't happen to lose it onboard a naval ship, did he?" Kes asked.

Her confusion at his comment couldn't have been more apparent, but she was also clearly amused. "As far as I know, my father has never been on a naval ship. Merchant ships, certainly."

"This was left on a naval ship, though I do not know how long ago. Its owner could not be identified, but my name was found scratched into it."

"Your name was on it, but it's not yours?"

He shook his head. "The Admiralty seemed perfectly happy to pass the infuriating mystery along to me."

She bent her right elbow on the tabletop and rested her chin against her upturned hand. "Did the contents of the box offer any clues?"

"The box did not arrive with its key," Kes said. "I haven't the first idea what is inside."

Violet watched him closely, biting her lips closed.

"What is it?" he asked.

With a bit of a wince, she said, "I worried my revelation yesterday would severely lower your opinion of my family. But what I am about to tell you now *absolutely* will."

"Now I am too intrigued to resist begging you to explain."

A corner of her mouth tipped upward. "My father can almost certainly open your strongbox."

Confusion and excitement bubbled inside. "He can?"

She nodded. "As I said, he had a box very much like this one, and the key was lost at one point. He learned how to open it without the key."

"Would you ask him if he would try?"

Violet smiled. Oh, how he loved that smile. "I believe he is in your library. We can ask him together."

Time spent with her was always a wonderful prospect. Far be it from him to turn down the opportunity.

They rose. He held her cane out for her.

Violet took it in her right hand. "Someday, should I need a cane again, I may be able to hold it in my other hand. Wouldn't that be wonderful?"

"I intend to keep spinning my thoughts around that until it's not merely possible but reality."

"And you don't mind keeping the secret?"

He took up the strongbox. "On the contrary, I'm touched that you've trusted me with it."

"Especially knowing I come from a family of picklocks?" she asked with a laugh.

He nodded emphatically. "*Especially* knowing that."

They laughed as they stepped out into the corridor. Spending time in her company was easy in a way it was with no one else other than the Gents, and sometimes not even with them. They talked comfortably about any number of topics. They laughed when they were together. He didn't yet know how she felt about his tendency toward introspection and isolation after hours of social interaction. He was choosing not to think about that. Few people understood or respected that need in him, and he wasn't ready to discover she didn't either.

"You aren't limping as much as you did yesterday," he said. "I hope that means your foot feels better."

"Much better," she said. "I predict I will be triumphant in our next attempt at move all!"

"Perhaps we could suggest a cutthroat game of lawn bowls."

"Excellent," she said with theatrically wide eyes.

Mr. Ridley was indeed in the library. As were Julia, Henri, Aldric, and Digby. Julia's appearance was unexpected, as she was dressed all in black, something seldom seen in a person not in mourning. Digby's *presence* was even more surprising. He wasn't unintelligent, neither was he opposed to the idea of quiet study, but he simply didn't choose to do so often.

The gentlemen got to their feet, Violet having arrived in the room.

Digby's eyes settled quickly on the strongbox in Kes's hand. "Ah, the mysterious box has reemerged."

"Still unopened," Aldric added. "That is a maddening riddle."

"One we may soon have an answer to." Kes dipped his head to Violet.

That brought Julia into the discussion. "Violet, you have sorted the origins of our mysterious box?"

"I have not," she said. "But I do know how to get it open."

"Without the key?" Aldric was clearly intrigued. "How?"

"By asking *me*, most likely," Mr. Ridley said, crossing to where they stood.

Violet leaned against her father, who set an arm around her. "It reminded me of the one you had in your offices in Portsmouth."

"Let us hope it can be opened in the same way." Mr. Ridley motioned toward the large desk. "Set it down, and I'll have a look at it."

"What else are you likely to need?" Kes asked as he laid the strongbox on the desk.

"A key, perhaps," Digby suggested with his perfected air of foppish ineptitude.

"Pay him no heed, Mr. Ridley," Julia said. "Mr. Barrington is far more likely to be cooperative."

"I resent that," Digby said with a tsk.

"You deserve that," Aldric countered.

"*Chut*," Henri said, softly but firmly.

Violet stepped up beside Kes. In a whisper, she said, "I don't speak French."

Kes leaned a touch closer and lowered his voice to the same level as hers. "He told them to hush."

"I am never going to fit in Society." She sighed in obvious frustration.

"Julia speaks multiple languages, and I am certain she would be delighted to teach you whatever you'd like to learn."

"And in return," Violet said, looking lighter already, "my father will teach you how to pick a lock."

Kes looked to Mr. Ridley. He was closely examining the seam and keyhole in the strongbox.

"Do you have access to a very narrow needle file and something similar but with the tip bent at a right angle?" Mr. Ridley spoke as he continued his examination.

"There are a few things like that amongst my tools," Kes said.

"I can fetch them," Henri offered. "In your tool room or in the outbuilding?"

All the Gents knew of Kes's projects and the places where he undertook them. Indeed, it was one of the reasons he got so little done when they were at Livingsley Hall—they knew where to find him.

"The tool room inside the house," Kes said.

Henri bowed. "*Je fais vite*."

"*Merci*," Kes said.

In another whisper, Violet asked, "Does everyone in Society speak French?"

"Most people do, at least a little. The Gents speak it well and often on account of Henri, and also because Aldric's family has connections to France, so he speaks almost perfect French."

"The language I ask Julia to help me learn had best be French, it seems."

Kes offered what he hoped was a reassuring smile. "I can help you with that as well."

"I was teasing you early in our stay here when I said I meant to visit every single day. If you keep offering to help me with more and more things, I will have no choice but to make good on that threat."

He found he wasn't as worried about that possibility as he had been weeks ago. Having her visit would be delightful.

Julia came and stood beside them. "How is your foot today, Violet?"

"Much better, thank you. How is your book?"

"Fascinating." She looked to Kes. "I found a volume in here a few days ago that analyzes the chemical aspects of fire."

"Ah, yes. I found that in London a few years ago, but I haven't read it."

"You should," Julia said.

"Kester volunteered you to act as my French tutor," Violet said. "Was that not presumptuous of him?"

"Terribly presumptuous." Julia matched her teasing tone.

"And everyone wonders why I grow so quickly grumpy."

Both ladies laughed. Heavens, he was not used to being the entertaining person in the room.

"Were you able to find where your name was scratched into the box?" Julia motioned to the strongbox now being looked at by Aldric and Digby as well as Mr. Ridley.

Kes nodded. "I did my own rubbings of all the sides. 'K. Barrington' is etched into the bottom but clearly not by a professional engraver. And there were other letters, as well, amongst all the gouges and scratches. I suspect there used to be a lot more written there."

"Do you have any theories about why your name is on a box you've never seen, found on a boat you've never been on?" Violet asked.

"To tell you the truth, I am all but convinced the K. Barrington scratched into the bottom is a different K. Barrington."

"Perhaps the contents will help us identify this other Mr. Barrington," Violet said. "You might discover family you didn't know you had."

"More people to visit." Julia gave him a teasing look that contained an unmistakable degree of empathy. She understood that he struggled with the never-ending demands on his time.

"I'll suggest they gather at Everett's home instead," he said dryly.

"Who is Everett?" Violet's sincere curiosity about his life and genuine enjoyment of their conversations was a boost to his sometimes-flagging confidence.

"My older brother. He lives in Norfolk at the family seat. And he enjoys having company."

She set her hand lightly on his arm. "I know you don't. I do feel a little guilty that we've all descended upon you."

He took that hand in his and pressed a light kiss to her knuckles. "Please, do not feel guilty. Your family is always welcome here."

"And you will always be welcome at Irthing Grange," Violet said. "Assuming we don't burn it to the ground."

Kes and Violet both laughed. Julia, however, watched them with narrowed and curious eyes. She always saw far too much. Henri returned in the next moment, likely saving Kes from an embarrassing explanation.

Archbishop set a handful of tools on the desk, all of which matched the descriptions Mr. Ridley had given but in various lengths and widths.

Everyone gathered around the desk as the one-time shipping merchant selected two items from amongst those Henri had retrieved and slipped them with precision into the keyhole. The man was deeply focused on his work. Everyone in the room held their breath.

Several minutes passed. Mr. Ridley did not seem frustrated, so the passage of time must not have been a bad sign. He made the tiniest adjustments to the tools he held, leaning ever closer to the box. Everyone was concentrating on his efforts, perhaps even more than Mr. Ridley himself.

The room was so quiet that the click of the locking mechanisms echoed loudly around them all.

He had unlocked the strongbox.

With a grin of delight, he motioned to the box. "The contents await, Mr. Barrington."

"As anxious as I am to see what is inside, if I do so without Lucas and Niles present, they will murder me. And I think Miss Georgie would enjoy watching the mystery unfold as well."

"She would indeed," Mr. Ridley said. "Thank you for thinking of her."

The man's gratitude was kindly offered, but Violet's smile of approval fully eclipsed it. He would do almost anything to see that smile over and over again.

Chapter Seventeen

"I CANNOT COMPREHEND HOW YOU'VE resisted looking inside the box for two hours." Lucas sounded and looked exasperated. "I would not have lasted five minutes."

"Five *seconds*," Digby corrected.

Everyone had gathered in the drawing room after dinner, including little Georgie. She looked tired, but she was also clearly excited. Kes was glad she'd been included. Solving mysteries and undertaking adventures with the Gents had helped him stay afloat during the painful years after his parents died. Offering a bit of that to this girl who was grieving as well was a privilege.

A table had been set in the center of the room. Kes stood at it, the strongbox waiting, unopened on top, his hand resting on the lid. "We might open it to find the contents are utterly boring."

"Or it might be a treasure," Georgie said, leaning against the table with her chin resting on her folded arms. She was watching the box with every expectation of being amazed by what they found.

"Shall we?" Kes asked the room.

Everyone nodded enthusiastically.

He met Georgie's eyes. "I hope it's a treasure."

She grinned at him. "So do I."

Kes tipped the lid open. The lid's underside was a maze of rods and levers, just as expected. He spent less than an instant eyeing it though. His attention fell on the box's contents.

It was a mess of papers and leather pouches and odds and ends. On the top, at one corner was a small brass pin that Kes recognized.

He pulled it out. "Look at this."

Declarations of amazement and excitement spilled from the Gents.

"What is it?" Georgie asked.

Kes set the pin in her hand. "It is a membership pin for the Travel Society at Eton. Three of us in this room belonged to that society when we were in school."

Georgie was entirely engrossed with the pin. Kes returned his attention to the box. He pulled out a few of the papers, spreading them on the table. There were a number of drawings but not of the variety anyone would have expected. They were very detailed renderings of carriages and carriage lanterns, with notes about measurements and angles and such. Among the drawings were sheets of notes about mirrors and candles.

"Are you certain this isn't your box?" Lucas asked, eying the papers. "A Travel Society pin *and* a detailed study of something shockingly specific and vaguely scientific . . . That sounds remarkably like you."

It did, actually. But he knew the box wasn't his.

"What else is inside?" Aldric asked.

Kes removed the remaining papers, some of which were blank. He pulled out the two leather pouches and set them on the table as well. That was all the box held. Not precisely the treasure Georgie had hoped for or the clear indication of ownership Kes had hoped for.

"It is odd that a collection so focused on carriages would be found in a box left onboard a naval ship." Aldric flipped through a few of the papers.

Niles took up one of the leather pouches. Julia took possession of the other.

"Perhaps the box belonged to someone who knew you through the Travel Society at Eton," Lucas said, motioning toward the pin Georgie was still studying.

"Perhaps." Kes had fewer answers than he'd expected and far more questions. Nothing in the box's contents told him who it had belonged to, what connection the person had to him, or when or why it might have been left on whichever ship it had been found on.

Violet stepped up beside him. "It didn't contain gold and jewels. That was my theory."

"I think it was your cousin's as well." He pushed out a frustrated breath. "I wasted everyone's time pursuing this, especially *yours*. We could have been working on more important projects."

She set a hand on his arm. He loved when she did that. It was friendly and comforting.

"Lead pencils." Niles made the announcement without warning, and for a moment, Kes wasn't certain what Puppy was referring to.

He pieced it together though: the leather pouch had contained pencils, which Niles had dumped into his hand. The box's owner had, no doubt, used these writing implements to make his sketches and notes.

"My apologies, everyone." Kes felt like an utter fool. "I was so certain this would prove an exciting discovery." Another mistake he'd made often enough.

Julia peeked inside the leather pouch she had taken from the table. She reached in and pulled out what looked like a miniature. The color drained from her face as a gasp escaped her lips.

Digby, the one standing nearest her, set a supportive arm around her. "Do you need to sit?"

Lucas was there in the next instant. "What's happened?"

She was shaking, her grip on the miniature white-knuckled. What about it could possibly have upset her so much?

Lucas and Digby looked down at it. Both their mouths dropped open, even Digby's, who generally refused to assume so undignified an expression. Julia crumbled into her husband's arms. He handed the miniature to Kes.

What could it possibly be to have had such an enormous impact on the three of them?

He looked at it, and every ounce of air left his lungs.

Two little girls, about Georgie's age, and a young man nearly grown.

A young man he knew on sight but hadn't seen in years.

Stanley.

"Why is everyone sad?" Georgie whispered. The Gents had dispersed, Julia and Lucas retreating from the room altogether, the others wandering to the corners of the drawing room.

"I'm not certain," Violet said. Everyone had grown quiet and distant so quickly upon seeing the miniature that she'd not had the opportunity to ask who the painting depicted. Was it a friend or foe, loved one or enemy?

"I don't like that they're all sad." Georgie's gaze fell on Kester standing at the blue-draped windows in the bay alcove. "Mr. Barrington thought he was going to find a treasure. He must be very disappointed."

There had most certainly been emotion in Kester's face, but Violet didn't think it was disappointment.

"Would he be angry if I talked to him?" Georgie's voice had dropped to a low and uncertain note.

"I'll go with you, dear. We'll talk to him together."

They crossed the room, Georgie tucking herself against Violet's side. Kester looked over at them when they arrived. The sadness in his eyes struck painfully at Violet's heart.

"Mr. Barrington?" Georgie spoke hesitantly. "I'm—I'm sorry your box—I'm sorry you didn't like your box." She held her hand out to him. "I still have the Travel Society pin. I didn't know who to give it to."

Kester allowed her to set the small trinket in his hand. "Thank you, Miss Georgie."

She offered a quick smile, then rushed off to where Violet's parents sat on the far side of the room. Violet herself remained at the windows.

"I will understand if you do not feel equal to talking about it," she said, "but clearly, whoever was depicted in that miniature was known to all of you."

Kester reached into a pocket of his blue-silk frock coat and pulled out the very miniature that had caused such immediate emotion in all the Gents and Julia. He held it out to her. She took it with great care.

Three people were portrayed in the small painting: two little girls and a young gentleman.

"Who are they?" she asked gently.

"The little girl with the red hair is Julia."

The resemblance was obvious now that Violet looked closely.

"The girl beside her is her twin sister, Charlotte, who died very near the age she is in that painting."

Oh, merciful heavens.

"They are sitting with their brother, Stanley."

Stanley, whom Mr. Fortier had said Kester still deeply mourned. Whom all the Gents grieved for. Whom Julia had grown teary simply talking about weeks earlier. The emotion in the drawing room as this miniature had been revealed now made complete, utter, and heartbreaking sense.

"We weren't upset at seeing him in this painting," Kester said. "We simply weren't prepared for it, or for what it meant."

She stepped closer to him, near enough that he could lower his voice if he chose, near enough that, she hoped, he would feel supported. She wasn't certain what more she could do to help her friend.

"The box was his," Kester said. "The handwriting on those papers is his. The Travel Society pin was his. We had a piece of him with us these past weeks, and we had no idea."

"How do you suppose it made its way onto a naval ship?"

A poignant sadness entered his already sorrowful eyes. "Naval ships took soldiers to the colonies during the war. And a naval ship . . . brought him back."

Stanley had died in that war. His remains, it seemed, had been returned to his family, something that did not often happen. This box had likely been lost during that sorrow-filled return journey.

"I am so sorry, Kester," she said. "This was a blow you were not permitted to prepare yourself for."

"We solved the mystery of who the box belonged to, but all that did was leave me with an even heavier question: Why did he scratch *my* name into the box?"

Chapter Eighteen

VIOLET HAD HEARD ABOUT ARISTOCRATIC picnics. They little resembled those she and her family had undertaken in their days in Portsmouth. In those days, the Ridleys had fetched a blanket and spread it out in an open grassy area near the seashore, bringing along cushions for added comfort, and had enjoyed a light repast.

The picnic held at Livingsley Hall several days later was a sight to behold. And while a blanket was spread out and cushions provided, those were generally meant for the gentlemen to lean back on. Chairs were carried out for the ladies, along with a couple extras. Food was set elegantly on a table. It was almost as if the breakfast room had been relocated outside.

While Violet had enjoyed the freedom inherent in sitting on the ground and watching the waves crash against the shore, she had to admit that having a chair to sit on whilst wearing panniers was nice. Getting up off the ground in current fashions, no matter that her version of it was subdued, would have been a difficult thing and might have been more than a little embarrassing to attempt with witnesses about. And though she no longer needed to use a cane, her foot feeling much better the last day or two, there was every possibility it might prove too delicate yet for repeatedly rising from and sitting on the ground.

She sat next to her mother, who was watching the goings-on with delight. Father sat on a cushion next to Lord Aldric, the two of them, no doubt, discussing matters of politics and finances. He'd found in Lord Aldric a gentleman of similar interests. Both men were quite attentive to the affairs of the nation. Both were business-minded. It really was little wonder the Gents called Lord Aldric the General. He was decidedly inclined toward strategy and problem solving.

"Seeing them all a bit lightened has done my heart good," Mother said. "Their grief has been palpable these last couple of days. I have wished I could do more to ease their sorrows."

Violet hadn't known what to do either. *Be sunny or be silent.* In the end, she'd mostly tiptoed around them all. She'd not known how to implement the vicar's exhortation in the face of their grief. She'd failed them utterly. Being sunny was often tiring. Being silent was sometimes worse.

In the expanse of grass separating their picnic area from the glassy water, Lord Jonquil and Mr. Greenberry were teaching Georgie how to play cricket. The three of them appeared to be thoroughly enjoying themselves. Lord Jonquil rushed around fetching the cricket balls, applauding and cheering Georgie on. Mr. Greenberry praised her efforts wholeheartedly. She looked happier than she had in ages. And the two gentlemen seemed to be benefitting from the joyful undertaking as well.

"They have been good for her," Mother said, apparently having noticed where Violet's attention had settled. "I worry for her. There's still so much sadness in her eyes. She will never stop mourning her parents, but I wish I knew how to lift some of the burden she carries."

"And I worry what will happen to her spirits when all of these visitors leave Livingsley Hall. And when *we* leave."

When the fire had first forced them out of Irthing Grange, Violet would not have believed she would ever feel reluctant to return. But she would dearly miss the people she was spending time with here.

At least Kester would still be nearby. She would not be entirely without friends, and he had proven a particularly delightful one.

She had heard from the staff at Livingsley Hall that he was not often home. He traveled a great deal with the Gents. Once he was gone, would he forget all about her?

In that moment, he was sitting on a cushion with his back against a tree, a bit apart from everyone. Resting against his bent knees was a small journal of sorts. He was writing in it, though she didn't know what. He continually pushed his spectacles back into place as they slid down his nose.

He often seemed eager to be on his own, but he never insisted upon it. He always joined his friends in their undertakings and activities. If he wished so much for solitude, why did he not fully claim it more often?

Mr. Layton turned his attention to those nearby. "I have heard from a reliable source that the assembly rooms in Carlisle will be holding a ball at the end of the week."

"I was not aware there was an assembly room in Carlisle," Mother said. "How did we not learn of it during our time there?" She looked excited, which wasn't surprising. She thoroughly enjoyed gatherings and had been eager since their arrival to find a means of joining the local society.

"It is not so large or grand as one would find in larger cities," Lord Aldric said. "But they do hold gatherings now and then, and they are well worth the effort of attending."

"Especially as *I* will be in attendance, having made every effort at somehow improving upon perfection." Mr. Layton tugged foppishly at his cuffs. "I would never deprive local society of the pleasure."

Mr. Fortier and Lord Aldric chuckled. Violet smiled as well. She had come to know Mr. Layton a little in the time she'd been at Livingsley Hall and recognized that he tended toward dramatics but was not actually arrogant.

"It wouldn't be difficult to arrange a trip to Carlisle," Lord Aldric said. "We could send word as early as today, requesting that rooms be held for all of us at the Dappled Chicken."

"Not all of us," Julia said. "As much as I would enjoy attending and watching you gentlemen make fools of yourselves, I know perfectly well that ladies so obviously in my condition are not meant to attend such things. I, therefore, will remain here."

"Do you not think you could at least travel to Carlisle with us?" Violet asked. "You could remain at the inn the evening of the ball. Then you needn't miss out on every single bit of it."

"And if *you* don't go," Mr. Layton said, "*Lucas* won't go, and who will we poke fun at all night?"

In perfect unison, Mr. Fortier and Lord Aldric said, "Kes."

That brought on another bout of laughter from the Gents who were nearby and even from Julia.

Lord Aldric immediately began a discussion with Father about the complications of planning another journey to Carlisle.

Mother bent closer to Violet. "This could be a lovely opportunity to meet the other families in the area. Yet, I cannot help but be a little nervous."

Violet was more than a little nervous. She was fully worried. But if Mother was in need of reassurance, Violet would offer it. "I'm certain all will be well."

Mother patted her hand. "Of course you are."

"We can always retire back to the inn if we find our reception at the assembly rooms colder than we would wish for." Violet hoped it didn't come to that.

Mother loved having friends and people to call on and take tea with. If she didn't find that in this corner of the country, she would be miserable.

Violet understood that wish herself. But she knew there was an additional reason for her to be rejected by the people they were soon to meet. There wasn't a single dance that didn't require the touching of hands or linking of arms. It would become immediately apparent to a dancing partner that her left arm was not what it seemed.

She wasn't certain how to proceed. Mother would want to go. Father looked eager. If Violet refused to attend, they would as well, and she didn't want that. Would it be too much a violation of her promise to be cheerful in the face of difficulties if she told them how unsure she was? If she asked to be left out of the festivities? She didn't think she could manage to obtain permission to do so without being more gloomy than sunny.

No. She would do better to keep a smile on her face and pretend the weight of her worries wasn't growing a bit crushing.

Perhaps Julia would decide to make the trip to Carlisle, after all, and remain at the inn the evening of the ball. Violet could cry off at the last minute and insist on staying with her friend. Mother and Father could still attend. She could have her escape without dampening Mother's spirits.

Mr. Fortier crossed to where she sat and asked if he might take the seat beside her. She, of course, agreed.

Mother quickly squeezed her right hand and offered a thin excuse about wanting to go speak with Julia, but the eagerness in her eyes gave her away. She and Father were delighted with their idea that Mr. Fortier and Violet might find they liked each other.

"Forgive me if I am wrong in my evaluation," he said, "but you seemed uneasy when the assembly was spoken of."

She thought she'd hidden it. "It does make me nervous. My family is not known in this area, and we have quite often experienced people dismissing us before they know us." *Be cheerful.* "While there is some possibility of that happening, I don't choose to assume it will. One mustn't, after all, anticipate trouble when there is every possibility of joy." *And,* she silently added with an inward sigh of weariness, *one mustn't burden others with those troubles.*

He nodded. "Your mother wishes to attend, *oui*?"

"She longs to come to know the people in the area. I hope that among them, she will find friends."

"And I hope you know that you have found friends among us," he said.

"I do, and I'm grateful." Her gaze wandered back to Kester, still sitting apart from them all, under the same tree, writing in the same journal. "Mr. Barrington will likely not enjoy the outing, though I suspect he will make the journey, nonetheless. He clearly prefers solitude. Why does he not claim it?"

"We have many theories, *mademoiselle*, but none of us is certain."

It was not at all the answer she'd been expecting. "What are your theories?"

"They range from worry over being forgotten by us if we are apart too long to feeling an obligation to make certain we do not get ourselves into too much mischief."

She could smile a little at that. "Does he not think the presence of an archbishop would keep his friends out of trouble?"

Mr. Fortier acknowledged that with a quick upturn of his lips. "Alas, it has not always proven enough."

She did enjoy Mr. Fortier's company, but her parents' hopes where he was concerned did not seem destined to come to fruition. Violet felt nothing beyond friendship for him.

"The Gents have known our Grumpy Uncle half his life. We have walked with him through sorrows and loss, through triumphs and joys. He has a brother, but I suspect even that gentleman does not know Kester Barrington as well as we do. And yet, he presents us with such a mystery."

She looked to Kester once more. Georgie laughed at something. The sound pulled Kester's attention from his writing, and he looked up, adjusting his spectacles in that endearing way of his. He watched the cricket instruction for a moment. He appeared genuinely pleased. After a brief moment, he looked back at his book. He was a riddle, for certain.

"Will you excuse me for a moment?" she asked Mr. Fortier. "I find myself needing to undertake a mission of mercy."

Mr. Fortier motioned for her to do precisely that. "Far be it from me to interfere with a charitable act."

She rose and crossed to the table where the repast was spread. She didn't remember Kester obtaining any food for himself. He had been in the spot he now occupied through most of their time outside. He'd helped arrange the chairs and such but had immediately thereafter retreated. She set a plate on the tabletop and placed a few finger sandwiches and pastries on it. She took it up in her right hand and made her way to where he sat. Taking care not to spill the contents of the plate, she lowered herself to her knees on the small blanket his cushion rested on. She was grateful her foot felt so much better. Managing this food delivery would have been impossible otherwise.

He looked over at her.

"Do not let me disturb you." She set the plate down. "I thought you might be hungry, and if you had a few things here, you could eat without needing to pull yourself away from whatever it is you're doing."

"You brought me food?"

She nodded. "I suspect if you were to obtain it yourself, our well-meaning friends would prevent you from returning here."

"Then you don't mean to insist that I join them?"

"Do people often insist on that?"

He shrugged. "Some. Most simply express confusion or disappointment."

Perhaps the reason he forced himself to participate in activities despite his exhaustion was worry over disappointing people.

"Julia seems in better spirits today," Violet said. "I've been concerned about her since the night the strongbox was opened." She'd been concerned about Kester as well but wasn't certain he was ready to talk about his own reaction.

"Stanley and Lucas were brothers to each other in every way but blood. He understands Julia's grief and she his."

"Does anyone understand *yours*?" she asked quietly.

He looked away but not at anything in particular. There was so much sadness written in the lines of his face, so much heaviness in his eyes. Violet's heart broke to see it.

He did not, however, answer her question. "Thank you for bringing me food. That was very thoughtful of you."

If he was not yet ready to talk about Stanley, she would not force him to.

"If, as the afternoon wears on, you find yourself hungry again, you need only meet my eye. I will make another clandestine delivery and save you from the Gents and their nosiness." She rose, a little awkwardly but successfully, and turned to leave. His voice, however, stopped her.

"You would have liked him."

"Stanley?"

He nodded silently.

"Someday, I hope to learn more about him."

With an exhale so heavy she could hear it, he returned his gaze to his small journal.

Mr. Fortier said the Gents didn't know the reason for the contradiction between what Kester needed and what he required of himself. Though she knew it wasn't the entirety of the answer, Violet felt certain a piece of that puzzle lay in the raw pain of grief.

Chapter Nineteen

Kes wandered toward his workroom on the ground floor of his house the next day. His thoughts were a jumbled mess. Discovering that the mysterious strongbox had, in fact, belonged to Stanley, of all people, had dealt a blow. Julia and Lucas had already come to think of the box as something of a gift, a bit of their brother and friend that they'd been unexpectedly given after a decade. Kes, though, was struggling to see it in such a positive light.

He stepped into the workroom and, to his utter delight, found Violet inside. Her presence was soothing in a way she likely didn't even realize. That she had sat by him for a time during the picnic the day before had done more to lift his spirits than anything else he had tried since opening the strongbox. She hadn't attempted to force him to join in the activities going on around them. She hadn't scolded him for not participating. She'd simply let him sit and think and breathe.

When she looked up at him upon his entrance, however, she looked anything but peaceful and at ease. There was no mistaking the frustration in those beautiful eyes of hers.

"I had hoped you would make a visit to this room," she said.

It was quite possibly the best way he had ever been greeted. "I'm glad I chose to wander in this direction."

She motioned with her right hand toward the small pegboard on the tabletop and the gears and wires she had arranged on it. As always, her left arm was tucked under her shawl and was well hidden beneath her long undersleeves. "I've been experimenting with this. Turning the crank lever with it connected to the gears like this does make the gears turn, as I had hoped, but as near as I can sort, when it is attached to the fingers, making them bend would require wire from the fingertip back toward the crank. I couldn't wear gloves, and I wouldn't be able to hold anything because the wire would get in the way. I've found a means of bending the fingers, but they would still be entirely unusable."

He sat in the chair next to hers. "It likely isn't a great deal of comfort, but discovering the failure in this approach is a good thing."

She looked at him with clear doubt in her eyes. "How is it a good thing?"

"We know that using a metal wire to bend the fingers is not the right approach. You discovered that without having to alter your prosthesis first."

Some of the tension in her posture eased. "I suppose that's true," she conceded. "Though I do wish I had discovered a *solution* rather than having merely *eliminated* one."

"If the Royal Society accepted members based on how often they have spoken that exact phrase, I would have become a member long ago."

"Have you been petitioning for membership?" Violet sounded excited, but she was about to be disappointed.

"I have been making the attempt for years now. Thus far, my efforts have proven unsuccessful."

She smiled a little. "And all this time I had heard they were quite bright, the Royal Society. Imagine my shock to learn how very dull-witted they actually are."

For the first time in years, he found he could laugh a little at his ongoing failure to achieve a lifelong goal.

"Have you tested any other hypotheses regarding the improvement of your prosthesis?" he asked her.

"I've thought of a few, but this was the first I'd implemented. Many of the things I've thought of would require testing on my actual arm, and I can't risk destroying what I have now in the hopes of gaining something better from it."

He could appreciate that.

"I hope you don't plan to abandon the effort," he said. "I do think there's an answer. It simply might not be easy to find."

The twinkle of mischief entered her eyes. "I think you'll find, Kester Barrington, that I do not give up easily."

"Is that your way of telling me you are stubborn?" he asked with an upturn of his eyebrow.

"*Warning* you, Kester. *Warning* you that I am stubborn."

"Then allow me to return the favor and warn you that I am grumpy."

She shook her head. "I don't think you actually are."

"You've sorted me out, have you?"

"I am making a valiant attempt." Her smile didn't disappear even as her gaze fell once more on the gears and peg board. "Do you have any brilliant insights on this?"

He shrugged. "I don't know that I would call it 'brilliant,' but I have a thought that might at least be useful."

Violet looked intrigued.

"I think we would be wise to create some prototypes of wooden fingers," he said. "They needn't look perfect, simply be about the right size, shape, and weight. We can attach the components of our various attempts to those to see how well they work. Then we needn't make any alterations to the prosthesis you already have."

She nodded enthusiastically. "That would take a tremendous weight off my mind. There's no telling how long it would take to find the solution we are looking for or even if it's possible. I wouldn't want to be left without an arm while we are working."

She continually referred to *we*. That single word rested like a promise on his heart. She seemed to like having him around. And she had admitted that she'd come to this room in the hope that he would arrive. He'd not needed to maneuver himself into her company to continually remind her that he existed.

"Have you decided to investigate your friend's strongbox any further?" she asked him.

"I'm not entirely certain what to do with it." He'd not admitted that to anyone else, but he felt safe doing so with her. "Discovering it was Stanley's has proven . . . difficult."

"That is entirely understandable," she said. "You are grieving him. That would leave anyone unsure how to proceed."

Once again, she had offered him empathy without making him feel weak or silly.

"I haven't been intentionally thinking about the strongbox or its contents," he said, "but I do think I have solved part of the mystery."

Apparently, sensing there was emotion attached even to this very logical branch of their discussion, she set her hand atop his. "Which part have you sorted?"

"His interest in carriage lights." Kes shifted the position of his hand so he could weave their fingers together. "His family was in a carriage accident many years ago. The road was dark, and the coachman, though an experienced and careful driver, couldn't keep control of the horses. The carriage collided with another carriage, neither driver able to see the other well enough to avoid the collision."

She watched him with drawn brow. "The collision must not have been a minor one."

"Julia's mother, whom Stanley adored—his own mother died when he was very young, and his stepmother raised him and loved him as her own—was significantly injured. Julia sustained a number of injuries as well. Their sister, Charlotte, the other little girl in the miniature, was killed."

She didn't release his hand, neither did she press for more information. She was allowing him to decide how much or how little to share.

"I only knew Charlotte through what Stanley and Lucas told me of her," Kes said. "She was, from what they both said, soft-spoken and rather angelic. Stanley loved her deeply. Her loss devastated him. He seemed utterly lost for weeks and weeks. Though he rallied after a time, the sorrow never entirely left him."

"Do you think, with those sketches and notes about lanterns, he was trying to sort out a means of better illuminating carriages in the hope of preventing another accident like the one that cost him his sister?"

Kester nodded. "That is exactly what I think. He was so heartbroken when Charlotte died. And he was worried about Julia. Lucas was frantic, as they were like family to him as well. Stanley seemed to find his equilibrium sooner than Lucas did. But I suspect what he actually found was a purpose."

"And that would explain why the little miniature of his sisters was kept amongst the papers in the box. They were his reason for pursuing the answer, no matter that he'd been working on it for years."

"The passage of time doesn't lessen the pull of a pursuit that means so much."

She squeezed his fingers. "This is only a theory, but do you think it might be possible that Stanley scratched your name into his box so that if it returned without him"—Kester swallowed against the emotion dredged up by that simple phrase—"the box would find its way back to you? The other Gents know of your interest in inventions and improvements. I can't imagine he didn't as well."

In a quiet and somewhat broken voice, Kes said, "He knew."

"I think, Kester, in a roundabout way, he left this undertaking, this calling that he felt to protect his last remaining sister, in your hands."

Kes hadn't really thought of it in those terms. There was no way of knowing for certain if her hypothesis was correct, but he knew with certainty it was entirely possible.

He ran his thumb along the back of her hand, finding both comfort and pleasure in the simple touch of their fingers. "Stanley was, without question, the one who believed in my abilities the most."

"I'm certain it's hard to even contemplate the possibility of continuing his work, but I hope that, at least, you'll take some solace in knowing he believed in you enough to leave this to you."

"It took ten years for the box to make its way to me. I would think fate could work a little faster than that." He tossed her a quick, dry smile.

She answered with one of her breathtaking ones. "I think fate was waiting for you to be ready."

There was a tremendous amount of insight in that simple statement. He could not have taken up this task immediately after Stanley left to fight in the colonies, being too racked with guilt and regret. After Stanley's death, when the strongbox might have come to him, he was struggling even more.

"I have learned a lot over the years since he . . . since . . ." Lucas and Julia didn't struggle to talk about Stanley as much as he did. Why was that? "I've dabbled in a few more undertakings and gathered more tools and such this past decade."

"And you have obtained a rather lovely assistant, if I do say so." She struck a theatrically coquettish pose that pulled a laugh from him despite his heavy heart.

"There is that."

"Finding purpose in the midst of grief can be healing," she said.

He set his other hand atop hers, enveloping it between both of his. "How is it you are so wise in such things?"

"After my accident," she said, lifting her prosthesis a little, "I was plunged into the depths of grief. My aunt and uncle, Georgie's parents, died shortly thereafter. I was drowning in loss. But it was in the midst of all of it that I first began to ponder the possibility of improving my prosthesis. I didn't know if it was possible. I wasn't at all confident I was even capable of accomplishing it. But having that pursuit ahead of me gave me something to look forward to, something promising awaiting me outside the fog of mourning. It helped. I think this would help you."

"Stanley pondered this for years, and he wasn't able to sort it out."

"Perhaps he hadn't your inventor's mind," she said.

"A mind the Royal Society does not seem overly impressed with."

She rose from the table and squeezed his fingers one more time before slipping her hand free. She made her way toward the door, paused on the threshold, and looked back at him. "The Royal Society might not yet see your worth, but Stanley Cummings did. And I do. It seems to me you need to decide which of us you intend to believe."

On that challenge, kindly issued, she slipped out.

He remained seated at the table, his thoughts spinning in hundreds of directions. Stanley had believed in him. Even before the arrival of the strongbox and, with it, the possibility that Stanley had intended for it to come into Kes's possession, he had known that Stanley believed in him.

Violet trusted him with a fiercely guarded secret. She believed in him enough to invite his help with her own very personal and important project.

Finding purpose in the midst of grief can be healing. His purpose these last ten years had been being present in the lives of the other Gents, never risking losing his last moments with any of them. His purpose had been pushing himself to exhaustion.

It had never been enough. The grief remained, plunging him under wave after wave of sorrow.

It was time for him to start swimming.

Chapter Twenty

Kes wasn't generally one to reach out and instigate interactions, yet he eagerly approached Violet as she walked through the back garden of Livingsley Hall the next day. She was a joy to spend time with. The mere thought of it set his heart racing a bit and his mind spinning in wonderful ways. The more he knew of her, the more deeply he liked her.

He had seen indications that she, like he, had developed more tender feelings. The way she'd looked at him when they'd discussed the map at the inn. The smile she'd given him after he'd helped her with her turned ankle. The trust she'd shown him in sharing her history and her hopes for her prosthesis and the support she'd shown him in return. The way she'd held his hand the day before as they'd talked about Stanley and the box he'd left behind.

He guarded his more personal thoughts and concerns, but she had given him reason to believe he didn't have to with her.

Kes caught up with her as she turned a corner. Today, she wore a deep-green shawl that perfectly complimented her rich brown eyes. The happiness in her expression increased when her eyes met his. It was a fine thing, bringing joy to someone simply by arriving. He had seen that between Lucas and Julia, but it was a new experience for him.

"I fear I am disrupting your enjoyment of nature," he said, suddenly realizing she might not actually want to accept the diversion he'd come to offer.

"Distractions can be welcome if the one doing the interrupting is himself welcome."

He was a welcome distraction. That declaration repeated in his mind. A *welcome* distraction. He liked that very much.

"Would you like to see where I do most of my inventing and projects?" That had emerged utterly awkward, as was common for him.

She didn't seem bothered by his ineloquence. "I have wondered where you did your work when you weren't in your tiny room."

"I have an outbuilding filled with tools and useful items," he said. "You can come see it. If you'd like, that is. You certainly don't have to."

Heavens, he was rubbish at this. Some gentlemen, like Digby, came about it more naturally. The Gents had thoroughly roasted Lucas during his courtship of Julia for bungling the effort, but at least he'd had *some* social acumen. Kes couldn't honestly claim any.

Violet was either very patient or very curious. She accepted the offer without any indication of reluctance.

Eager and more than a bit anxious, he led her to his Cabin of Cleverness, with its large windows and open door. He sometimes drew the curtains and snapped the latch shut while he worked, but propriety would make such a thing inappropriate with the two of them there alone.

They stepped inside, and he waited, nervous for her evaluation of this space he was so proud of.

"You must be able to do a great deal of work in here," she said, looking over the equipment and supplies and bits and bobbles. "I can't imagine there could be anything you need that isn't here."

That was a bit of an exaggeration, of course. But he had come to realize that she often exaggerated in the name of rosy encouragement. He was known to exaggerate sometimes himself but usually when pointing out something already acknowledged as ridiculous.

"I've been adding to my tools and supplies for years, in greater earnest since I inherited Livingsley Hall."

"From whom did you inherit it?" she asked.

"My uncle," he said. "The estate was not entailed, and it went to him when my father inherited the Barrington family estate. My uncle never married and had no children, so he left it to me."

"Do you have any other family?" she asked.

"My brother inherited the family estate after my parents died. He and his wife and children live there. I have a sister who lives in London with her husband, who is a barrister, and their child. We are rather spread out, unfortunately."

"Do you miss your family when you're away from them?"

"I do. And I miss the Gents when I am away from them."

She set a gentle hand on his arm. "It seems you are always missing someone."

Her touch was as powerful as it had been in the workroom, as comforting, as heart-pounding. "There are a great many people I miss. Not a day goes by when I'm not lonely for someone."

She watched him with a hint of sadness. What was it about people who were perpetually happy that tugged at the heart when they grew sorrowful?

"Georgie misses her parents. I try to cheer her, but I'm not always very adept at it."

He rubbed her hand still resting beneath his and atop his arm.

Her expression pulled into one of deep pondering. "I was once told that happiness and cheer were the best possible approach to all difficulties. That if one could not manage to be sunny, one had an obligation to be silent."

Who had told her that? "If one never speaks of one's troubles, then one is left to bear them alone," he said. "That is an awful burden to require of anyone."

For a moment, she didn't speak. She didn't even seem to breathe. Without warning, her shoulders drooped and a heavy breath rushed from her. "It is exhausting," she confessed.

He took her hand properly in his and moved enough to look directly at her. "I will make you an offer here and now. With me, you need never choose silence when you are struggling to feel sunny. Please, share your frustrations or your disappointments. You need not carry those burdens alone."

She tossed him a look that was equal parts dry and good-humored. "You tend to do most things alone, lest you forget. Do *you* need to carry your burdens alone?" Her smile took any sting out of the words.

Violet was good for him. She maintained her cheer but did not avoid calling him to account when she felt it needed to happen. Time with her had quickly become intertwined in the best parts of his day.

And she was still holding his hand. No lady had done that before. He'd been intrigued by a few over the years and felt certain there'd been at least a couple who'd found him at least a little interesting. But nothing had ever come of any of it. He was too quickly and easily forgotten.

But not by her.

"What have you been working on lately?" Violet turned her attention once more to the tools and odds and ends around them.

"I took your advice and have begun pondering the question of Stanley's carriage lights. I even returned to the box and read through his papers."

"You did?" She sounded genuinely excited.

"I won't lie and say it was easy, but once I began reading what he'd done, the desire to finish something so clearly important to him buoyed me."

Improving the illumination of a carriage had been a matter of protecting Julia, Stanley's beloved and only remaining sister. It had been a homage to his much-loved stepmother, who had survived the accident that killed Charlotte but had died of a wasting illness only a few years later.

"Have you chosen a direction for your improvements?" Violet asked.

"Stanley tried mirrors, thinking it would intensify the light, but found his variations only narrowed the light. I believe a mirror set at the back at angles that reflect the light forward, combined with changing the convexity of the glass at the front of the lantern might be the better approach."

"That's brilliant." Violet's excitement did his heart a tremendous lot of good.

His tenderness toward her was likely incredibly obvious. He hadn't the social subtlety to keep it entirely tucked away. But when those feelings were mutual, there was hardly any need for doing so.

"I have also given some thought to your prosthesis." He led her to the table on which he had been undertaking that. "I was reading about Götz von Berlichingen—"

"Who is that?"

"A sixteenth century mercenary knight. He became known as Götz of the Iron Hand after a cannonball took his hand off and a metal one was fashioned to take its place."

"A prosthesis of metal? Wouldn't that be quite heavy?"

Kes took up the book he'd been reading and had kept there for reference. "Nothing in here indicated its weight, but it was hollow, which would have helped." He flipped through the pages to the diagram he'd found. "I was particularly excited to read that the fingers of his iron hand *moved*."

"They did?" She moved so close their shoulders brushed as she looked at the book he held open.

Kester took the length of a breath to appreciate the warmth of her nearby, the floral scent that hung about her, the simple joy of her presence.

"I've copied out the diagram the best I can and am sending it along to the apothecary in Northumberland to see what his father thinks. I haven't been able to make full sense of it, but he likely will."

She studied the diagram a bit longer before looking up at him. "The fingers curl?"

He nodded. "As near as I've been able to ascertain, they move all together, not individually."

She offered one of her overly cheerful smiles, the sort he'd come to recognize was a shield. He'd promised her she didn't need to pretend to be buoyant when her spirits were sinking.

"I know it isn't what you're hoping for, but this is merely a concept and not a final implementation."

"That's true." She took a little breath. "And knowing the fingers on his hand *did* move all those years ago means it can be accomplished."

"I found the discovery quite encouraging," he said.

She returned her focus to the diagram. "It doesn't look at all natural."

"No, it doesn't. Even under gloves, it would be apparent that the hand was an artificial one."

"I've no doubt even my shawl and undersleeves would prove insufficient in disguising that." Her dark brows pulled, and her mouth pressed in a tight line. "Perhaps we can think of improvements on this idea that look more natural. I would appreciate that."

Choosing when and how she shared this part of herself was important to her.

"What do you intend to do at the assembly at the end of the week?" he asked.

She wandered a bit away, her shoulders drooping. "In truth, I'm hoping to find a way to excuse myself from attending."

This was the first he had heard of that. He almost never looked forward to balls, but he did this time. He had thought about the opportunity of dancing with her, spending time with her, taking a turn about the assembly rooms with her arm through his. Why would she wish to avoid it?

"At this assembly, you could easily keep your gloves on all night," he said. "There's no reason you should have to remove them. And a fine silk wrap could take the place of your shawl." His mother had, at times, worn exquisite lengths of silk with her most elegant gowns. It was one of the things he remembered very clearly about her.

"Yes, but I can't think of a single dance which does not require the clasping of hands or the linking of arms. These are people I don't know, people who will be forming their first impressions of me and my family."

Kes was generally a calm and even-tempered person, but the thought of people treating Violet with rudeness sent tension through every muscle of his body. He couldn't deny that she was correct. Society could be vicious in the way it treated people who didn't fit the preferred mold.

"If the Gents claim your dances, then you needn't dance with anyone else."

"That would only address the difficulty if they also knew about my arm, but I haven't told them yet. Besides that, many dances involve clasping hands with people other than one's partner."

That was true.

"Whichever of us has claimed that dance could sit it out with you, perhaps take a turn about the room as the set progresses."

The tiniest glimmer of possibility shone in her eyes, but she was clearly still unconvinced. "What happens when each of you has danced with me already?

I know a second dance would be noticed, perhaps even speculated on. Poor Henri is already doing his best to avoid encouraging my parents' enthusiasm."

Mr. and Mrs. Ridley showed a decided interest in Henri. Violet, however, didn't seem to be encouraging it herself. For her to prefer Kes to the far naturally personable and quietly elegant Frenchman was unexpected but very welcome.

"We can spend part of the evening introducing you to those in attendance. The six Gents can claim your first six sets. After that, if you wish, you can declare yourself weary and ready to retire. You'd have a chance to participate in the evening without having to do so in a way that made you uncomfortable."

"I do believe that could work." She thought a moment longer. "And Father could claim a seventh set, which would afford me additional time. I do enjoy people and social events. It would be a terrible disappointment to miss it entirely."

"It would be an utter shame."

She could likely see how eager he was for her to attend. It was his nature to hide emotions and eagerness, but he hadn't done so with her lately. He wasn't doing so now. It was a risk he found himself confident enough to take.

"Do you have a favorite dance?" she asked.

"I am quite fond of the minuet." He watched for disapproval but saw only curiosity.

"I have not attempted a minuet since my amputation. I'm not entirely certain if it can be done with an uncooperative arm."

"We could quickly make our way through the steps," he suggested. "I realize there isn't any music, but this is only an experiment."

"I suspect there is never a time when you aren't eager for an experiment."

He laughed. "If the Royal Society is not willing to accept me with that recommendation, then I know they never will."

"They will not offer any further rejections," she said firmly. "Or I will have something to say to them about it."

Her defense of him, even offered laughingly as it was just then, was a salve to his soul.

He counted off the beats as they began walking through the steps. The opening involved an elegant unfurling of the arms, almost like wings fluttering on a breeze.

She eyed her left arm with dissatisfaction as it stretched out from under her green shawl. "People might simply assume I'm not very graceful."

He wasn't certain that explanation would be accepted. She moved with utter grace, which only made the stiffness of her arm more apparent. It was little wonder she never chose to leave off her shawl. But it was further apparent why even that distraction had not been enough to prevent him and Lucas and Julia from realizing something was different about that arm.

They began the flow of overcrossing circles that came next in the dance. In his mind, Kes followed the movements of the other couples who would be dancing with them. He suspected Violet was doing the same. The steps brought them to the other couples, sometimes even splitting them apart to dance beside someone else. But thus far, no one's hands touched.

She might feel comfortable dancing a minuet.

From the corner the steps had placed them in, Violet glided forward to the spot where the other ladies would meet for their portion of the next movements. She lifted her arms and bent them at the elbow on either side of her, palms outward.

In the next instant, she lowered them and spun back to face him. "We all press our palms together during this movement. There's no avoiding it."

He crossed to her. "The minuet might not be an option at the assembly, at least not until you're ready to share this with others."

She looked up into his eyes. "I will be eventually. But not yet."

"People have obviously been very unkind in the past."

She nodded.

"I am certain the Gents will claim all your dances and spend them sitting with you or walking with you or whatever you'd prefer," he said. "And you need only ask. No explanations required."

She pressed her right palm to her heart, a gesture he'd often seen her mother employ. How many of his mannerisms were ones he'd learned from his own parents?

Violet began to step around him, but her wide dress bumped against him. Her balance wavered. Kes darted out his arm, catching her about the waist to steady her. She was so close he could see the flecks of darker color in her brown eyes, every variation in her skin, every individual coil of hair. The sweet, floral scent of her filled the air. The warmth of her standing so near radiated inside him.

He didn't pull away immediately. Neither did she.

No words were spoken, no movement made for the length of half a breath. His heart pleaded loudly even as his mind grew entirely silent. He was holding her. She wasn't moving out of his arms and wasn't looking away.

He bent and pressed a kiss to her inviting lips. All thoughts fled, every sensation but her.

Then the world came crashing down on him again. She pulled away. He met her eyes and saw not pleasure, not enjoyment, not even approval. What he saw was shock.

Without another word, she fled, not quite at a run but approaching it. Shock. Running away. That was not the response of a lady who felt for him what he felt for her. It was not the reaction of a lady who was in love. Like he was.

He had misread everything.

Chapter Twenty-One

Kes had taken his supper on a tray in his room and cried off the evening's activities. He'd also made a point of eating his breakfast in his bedchamber the next morning. Only when he was certain the guests at Livingsley Hall had been awake long enough to be engaged in some activity or another did he emerge from hiding.

He didn't consider himself a coward, but he knew when to make a strategic retreat. Not only did he hope to avoid further embarrassment, but he hoped to avoid everyone as well. Violet and Julia had become friends, which meant Julia likely knew what had happened. And that meant Lucas likely knew. And if Lucas knew, all of the Gents knew. Kes wasn't certain he could face that. Worse even than the teasing he would receive at their hands, if Mr. Ridley had learned what happened . . .

And so Kes quietly made his way down to his ground-floor workroom and fetched the box he'd left there containing various pieces of convex glass, a large candle, two mirrors, and a carriage lantern he'd obtained from his coachman and from which he had removed all the glass. Having obtained ample supplies to keep him well and truly occupied, he retreated to his room once more. He managed the whole thing without being seen, a bit of luck he felt the Fates owed him after all that had happened.

His bedchamber at Livingsley Hall had been a little overwhelming when he'd first inherited it. The room was large enough and the floor-to-ceiling windows in the rounded alcove let in light enough that even the dark wood and heavy drapes didn't overpower the space. He'd come to like it, to feel it was truly his own. But in that moment, licking his wounds and drowning in waves of regret, the warmth of the room didn't envelop him as it usually did.

He was no stranger to regret. Ten years earlier, he'd endured a string of blows to his pride and his confidence. A young lady had laughed at him when he'd tried his hand at a few flowery words. His recent examination in mathematics hadn't gone well. His sister had been courted by someone he hadn't met, and he'd learned of it only by accident, a sure indication he'd been forgotten. Again.

He'd done then very much what he was doing now: avoided everyone. It was far easier to believe people thought of him when he didn't afford them the opportunity to prove otherwise. The family estate in Norfolk had offered ample isolation, and he'd clung to it fiercely. He'd been there when Stanley's invitation to join the Gents gathering, the second one they'd held in as many years, had arrived. Kes had refused.

And he'd regretted it ever since.

A small but insistent voice urged him to abandon this repeat performance and do as he had in the years since: never push the Gents away again, never ignore his obligations to them, never sulk so entirely that he would cost himself valuable time with the best friends he had ever had. That time could not always be reclaimed.

He sat in the large armchair in the alcove and set his box of items on the end table he'd set near it specifically for that day's undertaking, all the while ignoring the anxious pleadings of his worried mind. He'd managed to remove from the box only the lantern and candle when the door to his bedchamber opened and all the Gents came inside.

All of them. Heaven help him.

They didn't speak or laugh as they entered, which was not a good sign.

"Here you are," Aldric said. "We were beginning to feel neglected."

"You are entirely capable of entertaining yourselves." He looked back down at his box and removed the mirrors, focusing all of his attention on his work and not his company. The approach had sometimes managed to send the Gents on their way during their Eton years. But not often. And not ever when Stanley was involved.

"I've not been fooled by your 'I'm too busy making impressive discoveries to listen to you' tactic since we were boys," Lucas said. "I'm certainly not going to be now." He leaned against the fireplace mantel and watched Kes with every indication of not meaning to leave until he spilled his budget.

The other Gents gathered around as well. Digby had managed to station himself in the fall of brilliant sunlight spilling from the windows in a pose worthy of being painted by an Old Master. Aldric had claimed use of the other chair in the room, having positioned it to face Kes directly. Henri stood nearby, looking concerned. Niles was watching them all.

Kes would have to offer some explanation. "You know perfectly well that I prefer solitude. I finally managed to procure some, and here you are interrupting."

"Grumpy Uncle is living up to his name," Digby said. "That can mean only one thing."

"He is trying to get us to leave," Niles said. "When has that worked?"

"Never," they all said in near perfect unison.

With a sigh, Kes snapped his book shut and eyed them all with what he hoped was a clear look of warning. "I am in no mood for jesting. The only one of you whose teasing I was willing to endure when perturbed was Stanley. So don't even try."

"Do I look like I came to tease?" Aldric asked, his General expression firmly in place, his elbow on the arm of his chair, temple resting against his upturned fingers.

"We are to leave for Carlisle tomorrow." Henri's tone held a note too close to pity for Kes's peace of mind. "There will be no solitude to claim during that journey."

"You all can certainly go without me," Kes said. "Aldric could arrange the entire endeavor with his eyes shut and his hands tied behind his back."

"Bad advice, that," Digby said. "He would look an absolute quiz."

Rumbles of amusement rippled through the group.

Aldric had not lost his focus. "Do you really intend to cry off?"

"With everyone gone for a couple of days, I would finally have tranquility in which to do my work." He motioned to the items on the table. "And you cannot argue that it isn't important. It mattered to Stanley."

"Yes, but Stanley would not have wanted you to forgo the privilege of dancing with Violet." Lucas's fingers drummed silently against the mantel, not in a show of impatience but simply because of his constant need to be moving about and expending the energy he never seemed to run short of. "You cannot convince any of us that you wouldn't deeply enjoy being her partner for a set."

"I would not, in fact, enjoy that," he said, speaking as firmly and convincingly as he could.

"Bosh," Digby said. "Of course you would."

Kes kept his peace. Aldric was studying him. It wouldn't be long before he sorted the entire thing.

"Why the sudden change of heart?" Henri asked.

As it was Violet's objections that would make dancing with her both uncomfortable and, more than likely, impossible, he couldn't directly answer that question. He rose from the chair and paced away.

"You believe *Violet* has had a change of heart?" Aldric always had been far too perceptive.

Kes turned to look at him. "When did all of you start calling her Violet?"

"After the picnic," Lucas said. "She asked us if we would since we have all become friends."

If she had become close with this group and he was in her black books, it stood to reason things were about to get extremely awkward between himself and the Gents.

"Names aren't the current order of business. *Hearts* are." Aldric watched Kes with that all-searching eye of his.

There would be no avoiding the discussion. It was likely just as well. Catastrophic things happened when he grew inattentive in his connection to them.

"Hers wasn't so much a change of heart," Kes said. "It's more a matter of her heart never having felt what I thought it did."

That sent near identical looks of confusion across the group.

"You might as well explain," Aldric said. "We don't intend to leave until we know how to help, and we'll never sort that out if we can't make sense of anything you're saying."

"This isn't something you can fix." Kes paced away, feeling overwhelmed.

"This group managed to make sense of my predicament with Julia a year ago," Lucas said. "And that was a bumble broth if ever there was one."

He had a point. And yet . . .

"Trust us," Aldric said. "Even just a little."

Kes's shoulders dropped with the weight he bore. There was likely nothing they could do. And yet, as he'd told Violet, bearing a burden alone only made it heavier.

"As our resident monarch would say"—Kes motioned to Digby—"I'm in bad bread this time."

"How bad?" Aldric asked, his tone clearly indicating he understood the gravity of the situation.

"Violet was nervous about the assembly. She hadn't danced the minuet in ages and was concerned she'd not be able to do it correctly. We were undertaking a quick walk-through of the steps—nothing elaborate, merely a staid rehearsal. Before I knew it, we were standing close together, and—" He wanted to think back on the moment with some degree of pleasure, but he couldn't. A *shared* kiss made a loving memory; a *one-sided* kiss absolutely did not.

"*Quelle pagaille*," Henri whispered, dismay filling his face. "You kissed her, *oui*?"

Kes grimaced. "I did."

"And did she faint with sheer pleasure?" Lucas, blast the man, appeared thoroughly amused.

"She looked at me as if I'd suddenly sprouted extra heads and transformed into a hydra. Then she ran."

"Generally speaking," Lucas said, "tender moments that end with the lady one loves running away are not a good sign."

"Our Jester is an expert in such things." Digby gave them all a knowing look.

Kes was in no mood for laughing, even over decidedly funny memories. "I imposed upon her, however unintentionally. She's already nervous about the assembly. My presence would only make her worry more."

"Your professed concern for her is admirable," Aldric said, "but your explanation is not entirely honest or complete."

Kes met his eye with a raise of his eyebrows. Aldric mimicked the expression and didn't flinch. They watched each other for a long moment. It was a battle of wills, one Kes didn't often win. He didn't this time either.

With a growl that was half sigh, he said, "Also, I'm embarrassed. Avoiding further humiliation is extremely motivating."

"Ah, but humiliation is our specialty," Digby said.

"Violet deserves for her evening at the Carlisle assembly to be a success," Aldric said. "And that, no matter your objection, requires your presence." He didn't give Kes a chance to say any more. To Digby, he said, "Fashion him an ensemble that will reflect well on his guests."

With a trademark "Huzzah!" Digby leapt into action.

To Niles and Henri, Aldric gave the assignment of discussing with the coachman what the traveling arrangements were to be the next day. He took upon himself the task of subtly discovering whether Mr. Ridley had heard of the awkward business between his daughter and his host.

Then everyone but Digby and Lucas slipped from the room. Kes dropped into his chair once more, feeling tired already despite not having made the journey to Carlisle yet. Lucas sat in the chair Aldric had abandoned. Across the room, Digby was looking through the clothespress, no doubt with disappointment. Kes hadn't the King's eye for fashion.

"Julia told me what happened," Lucas said quietly. "I didn't tell the other Gents, wanting you to be able to say how much you wished, and when. But remembering what happened with Eleanor, I was worried. We didn't see you for quite a while after that. We missed you when you disappeared. Stanley especially."

Eleanor. The lady who'd laughed at his ham-fisted attempts at being quite debonair. "She embarrassed me, but I was not truly wounded. I didn't swear off love or anything afterward."

"You seemed to swear off *us* for a while."

Kes sighed. "A series of disappointments sent me into isolation all those years ago. I was feeling sorry for myself. I was most decidedly not nursing a broken heart."

"Yes, but Violet has touched your heart far, far more than any of the ladies you've ever had an interest in," Lucas said. "What if this is the disappointment that pulls you away from us again?"

Kes was falling short as a friend once more. Had he not learned anything in a decade? Hiding away, refusing to participate in their activities, was not something he could allow. That way held sorrow.

"I don't particularly wish to attend this assembly," he said, "but I won't hide myself away entirely."

"The Ridleys have reason to be concerned. Society places tremendous importance on a family's origins," Lucas said. "If you don't come to introduce them, you *particularly,* since you live here in this area, it would reflect badly on them. The others in attendance would see it as a sign of disapproval and reason enough to act on their own worst impulses."

He pushed out a tense breath. "I know."

"Then you also know that, regardless of how uncomfortable it will be, you have to be there."

"If it were only my discomfort in question, or even the wishes of the Gents, I wouldn't hesitate to be there. But my presence will cause her misery, and I don't want that." He took off his spectacles and rubbed at the pain pulsing between his eyes.

"If there's one thing we've learned from Niles, it's how to be supportive while also being unobtrusive. That is the approach you would do best to adopt until you know how much she is willing to accept of your presence."

Accept his presence. Such a far cry from what he'd let his heart imagine.

"Will the rest of you look after her and her family?" Kes pressed. "Make certain she isn't left to endure any cruelty?"

"I'm a bit offended that you think you have to ask." Lucas didn't often grow serious—there was a reason they called him the Jester—but when he did, like in that moment, the change was impossible to miss.

"I do trust you," Kes said. "I'm simply feeling a little—"

"Guilty?" Digby said, crossing back toward them, having left an entire ensemble laid out on Kes's bed.

"Yes," Kes said. "I feel blasted guilty about the whole thing. And I feel utterly stupid."

"For an academic like yourself, that must be a horribly unfamiliar feeling." Digby tugged at his lace cuffs as he always did when being a bit ridiculous. "Lucas, offer him your experienced insights."

They laughed. Even in the midst of his struggles, the Gents lightened him.

"Knowing how badly I've bungled things with Violet," he said to the other two, "will the Gents relax their attempts to steer my romantic efforts?"

"We will not cause Violet any distress," Lucas said. "We will honor her wishes in this. But we don't mean to abandon you."

"Not ever," Digby said.

He wanted to be annoyed. He wanted to protest. But hearing them say they hadn't given up helped. It helped to think that maybe he wasn't quite as forgettable and unnecessary to them all as he so often feared.

Chapter Twenty-Two

VIOLET HAD SELDOM BEEN SO perplexed.

She had found in Kester a particular friend, someone she thoroughly enjoyed spending time with. They had shared interests, had enjoyed varied and interesting conversations. She appreciated his dry humor and his intelligence. She liked the consideration he showed Georgie and that he treated her parents with respect and courtesy as well. She'd even found herself growing quite fond of him.

Then he'd kissed her, and everything had become confusing. She'd not thought of him in overtly romantic terms, but it seemed he had thought of her that way. He'd kissed her hand on a few occasions, but she'd seen Society gentlemen do that when greeting or acknowledging ladies they hadn't a romantic interest in.

He'd also held her hand quite often. That had seemed a particularly personal gesture. But he'd also done so when one or the other of them was speaking of difficult things. She'd seen that as offering comfort and receiving in return.

Now she didn't know what to think. She'd not meant to mislead him, but she could see that she had. She'd misled herself, truth be told, by dismissing the myriad clues she now saw so clearly. His feelings had been growing tender, and she'd not seen it. Perhaps she'd chosen not to, fearing what it would mean for their growing friendship if what he wanted was not what she wanted.

Now, it didn't matter. She didn't imagine they could ever go back to the easy friendship they'd enjoyed. But after the Gents and Julia returned to their homes, she would still be living near him. When she called on the Dalforths or Overtons, there was a chance he would be there. Should she attend future assemblies, he might very well be there as well. She had worried for weeks that she wouldn't make friends in this new area of the country. Now she feared every interaction would be punctuated by discomfort.

And blended in with all that was the curious realization that she missed Kes. It had been only a couple of days, yet she wished she'd seen him more. She wished she could visit his workshop and talk with him about what he was making and the things that interested him. She wished she could walk with him in the gardens again. She wished, knowing they were going to Carlisle, that they could wander back to the bookshop on the high street, to the clockmaker's shop, and generally just enjoy a pleasant afternoon.

She didn't doubt that many people would insist her longings were proof that she ought to have a romantic attachment to him. It was possible that in time she might have felt something more than friendship. She might have sorted out more nuance in their connection. But there was nothing between them now but discomfort and awkwardness.

"I do not wish to disrupt your thoughts," Julia said from across the carriage in which they were both riding to Carlisle. "I know you have been nervous about the local assembly and thought perhaps you could use a little reassurance."

"I wish you were attending the assembly," Violet said to Julia. "I would be more at ease with you there."

"Yes, well, Society has specific feelings on that matter."

"They have specific feelings about a lot of things," Violet replied dryly.

"The Gents will all support you in whatever way you need," Lucas said. "You're one of us now, just as Our Julia is." He smiled at the nickname they had all fashioned for his wife.

Violet had heard them use it again and again: *Our Julia*. Did they have a name like that for her? She didn't feel they *had* to craft one, but she found herself curious to know if they'd done so. They'd begun calling her by her Christian name, which was encouragement enough.

"The Gents are quite adept at navigating the often-miserable maze Society sets out," Julia said. "We need only tell them what you'd like them to do, and they will do it. They are as reliable as the mountains themselves."

"And just as dense," Lucas tossed back.

They all laughed, and it did Violet's heart good. Kester had sworn to her that the Gents would take her part and support her family. Though he was now an enormous question mark, she did not doubt the truthfulness of that. They would help her. They would help her family if doing so proved necessary.

Could they do so without being suffocating though? She suspected their enthusiasm often got the better of them, leading them to take over situations rather than simply assist in them. But if they understood the particular difficulties, especially with Lord Aldric's mind for strategy and Mr. Layton's tremendous charm, they likely could manage the thing with an impressive amount of finesse.

But only if they knew the extent of the difficulty.

They wouldn't if she didn't tell them.

The carriage continued rolling its way toward Carlisle. She pondered the dilemma in front of her. These gentlemen would help her if they knew what she was facing. Why, then, was she so hesitant?

She had found ways of being brave before, and this hardly held a candle to the life-altering troubles she'd faced in the past. So she rallied her courage and squared her shoulders and faced her traveling companions.

"You have, no doubt, sorted the most obvious barriers to my family's acceptance at the assembly. But there's one you're not aware of, one that may prove insurmountable."

They watched with patient anticipation.

"Two years ago, I broke my left arm. It was not a simple break, and though the doctors did their best, it took to infection. The putrification began spreading quickly. We were left with only one option." Understanding was dawning on their faces. She likely didn't need to keep explaining, but she chose to. "I am fortunate in that the doctors decided to undertake an amputation whilst the infection remained below the elbow. While I am grateful to have a prosthesis, I know not everyone will see it as admirable."

"I have suspected your arm was injured or had been in the past and hadn't healed well," Lucas said. "You seldom use it, and you keep it tucked very close to you most of the time."

She hadn't fooled them as much as she'd thought she had. "I learned early on that people caught unaware when they saw my false arm tended to respond in ways that were often unpleasant. I've experienced everything from disgust to laughter to cold dismissal. Though I would rather not hide part of who I am, I have found it is far less exhausting to do so."

"Which is why you always wear gloves and a shawl," Julia said. "It provides something of a barrier."

Violet nodded. She unbuttoned the edge of her sleeve, then pulled her glove off. Her left arm in all its stillness lay bare in front of them. "It will be covered at the assembly, but the moment I clasp hands with someone or they offer me their arm to escort me to the floor, this will become obvious."

"Ah," Lucas said with a nod. "And therein lies your dilemma. You are likely to be asked to dance, and you can't refuse without appearing rude, but you can't accept without revealing to all and sundry something they might feel gives them leave to treat you poorly."

"And I would worry less about that possibility if there weren't other obstacles to overcome. Most people have pebbles to step over or small hills to summit when arriving in Society. I feel like I'm attempting to climb Mont Aiguille."

Julia leaned forward as much as her heavily rounded belly would allow. "Then I have a perfect bit of encouragement for you, my dear friend. Lucas is a mountaineer. He has climbed that mountain."

"Are we still speaking figuratively?" Violet suspected the answer was no.

"Mountaineering is one of my passions." Lucas's leg bounced as he spoke. "I have, in reality, climbed Aiguille. And the Gents have figuratively climbed many others. If you have no objections to me sharing this with them, I believe we can help you navigate the coming assembly with maximum success and minimal embarrassment."

"Kester already knows," she said. "But I don't expect a great deal of assistance from that quarter."

"I do believe you can depend on him as well," Julia said.

"I *guarantee* you can," Lucas said. "Though he did not tell us about your prosthetic arm, he insisted the Gents make it our particular mission during the assembly to see to it that you and your family are not mistreated or unhappy and that your enjoyment of the evening should be our primary focus. He was insistent."

That was not surprising in the least. "That is certainly in keeping with his character. But surely all of you have noticed there's a great deal of awkwardness between us now."

"If there is one thing Kester Barrington excels at, it is awkwardness," Lucas said.

"Stop it." Julia swatted at her husband. "Kes does have a tendency toward clumsiness in his interactions, but he has a good heart, and he means well."

"Much of the awkwardness is my fault," she said. "I misunderstood so many things. I didn't see the many ways he was, honestly, very clear about . . ." Heavens, she was frustrated and confused. It was hardly in keeping with her credo to be cheerful. She attempted a less worried mien. "How long will he avoid me, do you suppose?"

"If he is actually avoiding you, I am certain it is because he thinks that's what *you* would prefer," Julia said. "He tends to default to what he thinks they want most, what they *need* most. He's considerate to the point of sometimes neglecting himself. Adding to that his bit of ineptitude with social interactions means he doesn't always know what to do when circumstances grow uncomfortable."

Perhaps kissing her without realizing that she didn't feel all the things he did was due to the social ineptitude Julia spoke of. He was not good at showing how he felt but didn't realize he did a poor job of it. But then again, the grief he felt for Stanley and the emotions attached to opening the strongbox had been very clearly expressed. Not easily though. And not quickly.

She herself had admitted he'd expressed, in his own way, his fondness for her. She hadn't seen it, hadn't recognized it. But it *had* been there. She had, however unintentionally, misled him. And it had cost her his friendship. She knew she would mourn that.

"We will do whatever you want us to," Lucas said.

What did she want? A great many things. But what she wanted most where the assembly was concerned was for her mother to find the acceptance and possibility of friends she longed for.

"I think you ought to tell the other Gents about my arm," she said. "I suspect I'm going to need all their help tomorrow night."

"I have every hope that the assembly will be better than you expect," Lucas said, "even if it is unlikely to be perfect."

"I can be content with that," Violet said.

"Georgie and I will have a wonderful time while all of you are off dancing and navigating and enduring," Julia said. "I will insist you ride in this carriage back to Livingsley Hall, then you and I can discuss the assembly at tremendous length."

How she had come to adore her new friend. And Julia and Lucas did not live terribly far from Irthing Grange. The journey, as she understood, took about as long as the one to Carlisle, though in the opposite direction. They lived almost in Northumberland.

Northumberland, where the apothecary lived, the one Kester had intended to write to and ask his thoughts on a mechanical prosthesis. His shop, as Kester had explained it, was just beyond the edge of the county. That might put it near Brier Hill, Julia and Lucas's home. Perhaps if Kester didn't mean to continue pursuing their project, she could pay a visit to Julia and seek out the apothecary herself.

Explaining the trip to her parents would be far easier if she had the excuse of visiting her friend. She didn't think Mother and Father would object to her attempts at improving her prosthesis, but something about telling them she was working on it before she knew if her hopes were unfounded didn't sit well on her mind. She wasn't an untrusting person, not at all. But her thoughts turned once more to the words of the vicar in Portsmouth.

"Be sunny or be silent."

It all went back to that, really. Talking about her efforts required that she mention the chances of failure and the discouragement she felt. It meant speaking of her frustrations. Doing that wasn't being cheerful. Kester had insisted she not force herself to appear lighthearted, at least not in his company, but she didn't know that she would ever have his companionship again.

No, she would keep working on her prosthesis on her own, and she would keep her frustrations to herself. She would continue putting forth a rosy front, and she would hope, silently, for the best.

Chapter Twenty-Three

The group had arrived at the Dappled Chicken with two hours to spare before supper was to be served. The Gents, other than Kes, had made their way up to the high street. Mr. and Mrs. Ridley were resting in the room reserved for them. Julia and Violet were spending time with each other. Kes took advantage of the inn's garden to take a few minutes for himself.

He knew the Gents were correct; he needed to be part of the upcoming assembly and show local society that the Ridleys were a welcome and worthy addition to their ranks. But, heaven help him, he was uncomfortable. There remained so much awkwardness between Violet and him, and he hadn't the first idea how to address it.

He generally addressed social discomfort by making himself useful but unobtrusive. Helping the Ridleys navigate the assembly would certainly be useful to them, but he didn't know how to be present without imposing upon Violet's peace. The Gents were certainly capable of assisting the family. Perhaps if he concentrated his efforts on keeping the Gents from acting on their all-too-frequent tendency toward mischief, that would allow him to participate without being *too* present.

He'd very seldom failed them in that. With a familiarity borne of experience, he pushed down the memory of his most monumental failure to save them from themselves.

He turned a corner and saw Georgie walking toward him. She somehow managed to look both focused and a little lost. No matter his awkwardness with her cousin, he had no intention of abandoning this little girl if she was in need.

He met her on the garden path. "Is anything the matter? You seem a bit downcast."

"Everyone is talking about the assembly. I can't go, so there's nothing for me to talk about."

He could appreciate the feeling of not being part of what everyone else was undertaking.

"Why can't I go?" she asked him.

He motioned her to the nearby wooden bench. "Because Society only allows people to attend balls and such once they are considered fully grown."

"Lord Jonquil doesn't act like he's grown up," Georgie said, setting herself on the bench.

"He certainly enjoys larks."

Georgie nodded. "If Lord Jonquil would stay back from the assembly, he and I could play games. He's excellent at games."

"He always has been."

She slumped on the bench, the posture providing further evidence that she was not yet ready for an assembly, no matter her insistence otherwise.

"Lady Jonquil will not be attending tomorrow night," Kes reminded her. "You can spend the evening with her."

"I do like her. She listens to me when I talk about the things I'm studying. She doesn't think I'm strange because I want to learn."

"Lady Jonquil has a love of learning herself. In fact, I can say without hesitation that she is one of the most intelligent people I have ever known."

That brought Georgie's gaze to him. "Truly?"

He nodded. "I suspect she enjoys listening to what you are learning because she genuinely shares your enthusiasm."

Georgie's ebony brow tipped in an angle of contemplation. "There's always a little sadness in her eyes though. I never know if that's because of something I said."

"It is not anything you've said or done," Kes assured her. "She misses her family. And though she's a happy person, I think that makes her heart a little heavy."

Georgie tucked her feet up onto the bench and wrapped her arms around her knees. The position made her seem even younger than she was. "Did her family die?" she asked softly.

"Quite a few of them did, yes."

Georgie didn't speak for a long moment. When she did, she kept her eyes lowered, and her voice was hesitant. "My parents died. I feel sad about that a lot of the time."

Oh, how his heart ached for this child and the suffering he knew all too well. "My parents died when I was only a couple of years older than you," he said.

She blinked rapidly, a strategy he had often adopted to hold back tears. "Then you know."

He tentatively put an arm around her shoulders. "I do know."

The little girl leaned against him, still curled in something of a ball, still holding herself in that self-protective way.

"Do you feel sad a lot of the time?" she asked.

"I still miss them, and I still wish they were here. But the sadness doesn't hurt the way it once did."

"It's better?" She spoke with a very fragile sound of hope.

"It does get better, Georgie. I promise you."

"You still seem sad though," she said. "You don't always want to sit with people."

Those two things were not entirely correlated, but how did he explain to her? "Sometimes I sit on my own because I'm sad. But sometimes I just like that it's quiet and I can take some time to think."

She shifted a little and looked up at him. "What do you think about when you are alone?"

Based on the clouds clearing from her expression, this was a topic she was interested in pursuing. He was more than willing to indulge her in it. "My favorite thing to think about is how to improve and change things."

"What sort of things?" She sat up a little bit straighter.

"When I was very young, I spent a great deal of time trying to discover a means of making pens drip less. In school, I thought very long and very hard about how to make traveling desks easier to travel with. I have contemplated changes to the interiors of carriages and ways to change the landscape of lawns and gardens to assist with drainage. I have very recently set my mind to making improvements to carriage lanterns."

"What are you changing about them?" There was no mistaking her eager curiosity. He saw in her expression so much of what had lit his face at that age when new ideas had been presented to him.

He explained the concept to her, avoiding words that might be confusing while making certain not to talk down to her. At her age, he had disliked when adults spoke to him as if he were an infant. She asked insightful questions and seemed to truly enjoy the discussion.

Georgie sat fully straight, bouncing a little in her spot. "You and Violet could work on this together. She's very smart."

"I have discovered that about her."

"And she's very happy," Georgie said. "That will help when your heart feels sad about your parents."

It did help, he could not deny that. But he remembered all too well how she'd been told and had taken to heart the admonition to not ever be anything but sunny and outwardly happy. He had offered to hear any less-than-sunny worry she had, but that wasn't likely to happen now. Would she give up on that entirely?

"Does anyone help your cousin when her heart feels sad?" Kes asked.

"Her heart doesn't ever feel sad." Georgie shrugged. "Uncle Ridley calls her 'a ray of sunshine.'"

The sound of footsteps on the path pulled their attention in the direction of the inn. Violet was walking toward them, her gloved hands, overly long undersleeves, and shawl identifying her as easily as did her beautiful coils of nearly black hair.

He missed the friendship and connection he'd had with her. He missed the hopes he'd cherished where she was concerned. He missed *her*.

"There you are, Georgie," she said as she approached. "Have you been bothering Mr. Barrington?"

Kes rose, as any true gentleman would at the arrival of a lady, and answered on behalf of himself and Georgie. "She has not been a bother in the least. We've had a wonderful conversation."

"Did you know Mr. Barrington likes to invent and improve things?" Georgie said.

"I did know that," Violet said.

"And his parents died when he was a little boy, so *he knows*." She repeated the declaration of their similar grief with less heaviness than she had the first time.

"Best go back inside, dear," Violet said. "Your aunt and uncle are looking for you."

Georgie climbed off the bench and skipped back inside. Violet, however, remained behind. "Thank you for showing her such kindness."

"It was my pleasure," he said.

He wanted to say so much more, wanted to offer an explanation, an apology. Anything. The air around them hung heavy with discomfort and uncertainty.

She must have felt it too; she moved about in that stilted way people did when terribly uncomfortable.

The least he could do was offer her an escape. "Please, do not allow me to keep you. I'm certain there is much for you to do before tomorrow's assembly. And you would likely appreciate resting as well."

Her countenance fell a bit, but she didn't object to the escape. Before he could make sense of any of it, she hurried off in the same direction her cousin had gone.

Kes watched her go with an increasingly heavy heart. He didn't know how to make any of this right, but he sorely wished he could.

She might never truly begin working with him again, but he would be forever grateful that she had given him the nudge he'd needed to open Stanley's box once more and take up the task of finishing what his friend had begun. In allowing him to face some of the grief he still felt, she had opened a door for him, one he had been unable to open himself.

Though the assembly would be uncomfortable and likely exhausting, he would be there, and he would do all he could to see her accepted by local society. *That* was a door he could open for her.

He still felt uneasy returning to the inn, but his determination pushed him onward. He had a purpose at the assembly the next evening. He had a way of being part of Violet's life without imposing upon her. It was not the role he'd imagined himself playing, but he would do all he could to fill it well.

Chapter Twenty-Four

Violet spent the day of the Carlisle assembly leisurely undertaking the necessary preparations. Powdering hair alone required hours, and there were a great many people in their group. Though Violet would have preferred to leave her hair its natural color, Mother had rightly pointed out that they hadn't the social standing to forgo a fashion still so widely accepted. Yes, there would likely be young ladies and young gentlemen who attended without their hair powdered, but they would be few and would be those whose standing was well established. Until the Ridleys had that degree of cachet, Violet needed to tread carefully.

Julia, Mother, Violet, and Georgie had all claimed the same room at the Dappled Chicken for the day's preparations. Julia had shown herself to have a knack with Georgie, allowing the girl to talk when she chose to and sit quietly when she needed. Georgie had discovered in Julia someone who was as curious as she about the world and who also would sometimes lapse into quiet reflection.

A room in which everyone present was aware of her prosthesis allowed Violet to leave off her gloves for the first time in weeks. There was something very freeing about not hiding this. She kept this part of her life secret to avoid being treated with unkindness. But that secrecy undermined her confidence and made accepting this change very difficult.

Julia's lady's maid saw to Violet's and Mother's hair. She was capable despite working for a lady who never powdered her own hair. And she was empathetic when Violet's lack of enthusiasm became apparent.

"Will I have to powder my hair when I'm grown?" Georgie asked.

Violet couldn't see anyone in the room, on account of the metal shield placed over her face to protect it from the fall of powder.

"I suspect," Julia said, "the fashion for hair powdering will have ceased by the time you are old enough to undertake it."

"Good," Georgie said firmly. "I don't like it. I like my hair as it is."

"So do I," Julia said.

"I *do* like Aunt Ridley's gown though. I should very much like to wear that when I'm older."

"This color would look lovely on you, Georgiana," Mother said. "The green would bring out the green in your eyes."

"My eyes never can decide what color they are." Georgie had often spoken of her frustration with that. "I wish they were brown like yours and Violet's or gray like Uncle Ridley's."

"Your eyes are precisely like your mother's were," Mother said to the little girl. "And she was the most beautiful woman I've ever met."

How Violet wished she could see Georgie's reaction to that. It was difficult to predict from day-to-day if Georgie would be pleased by reminders of her parents or grieved by them. Her discussion with Kester the day before on this very topic had seemed to lift her spirits. Violet was grateful for his compassion and caring.

"My father tells me that my eyes remind him of my mother's," Julia said. "It is a fine thing to carry about reminders of people who are not with us. But it can also make me feel a little sad."

"A person isn't supposed to be sad," Georgie said. "People are forever saying that: that being happy, or at least *seeming* happy, makes one a better person."

"Did you know, Georgie, that I have a dear little boy in my life," Julia said, "and he was told much the same thing. Do you know what I said to him?"

"To be sunny or be silent?" Georgie guessed, her voice filled with discouragement.

Violet winced a little at the reminder of the tenet she herself struggled to live by.

"No," Julia said.

Georgie offered another guess. "We have to try very hard to have hope?" It was another of Violet's regular sayings.

"I likely did say something similar to *that*, as it is a helpful philosophy. But what I told him, my sweet friend, is that it is good and necessary to let our hearts be sad sometimes. Having been sad, we can appreciate even more those times when we are happy. Feeling one thing rather than another does not make us good people or bad people. It simply means we are *real* people."

It simply means we are real *people.* The truthfulness of that weighed on Violet's mind as she sat, her hair being powdered. Feeling one thing rather than another did not make a person good or bad. She had come, over the last two years, to accept the fact that she felt many different things about the difficulties she experienced in life. Enduring and experiencing them was one thing. Fully sharing struggles with others, though, still eluded her.

Except for with Kester. She'd told him a lot of what worried her. He was kind and reassuring. He'd listened without dismissal, and he'd shared some of his own worries with her. A lump of emotion rose in her throat. She missed him. And she couldn't make the least sense of her contradictory thoughts and reactions where he was concerned.

"Mr. Barrington said that he is still sad about his parents, but the sadness doesn't hurt as much now." Georgie sounded as though she believed him. That, Violet prayed, might give the girl some much-needed hope.

"He is right about that," Julia said. "In time, the pain lessens. And you'll find more and more reasons to be more and more happy."

"Are you more and more happy, Lady Jonquil?" Georgie asked.

"I am."

More and more happy. It was what Violet longed for. But her determination to be sunny didn't seem to be bringing her that increase in happiness.

Eventually, the preparations were completed, and they all emerged from the room to join the gentlemen in the private dining room below. Violet was nervous. She took strength in her mother's regal bearing, Julia's glances of consolation, and the tender trust Georgie showed in their new friend.

All the Gents and Father were waiting for them. They were resplendent in their finery. Silks and lace, ruffles and highly polished buckles abounded. Father wore his best wig, something his generation still did. The younger gentlemen's hair was coiffed to perfection, powdered to varying degrees, and tied back in ribbons perfectly coordinated with their silk jackets and pantaloons. Their buckled shoes were polished to a brilliant shine.

Julia crossed to Lucas and shook her head with a playful sigh. "I still insist you are most handsome without the hair powder."

He pressed the back of his hand to his forehead, the very picture of dramatic suffering. "Alas, my dear, I must sacrifice for the greater good tonight."

Julia looked to the rest of them. "And all of you? Are you sacrificing as well, or do you still consider me daft for my dislike of powdering?"

"We beg to be permitted not to answer the question, as we are sure to offend someone," Lord Aldric said.

Julia's attention had already returned to Lucas. "I wish I were going to be with you tonight."

He set his hands gently on either side of her face and pressed a light kiss to her forehead. "I will remain here if you wish me to, my dear. You simply say the word."

"The Ridleys need you at the assembly," she said.

"But what *you* need will always be most important to me."

The rest of the group was making their way toward the door. Violet kept back, touched by Julia and Lucas's tenderness toward each other.

"Eventually, I won't worry so much when you leave." Julia sounded a little embarrassed. "Everyone must think I am utterly pathetic."

"I certainly hope you don't think that of yourself," Lucas said.

"I try very hard not to."

Lucas kept one arm around his wife and turned to face Georgie. "Thank you for keeping my Julia company while I am away."

Georgie curtsied deeply. "My pleasure, Lord Jonquil."

Lucas kissed Julia's cheek before dropping his arm away.

"We had best be off," Kester said, standing near the door. He didn't look directly at anyone in particular. His posture spoke of discomfort and dislike of the situation. If Violet had to guess, she would say he wished to be at home. Though she was certain some of his feelings tonight could be laid at her feet, a good portion was likely due to his discomfort around others and his preference for quiet.

The assembly rooms were not far from the Dappled Chicken, and the journey was accomplished quickly. Mother and Violet entered, surrounded by a bevy of impressive gentlemen. They were far from the first to arrive, though Violet suspected they would not be the last. Bows and words of acknowledgment were offered to the Gents. Violet suspected they were quite well known in Society, no matter where in the kingdom they might be.

In a whisper, Mother said to her, "Keep your head high, my dear. We are as worthy of being here as anyone."

The declaration was made with pride and purpose and encouragement. Mother was not at all dismissing their legitimate reasons for concern but rather reminding her daughter that their worth was not determined by others' approval.

"Lord Aldric," a gentleman in garishly red silk said. "A pleasure."

Aldric acknowledged that with a quick nod. "I believe you know most of my company."

"I do," was the new arrival's response.

Kester stood among them but gave every indication of wishing he were anywhere else. His gaze was either on his feet or the distant dancers. Never on those gathered around.

"Allow me to offer introductions to our newest acquaintances," Lord Aldric continued with the gentleman who'd joined them. "Mr. and Mrs. Ridley, Miss Ridley, this is Lord Hettersham of Northumberland. Lord Hettersham, these are the Ridleys of Irthing Grange here in Cumberland."

"A pleasure." He offered the two-word greeting in precisely the same tone and inflection he'd used when first acknowledging Lord Aldric. Whether he was, indeed, as pleased to meet her family as he was to cross paths with the son of a duke or was merely offering the acknowledgment out of habit, Violet wasn't certain. Still, she chose to see it as a good sign for the coming evening.

Their introduction to a Mr. Adcock went equally well. Mr. and Mrs. Dalforth were present and pleased to cross paths with them. Sir Randolph and Lady Collington were not outright rude but neither did they give any impression of delight at seeing their newest neighbors.

How Violet wished Julia were in attendance. She was such a delightful source of reassurance.

A minuet was struck up to begin the evening. Violet made absolutely certain not to look at Kester. She rather suspected he was doing the same. Father accompanied Mother out to join the set.

Lord Hettersham approached Violet. Worry tugged at her mind.

To Henri, she whispered, "The minuet cannot be danced without touching multiple people's hands."

"Never fear, *mademoiselle*." He slipped her left arm through his, doing a remarkable job of showing no surprise at how awkwardly it laid there. Choosing that arm meant no one was likely to touch or reach for it in their interactions.

"Miss Ridley, are you engaged for this set?" Lord Hettersham asked.

"*Oui, monsieur*," Henri said. "I have been granted the honor of her company for this set, though I have quite adamantly insisted I have the opportunity to speak with her throughout rather than be continually separated by a dance."

The young baron looked a bit disappointed, which did Violet's heart a great deal of good. He bowed briefly and continued on his way.

"I fear you have now committed yourself to my company and will not be able to ask anyone to dance with you."

"While that is true, there is no reason for concern. I am pleased with the prospect."

She eyed him sidelong. "Can you honestly tell me that you would not enjoy dancing with a lady?"

"I do enjoy dancing," he said. "But, no, there is no one at this present gathering I would be utterly heartbroken to miss a dance with."

There was an undercurrent in his answer that struck her as intriguing. *No one at this present gathering.* Did that mean there was someone who did meet that description but who was not in attendance? How very intriguing.

They took a slow circuit around the room, speaking easily and with none of the discomfort that often accompanied such arrangements. That was one of the benefits of having arrived in the company of friends.

Henri stopped their forward progress now and then to offer a word of greeting or conversation with those present. If the person was unknown to Violet, he made the introduction. With those she had already met, he made certain to include her in their discussions.

"Your mother is an elegant dancer," Henri said as they began their second circuit of the room.

"She is. My father has always said so, though he is quick to point out his own inelegance. He first saw her at a gathering where dancing was undertaken, and it was her gracefulness that captured his attention."

"I can understand why. The French are very particular about dancing, and I can find absolutely nothing to disapprove of in her execution of the minuet."

With a laugh, Violet said, "I notice you did not make the same observation about my father."

"What he lacks in grace he makes up for in his clear admiration of his partner. Your father chose well, and not merely in the context of this dance."

"Yes, he did."

They passed a group of young people, all likely about her age, who watched her as she passed. Their expressions she knew well. They did not truly approve of her but were hiding it. Snippets of their whispered conversation reached her, mentions of "merchant class" and "upstart." Sometimes people were vocal about their disapproval; sometimes they were extremely subtle. Most of the time, people fell somewhere in between.

Keep your head high, my dear, her mother's words echoed in her thoughts. And she obeyed them. She would not be made ashamed of herself.

The evening pressed onward, with each of the Gents taking their turn sitting with her or walking about with her. Digby accompanied her to the terrace at the back of the assembly rooms. It was well lit, and the doors leading to it were kept wide open. It was far from empty, and there was nothing untoward or scandalous about spending time there.

"I suspected you needed a bit of an escape," he explained. "The closeness of these gatherings can be a bit much."

"Especially when one knows one is being scrutinized and subsequently dismissed," Violet said.

"Oh, is Lady Collington still here?" He spoke a little too innocently.

"You are quite familiar with her, it seems," Violet said.

"Unfortunately."

There was comfort in knowing she wasn't the only one who found the judgmental lady unpleasant company. "I can't imagine she has voiced any disapproval of you, Your Majesty."

Digby puffed his chest out in a show of feigned arrogance. "She wouldn't dare."

After a moment, they returned to the ballroom. The set was only then coming to its conclusion. Mother was standing at the other corner of the room, with Father at her side, the two of them speaking with another couple about their age. The conversation appeared to be a pleasant one. Violet hoped that it was.

Digby walked with her back to where Lord Aldric and Lucas stood.

Lucas lowered his voice as she reached them. "All appears to be going well, but you need only say the word if you are ready to retire."

"You have all been gallant knights this evening. I appreciate that."

Lord Aldric shook his head. "You are one of us now, Violet. The evening has not been a strain on any of us."

"Except for Kester," she said. "Social gatherings are not his preference, and he has seemed particularly uncomfortable at this one."

The three gentlemen gathered around her did not offer their own evaluations, but she could sense what they left unspoken. His added discomfort came from her. She didn't know what could be done about that.

From among the gathering, a gentleman approached them. She didn't think she had been introduced to him yet. There was nothing familiar about him.

As he came near, the three Gents who were with her turned to look. In near perfect unison, surprise and more than a hint of disapproval filled their faces. This gentleman might have been a stranger to her, but he clearly was not to them.

"Mr. Finley," Lucas said. The acknowledgment was not one made in overly friendly tones, but neither was it dripping with disapproval. "What brings you to this corner of the kingdom?"

"I've been visiting a friend."

In a tone of perfect innocence but with a look that skewered, Digby said, "I didn't realize you had any of those."

Mr. Finley ignored the comment. He turned his gaze on Violet. There was nothing threatening in it, nothing lecherous, but the other gentlemen's reactions to him made her wary.

"I do not believe I've had the opportunity of being introduced to your beautiful friend." There was no determining which of her companions he was speaking *to*, but it was clear he was speaking *about* her.

Lucas took up the introduction, which told her he was the one most acquainted with this new arrival. "Finley, this is Miss Ridley of Cumberland, a particular friend of ours, and a lady we value highly." The last bit was added in a tone no one would mistake for anything but warning.

Mr. Finley offered a bow that was neither deferential nor an obvious slight. "I hope you have not been engaged for this dance," he said to her.

Panic began to swirl. She had already spent a set with each of the Gents except for Kester. Accepting a second would raise eyebrows. Her father might've claimed her for another set without whispers, but he was not nearby.

What was she to do? She could tell Mr. Finley was not a man she wished to spend the length of a set with.

She felt certain the Gents would be willing to endure whispers in order to save her from misery, but she couldn't ask that of them.

Before anyone, including Mr. Finley, could say anything, another voice entered the conversation.

"Miss Ridley, forgive me for the delay." Kester. His arrival immediately eased her worries. He would find a means of helping her. She knew he would. "I do believe this is the set you so graciously allowed me to claim."

Where he had come from or how he'd arrived so quickly and so quietly, she couldn't say. But she was deeply grateful.

"If you mean to take a turn about the room, as was done with every other gentleman who has engaged you," Mr. Finley said, "allow me to join. I'd like to get to know you better."

"I'm afraid that will not be possible," Kester said. "This is the allemande, and I am excessively fond of dancing it."

Violet turned worried eyes on him. She knew how to dance the allemande, of course, but she hadn't done so since her amputation. She wasn't certain what new complications might arise.

He held his left hand out to her, which allowed her to place her right hand in his. She did so and held more tightly than was likely necessary. He led her away.

As they approached the floor, she asked, "How do we free ourselves from this?"

"The allemande doesn't separate couples. You will never be holding any hand but mine."

He'd thought it through. That likely had not happened in the split second between offering to walk about with her and realizing they would need to dance to avoid Mr. Finley. He must have pondered it at some length in the days since they'd attempted the minuet.

"I haven't practiced the allemande," she warned him. "I will likely look an absolute quiz."

In a voice just loud enough to be overheard but not obviously raised, he said, "I hope you will be patient with me, Miss Ridley. I have been known to render even the most proficient partners a bit upended with my excruciating lack of grace."

He had created a ready reason for any awkwardness she displayed. Another act of compassion. Was it any wonder he had become such a quick and valued friend? He thought of others, just as Julia said. He did what he thought would help *them.* That compassion and consideration came as naturally to him as breathing.

If only he hadn't misunderstood her feelings and she hadn't misunderstood his. If only that unexpected and confusing kiss didn't sit between them.

The dance began with her left hand in his. He gave no indication there was anything unusual in the hand he held. They moved forward with the prescribed bouncing steps. They separated to undertake the small circles that came next. Forward and backward they moved. She didn't dare look at anyone else, afraid to discover that her efforts were being met with disapproval.

Kester smiled and nodded minutely.

The steps brought them together again. The arm placement for the next bit was complicated, even in the best of circumstances. She held her right arm out to the side, and she bent, as well as she could, her left arm behind her back. Kester did the same. The slightest tug of the straps holding that arm in place told her he had, somehow, almost miraculously, managed to clasp the wooden hand behind her though she was certain she had not placed it in quite the right spot.

They moved in yet another circle, arms entwined that way. She looked across at him, trying to breathe her way through the struggle of this unexpected undertaking.

"All is well," he said in a low voice. "Have faith in yourself."

They dropped hands and switched arms. Again, he helped make up the difference in her inexperience. And he, who forever looked uncomfortable in such settings, gave every indication of sincere pleasure.

What would she do if she lost his friendship? How she would miss his good and caring heart.

The remainder of the dance was a repetition of what they'd already done, with a few small changes. She moved forward with full confidence that he would see her through any difficulties encountered.

As the dance concluded, she offered the closing curtsy and he the bow. The required polite applause sounded around the room, and the many couples who'd stood to undertake this most elegant of dances accompanied one another away from the open floor to rejoin the onlookers.

Mother and Father and all the Gents were waiting for them. Mother pressed a hand to her heart, a shimmer of tears showing in her eyes.

"It is good to see you dance again," she whispered. "I hope you will continue to."

"So do I," she said.

She found that she meant it. She liked returning to those parts of life she had once enjoyed. She hadn't even realized how many of them she had cut herself off from. With the right partner, she could enjoy dancing again. She could enjoy games of an evening. That for the length of the allemande the "right partner" had been Kester Barrington likely should have astounded her.

But it didn't.

He was the first person she had trusted in this area of the world, the first with whom she had shared her concerns. He was the first outside of her family to whom she had spoken about the loss of her arm. He was the only person she had told about her dreams for her prosthesis.

She trusted him. Even with the monumental misunderstanding that had pushed them apart, she trusted him.

He was nearby still but not truly among them all. He stood there, no doubt willing to do what needed to be done to defend her, as uncomfortable as ever in company. He was her friend, and a valued one.

Kester had told her there wasn't a day when he wasn't missing someone. Violet could not imagine spending the rest of her life missing him.

Chapter Twenty-Five

"I WISH THERE WERE A more accommodating place to stop between Carlisle and Livingsley Hall," Kes said.

They'd pulled the caravan of carriages off the road at the edge of a meadow. Julia had needed a respite from the tasking experience of riding in her uncomfortable condition, but this was all the road had to offer.

"Julia isn't in need of anything special," Lucas said. "She benefits most from simply being able to stand up and walk around."

"Is she doing well otherwise?" Kes asked.

Lucas nodded. "As far as I know. I'm hardly an expert in such things."

"It might be best if you traveled directly to Lampton Park after the Gents gathering has concluded. I imagine you would like your child to be born at the family seat, as most of the Jonquils have been over the generations."

"That was Julia's suggestion as well," Lucas said. "If the two most intelligent people I know both offer the same advice, I would do well to follow it."

"I can't say that I still deserve the label of intelligent," Kes said. "I've offered ample evidence to the contrary of late."

Lucas was clearly holding back a laugh. "If missteps with women were a mark against intelligence, I would wager most anyone who ever loved a woman has been proven rather stupid."

Kes could laugh at that. Most of the Gents, but especially Lucas, had made fools of themselves over a woman at one point or another.

"I was grateful to all of you for stepping in when Finley made his unexpected appearance. What are the chances he would be in this corner of the kingdom when he doesn't live anywhere near here?" Fate had dealt them an unkind hand in that.

While Finley had not shown himself to be physically dangerous company for a woman to keep, there was something a bit rotten about him, and he did not treat women as respectfully as he ought. That he had already been making Violet uncomfortable had been apparent even from a distance. Kes had moved with all possible haste toward her, all the while pleading with the heavens to get him there in time to provide her with a means of escape.

"That is the way with parasites," Lucas said. "They always manage to emerge where they are least expected and least wanted. Whilst you were seeing to Violet's escape, Digby and I dropped a word of warning in the man's ear. I doubt he'll be bothering her again."

Kes hoped that proved true.

"Did Violet say anything to you or Julia about the assembly?" Kes asked. "I've been attempting to give her as wide a berth as I can, but that means I haven't the first idea if she was pleased with the evening."

Lucas studied him a little. "Are you hoping that she was?"

"Of course. She and I may be on difficult terms, but that doesn't mean I want her to be unhappy. I haven't much to offer, but I will do all I can when I can."

"You sell yourself short, my friend. Your rescue of her was quite possibly the most dramatic of the evening, and you afforded her the opportunity to dance, which likely helped quell some whispers. It did not go unnoticed that no gentleman had danced with her yet. I worried a little what the gossipmongers would make of that. Any assumption they might have made, you turned on its head."

He had enjoyed dancing with her. The allemande was a very personal dance, one that kept a couple near each other, almost always touching. Maintaining his neutrality had been a hard-fought battle. He didn't mind if other people saw his partiality for her; he simply didn't want to cause her distress by subjecting *her* to his feelings.

"I am all but convinced I won't see her again after the Gents leave. I'm grateful that she's found friends in all of you. A person could not hope for better."

"Do you mean we could not hope for a better friend than Violet or that Violet could not hope for better friends than us?" Lucas asked with his customary tone of teasing.

"Both," Kes said.

"And is that why you spend so much time with the lot of us?" he asked. "If required to wager on it, I would place my money on you wanting far more time to yourself than you have allotted in years."

"I do like peace and quiet," he admitted. "But we're not at school any longer. We don't all live in the same flat with endless time together like we once did. When we *are* in company, I choose not to waste that opportunity. That, however, means there isn't time for other things."

"There is never time for things we don't *make* time for," he said. "Julia taught me that lesson clearly and concisely. I was not making time for her, and I nearly lost her."

And therein lay the reason Kes always made time for these gentlemen who had saved him in so many ways. He knew from painful experience that time sometimes ran out.

"Have you sorted out how you mean to move forward with the awkwardness between you and your nearest neighbor?" Lucas asked.

"I haven't, beyond my determination not to impose upon her. I will keep to Livingsley Hall when I'm home and leave it to the Ridleys to decide how often we see each other. That seems the best approach. I have imposed upon her already; I don't mean to do so again."

Except, he knew he needed one more quick moment with her. He hadn't apologized for what had happened, and it was important that he do so.

Violet and Julia crossed their path a few moments later. Julia stopped beside Lucas, who immediately slipped his arm around her.

Kes did his best to study Julia without appearing to do so. She looked tired. And she was a little pale.

"Do you need to sit?" Lucas asked.

"I'm about to sit for hours," Julia answered. "At the moment, I'm simply grateful to have stretched my limbs for a few moments."

"And the baby?"

"Not particularly happy about being jostled in a carriage," Julia said. "And the little one has not hesitated to make that displeasure known."

"Well," Kes tossed in, "the child *is* either a future earl or a future baroness."

Julia looked immediately confused. "Baroness?" She looked to Lucas. "The Farland title will be absorbed in the Lampton titles. No child of ours can inherit my title on its own."

"Of course he or she can." Lucas shook his head a bit, appearing entirely perplexed.

Julia looked to Kes. "Do you know what he is talking about?"

"Lucas told me back when your engagement was announced that he insisted, during the negotiation of the marriage settlement, that the Farland title remain independent, to be inherited by whichever of your children comes next in line to you, excluding the one who inherits the Lampton titles."

She returned her attention to her husband. "Why did you never tell me this?"

Lucas rubbed at the back of his neck. "I thought I had."

"You did that for me? Even when you were still decidedly opposed to the idea of marrying me?"

He nodded. "I could do little to improve things for you, but I fought for every consideration I could secure on your behalf."

Julia slipped her arms around him. "You are a good man, Lucas Jonquil."

"And you are a patient woman. I truly don't keep things from you on purpose. I swear to you I don't. I simply forget things. Or I think I've told you, but I actually haven't."

"I know, and I'm learning to trust you."

He kissed her temple. "I'm infinitely grateful that you are." He led Julia back in the direction of the carriages.

The Gents teased Lucas about being something of an idiot where his wife was concerned. In reality, he was easily distracted and too often inclined to undervalue his generosity. It was the reason the Gents had needed to work so hard to help Lucas save his marriage; he tended to get in his own way.

Kes stepped a little closer to Violet but not so near that she would be worried that he meant to inflict himself upon her again. "Do you think Julia is unwell?"

"She seems tired," Violet said. "But she didn't mention anything more concerning than that. I didn't notice anything alarming."

That was a relief. He would hate for her to be suffering or struggling or unhappy.

"I have known few husbands as attentive as Lucas," Violet said. "I've even heard him tell her when he means to leave the house to go for a walk or a ride with one of the Gents. Not in a way that implies he's asking permission but clearly as an act of courtesy."

Kes motioned for her to continue walking, and he kept to her side. "That is an agreement between them. Julia endured a painful degree of abandonment as a child, and that left scars and fears that are not easily overcome. Lucas shares his plans with her because he recognizes the enormity of the pain she still carries. Perhaps over time, her concerns will grow less overwhelming and these reassurances will no longer be needed. But I haven't the least doubt, he doesn't begrudge her the need nor does he think less of her because she has been hurt." Discussions of needed acts of consideration brought his mind around to the next order of business. "I will not detain you, but if you will permit me the briefest of moments, there is something I need to say."

She looked a little wary but nodded her agreement.

"Miss Ridley, I owe you an apology. That afternoon in my workshop, I imposed upon you, and that is inexcusable. I am sorry, and I swear to you it will not happen again. The extent of our interactions will be determined by you, and I vow to abide by the limits you set. Please do not worry that you will be imposed upon again by me. I promise you will not."

He knew the words had rushed from him, likely a little faster than they ought, but she seemed to have understood.

"You place far too much blame upon yourself," she said. "The misunderstanding between us was not merely on your part. My lack of clarity, I am certain, compounded yours. I do not, I assure you, hold you in contempt or distrust you. I was surprised, but I wasn't offended."

"I have been racked with worry these past days that I caused you pain."

She shook her head. "Confusion, yes. But not pain."

"I was, as you have acknowledged, a little confused myself."

Violet fussed absentmindedly with one of her curls, her eyes darting about but not settling on anything. He did his best to clear his dry throat, but it didn't help.

"I should—" He motioned with his head toward the other carriages. "Everyone is likely anxious to resume the journey home."

"I suspect you are correct." Her eyes shifted toward the carriage she had been riding in.

He nodded slowly, stiffly. "Thank you for your graciousness with my obtuseness, Miss Ridley."

"You needn't stop calling me Violet," she said. "All the Gents do, and I don't mean to exclude you from that."

Again, he was the recipient of consideration he knew he didn't warrant. He would honor her wishes in this but would not let himself see it as an invitation to reclaim their former closeness.

They had arrived beside the carriages, where their fellow travelers were gathered. Everyone was ready to leave.

"Mr. and Mrs. Ridley suggested that Henri travel in our carriage," Julia said to Violet. "But Henri informed them that the empty seat had already been claimed."

That was a narrow escape on Henri's part.

"Unfortunately," Lucas said, "none of the hulverheads in this group immediately identified himself as the one who had claimed it. So we had to say Kes was the fourth occupant."

Good heavens. He looked to Violet, gauging her reaction. "I said a moment ago that I will defer to you in dictating our interactions. If my presence in the carriage will make you too uncomfortable, I will insist one of the other Gents take my place. I will think of some explanation for your parents."

But Violet shook her head. "I'm not bothered by it. Julia and I can take the forward-facing seat and gossip to our hearts' content. You and Lucas can sit rear-facing and discuss whatever it is gentleman discuss on long carriage rides."

"Mostly pugilists and horse races," Lucas said in his well-known tone of jesting. "Sometimes questionable humor offered with far too much confidence in our own cleverness."

"Pay him no heed," Julia said, hooking her arm through Violet's and leading the two of them to their waiting conveyance.

It didn't take long for everyone to be settled. The arrangements inside Lucas's traveling carriage were precisely as Violet had suggested.

"Will we reach Livingsley Hall before dark, do you suppose?" Julia cast a concerned gaze out the windows.

"I know we will," Lucas said, reaching across the carriage and taking hold of her hand.

Violet met Kes's eye, a question in her expression, one he had little difficulty sorting out. She wondered if he had continued with the carriage-lantern project.

"I am making progress," he said quietly.

In an equally low voice, she said, "I'm glad."

As they rolled along, Julia told Violet of the people they knew in London, of local society where she and Lucas had grown up. They spoke of the places the Gents traveled to, the places where they lived. Through it all, Violet showed every sign of being deeply excited at the prospect of meeting people and joining in these undertakings.

"You simply must come visit us at Brier Hill," Julia said. "We aren't terribly far away. You could come and stay for a time. I would deeply enjoy having your company."

"I would love that," Violet said. "I hope I can convince my parents to make the trip to London for the Season, though I cannot say how many invitations my family will receive to balls and other social gatherings."

"Oh, that won't be a difficulty," Julia said. "Your connection to the Gents will see you invited to nearly everything. Lord Aldric, being the younger son of a duke, knows and is connected to almost everyone. And Digby is welcomed everywhere. Arriving at any event in his company automatically gives any lady tremendous cachet."

"I daresay a connection to *me* is not terrible for a person's standing," Lucas said, feigning offense.

The two ladies laughed at his antics, and he was quickly pulled into their discussion of people and places and diversions.

Violet would likely be in London for the Season. Under any other circumstances, that revelation would have filled Kes with uncharacteristic excitement for the annual journey to Town. But attempting to strike the precarious balance he'd struggled with at the previous night's assembly day after day would make London even more exhausting than usual.

If he focused his efforts instead, he could, perhaps, have a redesigned carriage lantern ready to present to the Royal Society. He could petition for membership and be accepted this time. His days in London could be devoted to academic lectures and discussions and his lonely evenings to wishing he'd not ruined everything.

Chapter Twenty-Six

Both ladies had drifted off to sleep. The previous night had been a long one. Kes hoped Violet was resting well. She'd been so nervous the night before, and she'd likely not slept well in the nights leading up to the assembly.

"I didn't realize we were such tremendously boring company." Lucas motioned with his head toward their slumbering companions.

"*I* have never rendered a lady insensible with boredom," Kes said. "This must be your doing."

Lucas laughed and shook his head. But the amusement faded after a moment, his concern for his wife evident once more. "She is exhausted lately. I wish we were nearer my mother so I could ask her if that is to be expected or if it is cause for concern."

"Does Julia seem worried?" Kes asked.

"No, but she is shockingly good at hiding her worries. She tucks them so far out of reach that sometimes it is impossible to know what she is thinking." He sounded a little frustrated, but mostly, he gave the impression of hurting for her, of wanting to help. The Jonquils were a family driven to rescue people; Lucas was no exception.

"You are very patient with her struggles," Kes said.

"It doesn't say much for the human race that we find it so exceptional when someone shows kindness to a person who is grieving and afraid, when someone *doesn't* demand a person who has lived through traumatic experiences to somehow be immediately whole again and never be undermined by lingering pain. Patience with each other in times of suffering, however long those times might last, ought to be our default, not our exception."

However long those times might last. For Kes, they'd lasted more than half his life. He still struggled with his parents' deaths. His grief over Stanley was still raw after a decade. Lucas would likely be understanding, but Kes wasn't ready to talk about any of it.

"Julia still worries about traveling at night, it seems." Kes knew he'd taken the coward's escape by changing the topic, but he hadn't the strength for anything else just then.

Lucas nodded. "Not to the point of avoiding it or refusing to travel in the dark, but it does make her a little bit uneasy."

"I'm convinced that is the reason Stanley was so intent on studying carriage lanterns. I've looked through his notes and drawings, and I'm going to try to finish what he started."

"I think Stanley would like that," Lucas said. "He'd be relieved to know Julia will be safer when she travels."

"He would be even more pleased to know that she is loved and happy," Kes said. "And that has much to do with you."

Lucas smiled fondly. "She is easy to love."

"Fortunately for you, she returns that regard."

Amusement tugged at Lucas's features, though he clearly tried to keep it hidden. "You'd not be a Gent if your attempts at love didn't go terribly awry."

"This one certainly ended in disaster."

Lucas's gaze narrowed on him. "What makes you think it has ended?"

He pushed out a breath. "What reason do I have to think it hasn't?"

"Apparently, I am not the only one with a tendency toward stupidity in matters of the heart," Lucas said a bit under his breath.

The carriage jostled hard, not enough to cause worry for their safety but sufficient to awaken the ladies sitting across from them. Both appeared disoriented at first, but their confusion didn't last long.

"How long were we asleep?" Violet asked, stretching her neck.

"Thirty minutes or so," Lucas said.

Julia adjusted her position but didn't look any more comfortable. Indeed, she seemed decidedly *un*comfortable.

Before Kes could say a word, Lucas reached across the carriage and set a hand on her knee. "Are you unwell?" Lucas asked her.

"I fell asleep in an odd position." She tried adjusting again. "My back is sore."

Violet shifted to the edge of the bench she and Julia shared. "It will take some doing, but let us try to switch places, Lucas. I believe Julia would appreciate having you beside her."

The switch was made, though awkwardly and not without a bit of effort. Violet took the seat beside Kes and across from Julia, while Lucas took the place beside his wife. He held out for Violet the carriage blanket she'd left behind. As Violet was adjusting her gown with her right hand and was unable to grasp anything with her left, Kes accepted the blanket on her behalf.

Lucas set his attention fully on Julia, the two of them speaking quietly. Once Violet was settled, Kes spread the carriage blanket over her lap and legs.

"Thank you, Kester."

"My pleasure," he said.

"Do you still think we'll reach Livingsley Hall before dark?" Violet asked.

"I do," he said.

"With your lantern improvements, you'll not need to rush journeys in the future," Violet said. "That will be a fine thing, as I know you and the Gents do a lot of traveling."

"*Constant* traveling, it seems."

Violet dropped her voice even more. "Do you not enjoy constant traveling?"

It was not a matter of enjoyment. *Not* joining the Gents in their travels and gatherings was out of the question. "I enjoy spending time with them."

With a glowing smile, Violet turned more fully toward him. "So do I."

"I think Julia, especially, is grateful to have you among us." He was finding talking with Violet was less uncomfortable than it had been even earlier that day.

"That reminds me." Her eyes pulled wide with excitement. "Julia has finished reading the book she found in your library, the one about fire. If you aren't opposed to sharing your carriage-light project with yet another person, she likely now knows more about candlelight than either of us ever will."

Kes hadn't thought of that. "She might know how to make the flame brighter."

Violet nodded. "Between her flame, your convex glass, and the work Stanley already completed, you'll have the greatest carriage lantern ever created. I am certain of it."

Her encouragement and faith in him was heaven-sent. If only the dreams he'd had for the two of them had been as well.

Chapter Twenty-Seven

The group had arrived at Livingsley Hall without incident, though they had done so quite late in the evening. Everyone had retired immediately to their bedchambers, exhausted from the whirlwind journey.

The next morning, Father and Mother looked in at Irthing Grange, receiving a detailed report on the repairs. Upon their return, they informed Violet and Georgie that the time for leaving Livingsley Hall had arrived.

This was to be their last evening as Kester's guests. They gathered with the Gents and Julia in the drawing room for one final night of games and revelry.

Kester had been as good as his word. Violet had hardly spoken with him. Indeed, she had hardly seen him. He did not avoid the gathering altogether, but he kept very much to himself and was even quieter than usual. She wondered at that. Was he withdrawn on account of her, or was he simply at the end of his endurance again?

"What is to be the game of choice tonight?" Niles asked, watching them all eagerly. He always seemed excited for whatever lark his friends suggested.

"Hide-and-seek," Lucas said.

The Gents all laughed at the standing joke Lucas suggested every night.

"Perhaps we might play three kingdoms again," Henri said. "That was enjoyable."

"I think we would do well to choose a game we haven't played recently," Lord Aldric said. "Variety being the very spice of life, if Cowper is to be believed."

"We could play crambo," Julia suggested. "That also involves a skill with words, but it is also quite simple, which I think would add to the enjoyment while we are all weary from our recent journey."

Violet suspected the Gents saw what she did: *Julia* was the one who was still exhausted.

No arguments were posed, and they were quickly situated in a circle, ready to undertake this latest game. Crambo was easy enough. The one who began each turn chose a word, and it was the task of each succeeding person to think of a word that rhymed with it. The play continued until someone either repeated a word already given, offered a word that was not real, or could not think of a rhyme. That person was then required to undertake a forfeit. The only other rule was that the word chosen to be rhymed with could not be overly odd or unusual. Allowing words that had few rhymes or, worse still, none at all would mean the game was over as soon as it began.

When they had first begun their evenings together, Violet had worried about what forfeits would be chosen. She had come to trust them since then.

As Julia had been the one to suggest the game, she was given the task of beginning their first turn. "Apple," she said.

Lucas was seated beside her. He offered the first answer. "Dapple." No doubt everyone had thought of that as they had only just quit the Dappled Chicken in Carlisle.

Digby was next. "Grapple."

Kester sat beside him. In a voice not exactly teeming with enthusiasm, he gave his answer. "Chapel."

The game reached Father. With a chuckle, he said, "I can think of nothing else. I fear I will have to accept the forfeit."

As Kester was the last one to successfully rhyme, it was for him to determine the forfeit. "You are required to offer a kiss to the lady in the room whom you find the most beautiful."

Father chuckled once more; he'd done that a lot since they'd come to Livingsley Hall. Without hesitation, he kissed Mother, as everyone must have known he would. The room applauded and generally expressed their approval of his choice.

It was now for Kester to begin the next turn. He offered the word *cat*. Sometimes the trickiest words were the ones with an enormous number of possible rhymes. Play would go about the circle so many times that those participating would struggle to remember which rhymes had already been offered. Such was the case this turn.

Simple rhymes such as *hat* and *mat* and *sat* were offered, as were more complicated ones, like *pitter-pat*. In the end, Digby was caught out repeating *flat* and had to adhere to Lucas's forfeit. Lucas insisted that Digby muss his hair and leave it in a state of disarray. Digby declared that utterly underhanded, but he went along good-naturedly.

Violet would miss these gentlemen.

The game continued with new words tossed out and new forfeits invented. Laughter was general, excited, and enthusiastic. Through it all, Kester never did return entirely to the joviality she had sometimes seen in him during this house party. He had never had the overflowing energy of Lucas or the eager participation of Niles, but this amount of distance was new. Something more was weighing on him.

Though she was a little sad at the prospect of leaving this gathering to return home the next day, she couldn't help but recognize that Kester was likely to get greater enjoyment from the few days remaining with his friends if she were not nearby.

The game paused for a bit of tea. Mother stood beside Violet, looking as pleased as ever. "I am anticipating with great pleasure the promise of seeing these friends of yours in London during the Season."

It was the first Violet had heard that her parents were considering such a thing, and she was ecstatic. "Julia said she hoped we would make the journey. I believe it will prove a triumph and a success. Before you know it, Mother, you will have more friends than you know what to do with."

Father laughed. "Your mother does not believe there is such a thing as too many friends. If going to London will procure her even more, I will go the moment she says we should."

Lucas called them all back to the game. This time, Kester didn't join them. He kept to the other side of the room, bent over a book. He remained among them even when he clearly longed for the serenity of isolation.

Lord Aldric was the last one to have successfully stymied another player. As such, he began this newest turn. "The word I choose is *steep*."

Niles was beside him and offered the word *deep* as his rhyme.

Violet was next and suggested *weep*.

Mother quickly said, "Keep."

Around the circle play went, with each person managing to think of a rhyme.

Play reached Julia for the second time. The answer she offered was, "Oh, dear."

It was so desperately wrong that the group burst out in laughter.

"I'm afraid we cannot accept that one," Lucas said through his chuckles. "And it seems Mrs. Ridley is charged with giving you a forfeit."

Julia shook her head. "Stubble it." She had not objected to the game, which made her call for silence now all the more strange.

"You can't end the game simply because you can't think of a word, sweetheart." Lucas smiled at her. "I can't imagine Mrs. Ridley will choose an unpleasant forfeit."

"Unless that forfeit is to deliver a child right here in this room, I'm afraid it is going to have to wait."

One look at her face and the truth of the situation became clear: Julia was in labor.

Chapter Twenty-Eight

Lucas was in a frenzy. All the Gents were talking at once. Even Aldric seemed to have misplaced his usual focused and unruffled manner.

Though Kes was, of course, concerned, he was not panicking. He had been preparing for this possibility from the moment Julia had arrived at Livingsley Hall. "Mrs. Ridley, would you be willing to assist Julia to her bedchamber while I send for the midwife?" It was, after all, the purview of married women, particularly those who had children of their own, to assist at a lying-in.

"Of course." Mrs. Ridley was calm and collected, precisely what Julia needed in that moment. She laid an arm across Julia's back and guided her slowly and gently from the room.

Lucas followed close on their heels. He would be tossed from the room the moment the midwife arrived or Julia's labor pains began in earnest, but he could help see her settled in the meantime.

Kes tugged at the bellpull. While waiting for the summons to be answered, he addressed the rest of the group. "We all know Lucas will be a mess tonight worrying about Julia. All of us care about her and will have concerns of our own, but he needs us to be rocks in this storm. If any of you do not think yourself equal to it, now is the time to slip out."

The Gents all indicated their ability to take up the assignment.

Kes turned to Mr. Ridley. "As you are the only one among us who has experienced what Lucas will, please tell us what you think would most help him. And we would be much obliged if you would lend your support as well."

"Of course," he said.

That left Violet. Kes turned to her. "You'll be left out of the room where the ladies are, but that will mean either being on your own somewhere or being in here with a group of gentlemen who are pretending not to be frantic and entirely out of our elements. As I promised you before, your autonomy will always be protected in this house. You do what you feel best, and please let us know if there is anything you need."

"I would very much like to stay," she said. "I realize I will be terribly unhelpful, but I will worry for her as well. There is something comforting in being with other people who are also traversing the same worries."

"And she is remarkably good at keeping spirits up," Mr. Ridley said. "You couldn't hope for a more potent ray of sunshine in the midst of dark clouds than you have with Violet nearby."

How much of that was her natural cheerfulness, and how much was the advice she'd once received to keep silent if she meant to share any emotions or feelings other than joyful ones? She deserved to be her whole self.

The butler stepped inside. "How may I be of assistance, Mr. Barrington?"

"Please send a rider to Mrs. Cobb. Lady Jonquil is in need of her immediate attendance."

The butler moved with more haste than usual from the room. The midwife, unwaveringly dependable, would arrive quickly.

Kes had seen to all he could; the rest lay in the hands of fate.

Within half an hour, Mrs. Cobb was overseeing Julia's care. The soon-to-be mother was settled and ready to begin her travail, Mrs. Ridley was there to offer support, and Lucas had been tossed out to join the others anxiously awaiting the new arrival.

Lucas had been with them only a few minutes, but he hadn't stopped pacing. After one particularly frantic circuit of the room, he muttered, "She's before her time. It's too early. What if something's the matter?"

Though it was apparent he was speaking to himself, everyone overheard.

"Do sit down, Lucas," Aldric said. "If you walk any faster, you'll collapse in a dizzy spell, and then you'll be utterly useless."

"Not to mention inexcusably rumpled," Digby added.

Lucas dropped into a chair, slouched and bent but not appearing the least at ease. His brows were drawn, and his head rested against his upturned fist. The fingers of his other hand tapped the arm of the chair he sat in. One foot shook in a quick and worried rhythm.

Violet moved to stand next to Kes. She lowered her voice, "I wish I knew what to say to reassure him. I haven't enough experience with this."

"I have extensive experience with Lucas and settling his worries, yet I'm at a loss as well." And that was frustrating. "If Stanley were here, he would know what to do."

"Is Julia really so far before her time?" Violet asked.

"From what I understand, they weren't expecting this arrival for another month."

Violet's forehead creased, and her mouth tightened. He'd not meant to add to her concerns.

"These things can be miscalculated, of course," he quickly added. "It is entirely possible she was closer to her confinement than she'd realized. She might be only two or three weeks early."

"She wasn't feeling well during the journey back from Carlisle, and she was in a little bit of pain. Do you suppose that trip was too much strain for her?"

The thought had occurred to Kes, though he'd kept it unspoken. He led Violet a little farther away from the Gents, who were doing their utmost to distract Lucas from his own thoughts. "That may be the case, but she herself didn't seem to think so."

"She wasn't going to make the journey," Violet said. "She had considered it but was inclined not to. Then I told her how I would miss having her there and how I wished she would come and how nice it would be for Georgie to spend the evening with her. What if I pushed her into this? What if my insistence is the reason she joined us and the strain of it is why she's now delivering sooner than she ought?"

He took her right hand in his and held it gently, careful to otherwise maintain a distance between them that was appropriate for mere friends. "You are relatively newly acquainted with Julia. Let me tell you this: she is amiable and generous but also fiercely independent and precisely the sort of person who cannot be forced to do anything she doesn't wish to do."

Violet shook her head. "I heard from her own lips that she and Lucas had not originally wanted to marry but were forced into it."

"That sort of entanglement is not undone by stubbornness. Did she tell you she did not simply shrug and accept her fate? That for the small amount of time she was granted between the betrothal announcement and the wedding, she exhausted every avenue available to prevent it? Did she tell you she arrived at her own wedding dressed in full, unrelieved mourning so that no one in attendance would doubt precisely how she felt about it?"

Violet's eyes pulled wide. "Did Lucas tell you that?"

"He didn't have to. I was there. It is a wedding I will never forget."

Across the room, the Gents had started a game of cards. Lucas appeared to be participating under duress. Kes hoped it would prove the needed distraction.

"Lucas and Julia do seem to love each other quite entirely now," Violet said.

"They do. Utterly and completely. They were friends as children, then had a falling out, but regained the friendship between them. What they have now is built on that foundation."

"Of friendship?" Violet asked.

"If there is one thing this group has discovered over the years, it is the life-altering power of loyal and dedicated friends."

Violet slipped her hand free from his. It felt so natural there that he'd forgotten he was still holding it. He studied her quickly, hoping he hadn't upset her. She didn't look the least distressed or unhappy. But, then, she seldom did. She seldom allowed it.

"I have been so pleased to be part of this group of friends," she said. "They adopted me so quickly and so entirely. It is one of the greatest gifts I have ever been given."

"You are a wonderful addition to the group. With both you and Julia part of us now, I'm not certain what the Gents will begin calling ourselves. We had been 'the Gents and Our Julia' the last few months. That is insufficient now."

She looked at him with a stunning smile. "Am I accepted enough that the Gents would even consider incorporating me into your group name?"

"*Our* group name. You are permanently one of us."

She pressed her hand to her heart. "That means the world to me." On that happy declaration, she moved back toward the others.

In a whisper no one would overhear, he said, "*You* mean the world to me."

Two hours had passed, and only the most cursory updates had arrived. Julia continued to labor. The midwife was no more concerned than was generally the case. Mr. Ridley insisted again and again to Lucas that two hours was not an overly long time for a child to be delivered and was no cause for alarm. Even his experienced evaluation did not set Lucas's mind at ease. The tiniest sound, the tiniest movement, pulled his eyes away from every distraction they undertook and directly to the doorway, no doubt anticipating word of his wife and the child she was bringing into the world.

Kes was at a loss. He knew he couldn't take the worry away entirely, but he did wish he could offer some relief. He was running out of ideas.

After Lucas had shown absolutely no interest in any of the games the group undertook, Kes exchanged looks with the other Gents. They all appeared as baffled as he was.

Violet rose to the occasion. "I was touched by the miniature in the strongbox. But I hadn't realized how much older you all are than Julia. That age difference must have made it difficult for Lucas and Stanley to include her in their larks growing up."

"On the contrary," Lucas said. "Julia gave us no choice."

Looks of hesitant relief began to trickle across the group. Perhaps Violet's strategy would work.

"And the two of you were not annoyed at having a little sister tagging along?" Violet asked.

"Had she been the only one, it might've been a little annoying. My brother James joined in as well. He was nearer to our age. Julia led the charge for herself, Charlotte, and my little sister, Harriet. My youngest brother Philip, while he was still alive, was part of the adventures as well."

"What a merry group you must have been," Violet said quickly. Perhaps she had noticed that speaking of his siblings was weighing down his spirits. She likely didn't know that every one of them had died. Every last one except Lucas and Julia.

"We ran our parents ragged. I'm certain the entire neighborhood dismissed us as a ragamuffin collection of troublemakers." Lucas shook his head and sighed. "Those were grand days."

"When did the rest of you meet Stanley and Lucas?" Violet asked the Gents.

"I was the first to make their acquaintance," Digby said. "It was during our first year at Eton. Kes was a year behind us, and we met him when he began there. It took a couple of years, but we eventually forced him to be part of our group of particular friends."

Violet looked to him. "Forced?"

"That is the only accurate description," Kes acknowledged.

The other Gents chuckled. Violet took obvious pleasure in hearing their stories.

"I began at Harrow rather than Eton," Aldric said. "Much to my father's disapproval, I broke with family tradition and followed my Harrow years with Cambridge. Upon my arrival, Stanley quickly made me his friend. Henri was the next to join our group, followed shortly by Niles. By our second year at Cambridge, when Kes joined us there, ours was a friendship as permanent as the mountains themselves."

"And I'm assuming you were all very well behaved," Violet spoke in a tone of overdone seriousness. "Surely by then, Lucas and Stanley had outgrown their tendency to be 'a ragamuffin collection of troublemakers.'"

"Not in the least," Lucas declared proudly. "Stanley was known amongst us as the Highwayman. He never outgrew his longing for adventures and excitement."

"But you mustn't think he was irresponsible or caused actual grief to anyone," Niles added quickly.

"Having known Julia, I could never think ill of her brother." Violet's pretended teasing had dissipated, replaced by a firm conviction.

"He loved his *sœur cadette*," Henri said with a hint of sorrow. "Were he here now, he would be as pleased and anxious as we are."

That was true. "But he also would find a way to entertain all of us while we waited," Kes said. "He had a knack for it."

That led them to recounting various adventures and deeds they had undertaken. They laughed at stories they'd told hundreds of times. Violet posed countless questions. Even when they spoke of some slightly shocking things—the time they "stole" horses or the day they broke into the London home of Lord and Lady Hardford—she simply laughed along with them, apparently having realized that while they did cause trouble, their larks were generally harmless.

Through it all, Kes watched Lucas. This approach to distraction was working. There was no doubt he was still concerned for his wife, still anxious for word of her, but he did not appear as ready to burst with worry as he had throughout the evening.

Reminders of Stanley were often heavy in this group, for Kes especially, but in that moment, it was precisely what they needed. Stanley, who had lifted them from sorrows and worries time and time again, was somehow managing to do it even now. He had created this group, and his influence was felt still. In a small way, doing what he could for Julia that evening and for Lucas as he waited felt to Kes like offering Stanley a bit of the caring support he had offered to all of them.

In the midst of their storytelling, Julia's lady's maid arrived in the doorway. All eyes turned to her, and every voice became immediately silent. Lucas was on his feet on the instant. He took a single step toward the door, and there was fear in his face. Fear mingled with hope, mingled with uncertainty.

Kes joined him where he stood and set a supporting hand on his shoulder. The other Gents surrounded him in the next instant.

The maid smiled softly. "Lord Jonquil, your wife wishes for you to meet someone."

Chapter Twenty-Nine

The Gents had been made to wait for more than half an hour. They understood—the new parents ought to be permitted time alone with their child—but the group was growing impatient. All they had been told was that there was no concern from the midwife that either mother or infant was in any danger. That had offered some relief from their worries but had not at all satisfied their curiosity.

Mr. Ridley had left to join his wife, who had retired for the night, having stayed with Julia until the moment Lucas arrived. Kes meant to offer his effusive gratitude to her before the Ridleys departed the next day. It had been fortuitous that she had been present when Julia's labor had begun, but he would not have hesitated to send for her had the family already returned to Irthing Grange.

Violet had remained in the drawing room with the Gents. She was being regaled with various stories of their early exploits, and Kes was taking great delight in watching her. Her smile, as beautiful as it had ever been, had become a source of peace and reassurance to him. It warmed him through and calmed his own concerns. Her father had called her a potent ray of sunshine. She was something more than that to Kes. He couldn't put it in words, couldn't capture the right analogy, but she offered tranquility in addition to cheer. He had never known anyone like her.

A summons finally arrived for the Gents and Violet to meet Lucas in an unoccupied bedchamber in the guest wing. They were soon ensconced in a moment Kes knew he would never forget. His best friends in all the world were gathered around Lucas as he held in his arms a perfect little baby, looking at the infant with all the pride, love, and joy a father could possibly possess.

When he spoke, Lucas kept his voice quiet, no doubt, on account of the child he held, "Gents, this is my son. Julia, I am sure, would have liked to have been part of this introduction, but she is exhausted. She was only half awake when I left. I couldn't bear the thought of keeping her from the sleep she so desperately needs."

They all agreed he'd chosen rightly.

"We had originally planned to name the child Stanley if he proved to be a boy," Lucas said. "But Julia and I sat looking at this little bundle and knew it wasn't the right name."

"I'm assuming you settled on Digby," the King said with feigned arrogance.

Smiling, Lucas said, "No."

"Then you must have chosen Layton," he quickly amended. "Either one would make quite a dignified name."

Lucas laughed, the sound startling the baby enough for him to squirm a bit, though he didn't fuss. "When I first saw him"—Lucas's eyes dropped to his son again—"I was struck by how much he looks like my memories of my littlest brother. I felt as though I was seeing Philip again for the first time in twenty-five years." His voice broke with emotion. For a moment, he didn't speak. It didn't seem as if he could. Lucas had talked about each of his siblings when he and Kes had been on the Continent. That he mourned them deeply had been apparent. That grief surfaced again now but was lightened by the hope in Lucas's face.

"When I suggested to Julia that we name this little boy for the one we lost so long ago, she agreed in an instant." Lucas blinked back tears.

"You made the right choice," Aldric said.

"The perfect choice," Digby insisted.

His voice quivering a little, Lucas said, "My friends, this is Philip Kester Jonquil, Lord Fallowgill."

Kes swallowed back the lump that formed in his throat. Philip *Kester*. He'd not been expecting that.

"I fully expect you to fawn over Philip as if he were the most perfect child ever born," Lucas instructed.

"I wholeheartedly agree to do so." Digby reached out and was granted the honor of being the first of the Gents to hold the tiny lordling. "I declare here and now, Philip, that you will have a far better fashion sense than your father, even if I must invest the rest of my life making certain of that."

Digby held and talked to the little baby for several long minutes before being forced to relinquish his armful to Henri, who spoke exclusively in French to the infant, extolling how beautiful a baby he was. When Niles's turn arose, he made promises of grand adventures.

Aldric had his turn. The man could be intimidating and fearsome, but Kes had seen him with his nephew, Roderick. There was a tenderness to him that spoke of a father's heart.

Lucas had wandered to where Kes patiently awaited his opportunity.

"You could have picked any of the Gents to name the baby for," Kes said. "Why did you choose me?"

"Maybe we like you best." Lucas jabbed him with his elbow.

Kes didn't believe for a moment that that was true. They were all the closest of friends. "Whatever the reason, I am honored. I truly am."

"If he could not have been born at Lampton Park," Lucas said, "I could not imagine a better place for him to make his debut in this world. Thank you for hosting this gathering. I know it wasn't easy on you—weeks of forced socializing never is."

"This was not how I expected the annual Gents gathering to play out," Kes said. "But I suspect it will go down in history as the best one we've ever had. For the first time in ages, it feels like Stanley is with us again. He would've wanted to be here for this."

Lucas set a hand on his shoulder. "I suspect the heavens are closer than we realize. And I wouldn't doubt he's here now, likely fuming at the fact that we did not name this child after him. He shall simply have to be patient."

"I don't know how patient Digby is going to be. You might consider naming the next child after him, boy or girl."

Lucas called out to Aldric, "It's Kes's turn. Hand over the bundle."

Aldric was reluctant but obedient. The transfer was carefully made, and Kes had his turn meeting this newest addition to their group. How easily he could picture all of them gathering to meet each other's children over the years. Looking into the face of this tiny child, seeing Lucas's joy and imagining Julia's, Kes couldn't begrudge the disruptions that would come.

He ran a finger over the child's soft cheek. Bits of wavy golden hair peeked out from beneath the blanket, resting against the tiny forehead. He was, no doubt, going to look a great deal like his father. What a delight it would be in the years to come to discover which bits of each parent showed up in their children.

The Gents were gathered close to Kes, all talking, all commenting enthusiastically. He ought to have been grateful for them nearby, but he found himself growing a little frustrated.

Violet spoke, firm and insistent. "Kester has earned the right to enjoy his moment with the baby. He, after all, proved to be the only one of us prepared for this possibility. You are perfectly aware of the fact that he needs a little space, and he needs a bit of quiet."

Looks of amused acknowledgment flashed over the group.

"You are, of course, correct," Aldric said. "I fear we too often need the reminder."

Without argument, his friends made their way to the other side of the room, quite at their leisure and not appearing at all offended. That left Kes standing near the window in a cocoon of peace even while in the company of others.

Violet stood a few paces away, watching the Gents. She pointed at each of them in turn, a comical version of a threat. "You stay over there until he's ready."

Again, they laughed and held up their hands in shows of innocence. While she clearly was exaggerating for the sake of humor, Kes felt certain she was, to a degree, in earnest. She meant to give him the moment of communion he needed, and she intended to see to it that he was not interrupted. He was not always good about insisting upon that for himself.

Kes held little Philip close to him, not wanting his time with Lucas's child and Stanley's nephew to end too soon. Those two had saved him from his grief and loneliness long ago. They were like brothers to him. His time with Stanley had been cut short, and he meant to cherish this moment.

And yet, he found himself pulled to Violet. He moved a bit closer to her. "Would you like to meet him?"

"I will have an opportunity to do so. You need a moment of your own."

He nodded. "You've given me that. Thank you. Thank you for seeing what I need, for helping me claim it when I don't manage to do so myself. You've done that before, and I cannot tell you how much it means to me."

She set her right hand on his arm, a gentle and friendly touch. He'd missed that.

Her gaze dropped to little Philip. "He really is a beautiful baby. Considering his parents, I suspect he has blue eyes." Such was not clear, as the baby was sleeping.

"I'm certain he does. I, for one, have always been rather partial to brown."

"So have I."

He told himself not to read too much into the declaration. He had been wrong where she was concerned before. He still had some hope of regaining her friendship; he wouldn't ruin that by pressing for more. Again.

Violet gently touched one of the little golden curls. She cooed a bit over the baby, the singsong words people often used when speaking with infants.

"You should have a chance to hold him," Kes said.

"Not until you're done."

"Let me stay beside you while you hold him, and I will be perfectly content to watch the baby sleep."

Eagerness twinkled in her eyes. "I have been incredibly anxious to have my turn."

"That settles it, then." He carefully set little Philip in the crook of Violet's right arm. Her left was laid against the baby's side to steady him.

She looked to Kes once more. "If we do manage to design a prosthesis that can hold things, I could someday hold a baby and a rattle at the same time."

She spoke of their one-time project in the present tense, referring to the undertaking as something they were still doing together. She hadn't, then, decided to entirely sever that connection to him. It gave him hope he hadn't felt since the day she had run from his workshop.

"I haven't the least doubt in our ability to solve that riddle," he said.

With contented happiness written on her face, she looked back at the baby once more. Kester stood beside her as she rocked Philip gently. They talked about the child, about their inventions and interests. She was as easy in his company as she had ever been. Conversation between them flowed as if nothing difficult had ever occurred.

In that room, holding this new little life, having been defended by her and having felt a bit of the healing he had needed for years, a calming sense of relief settled over him.

She was willing to be his friend again. And though he suspected his heart would always long for something more, he would not waste the chance to have her be part of his life in whatever way she would allow.

Chapter Thirty

Violet walked with her hand in Georgie's from the shore of the lake to the front door of Livingsley Hall. They had been back at Irthing Grange for two days. She and her cousin had taken advantage of Kester's generosity and spent time on the lakeshore during both of those days. They'd also used the map he'd drawn to explore a bit of the surrounding countryside. Though she'd not had the pleasure of Kester's company since leaving his home, she felt almost as if he'd been with them. That feeling had added to her enjoyment of the outings.

Georgie wished to see little Philip, so Violet had agreed to forgo further adventures in order to make the introduction. They were ushered inside and made their way to Julia's bedchamber.

"Is the baby very small?" Georgie asked as they climbed the stairs.

"Newly born babies always are," Violet said. "Little Philip is small, but he is the right size for how old he is."

"Isn't he only two days old?" Georgie asked.

"Yes. And he is two-days-old small."

The door to the bedchamber was open, so Violet peeked her head inside. Like every other bedchamber at Livingsley Hall, it was beautifully appointed. The tall half canopy above the bed perfectly matched the golden-tapestry window curtains and complemented the cream silk hung on the walls. But the loveliest sight of all was Julia sitting on the bed, looking down at the bassinet beside her. There was no mistaking the love in her eyes.

"Are you equal to having visitors?" Violet asked.

Julia looked up and waved her inside. "I had hoped you would call."

"I've brought Georgie with me," Violet said, allowing herself and her cousin inside. "She has been anxious to meet your son."

"Oh, Georgie, I'm so pleased you've come. Philip is in the bassinet. Climb up here next to me, and I will introduce you."

Georgie did so eagerly. She had changed a lot recently. Her heart was lighter, and her trust in people had grown. Julia had become like another family member to her.

"Violet told me he was small but that he was the right amount of small for a baby that was only two days old."

"Yes, he is just the right size." Julia reached into the bassinet and carefully lifted the baby out. He fussed a little and squirmed. Julia held him and rocked him. "He can be shockingly vocal," she said. "When he has an opinion about something, he makes it known."

"And what is his opinion about being lifted from his bed?" Violet asked, sitting in a spindle-back chair next to Julia's bed.

"He does not approve," Georgie said firmly.

Julia nodded. "He'll settle quickly, then I'll let you hold him," she said to Georgie.

"I've never held a baby."

"The easiest way to manage it," Julia said, "is for you to sit with your back against the head of the bed with your legs stretched out in front of you. Put a pillow on your lap and your arms on top of the pillow."

Georgie did precisely that.

"I will sit beside you and help in any way you need." Julia spoke encouragingly. "But I'm not worried. You'll be careful with him."

Georgie's brow furrowed in fierce concentration. After a moment, Philip was contented again, no longer complaining about the change in situation. Julia took great care in setting the baby in Georgie's arms. She kept her hands there as well, adding support and strength to the arrangement.

Philip was awake, something that had not been the case when Violet had seen him before. She leaned a little closer, studying his angelic face.

"Kester and I were certain he would have blue eyes," Violet said.

"And he has his father's golden waves," Julia said.

"I have my mother's eyes," Georgie said with pride and excitement. "I don't know whose hair I have."

"Your father's," Violet said. "His hair, like my mother's, curled in tight coils, just exactly as yours does."

"Yours does too," Georgie said.

Violet's curls were a bit looser than Mother's and Georgie's but not unsimilar.

"Is my hair the same color as my father's was?" Georgie asked.

"Your father's was darker than yours." Indeed, his hair had been the same nearly black shade that Violet's was. "The color of your hair is nearer your mother's. Your nose and your smile, as well as your eyes, are exactly like hers. There are bits of both of them in you."

In the past, talk of Georgie's parents had often led her to be melancholy, but this time, she seemed pleased. She studied the little baby once more. "Whose nose does he have?"

"I think it is too early to tell," Julia said. "It will grow and change a lot."

"I hope he has a lot of things that are yours," Georgie said to Julia. "He would like that. It's nice to have things that are one's mother's."

"Yes, it is," Julia said.

Violet didn't doubt Julia wished for this little boy to have some of his father in him. But Georgie was clinging to the joy of resembling her mother, and Julia did not seem intent on undermining that. Violet had come to treasure Julia's friendship. A lot of that grew from moments like this when she might have offered correction or contradiction but understood that sometimes a person simply needed to be heard.

What a blessing it was to have Julia in her life. *The Gents and Our Julia.* Kester had said they were contemplating changing the name of the group yet again to include her somehow. But she wouldn't be bothered if they didn't. She treasured them all and would likely always think of them by the name they'd used when she first met them.

"Philip will change a lot over the next year and continue to do so after that." Julia looked to Violet. "Which means you simply must come visit Brier Hill often so you can see him growing up."

"Do you mean to bring him to London when you go for the Season?" Violet asked.

"We do. He, obviously, will not attend balls and such with us, but he will be at our London home."

"Mr. Barrington says there are bookshops in London bigger even than the one in Carlisle." Georgie bounced a little, prompting Julia to hold the baby more firmly. "He said some of them have many rooms of books."

"When did you talk to Mr. Barrington?" Violet asked.

"I went to the lake again yesterday while you and Aunt Ridley were doing your sewing, and he was there. We talked about bookshops. He said he was still trying to find a book about John Blanke, but he hadn't yet."

He was still looking. Of course he was. Kester was one of the most thoughtful people she knew.

"London boasts many bookshops," Julia said "As well as sweetshops and a very large, lovely park. I think you will love London."

"Do you have the book we were reading before I went back to Irthing Grange?" Georgie asked her.

Julia nodded and motioned with her head toward the small table and wing-back chair next to the window. Georgie climbed off the bed and crossed to it. She took up the book, crawled onto the chair, and curled herself up there with the book open on her knees.

"Are you truly going to London for the Season?" Julia asked Violet.

"On the heels of our success at the Carlisle assembly and confident in the support of the Gents, my parents think it worth the excursion."

"For entirely selfish reasons, I am particularly glad you're going to be there," Julia said. "I love the Gents. I adore them. But there's something wonderful about having another lady in this group, especially one with a good head on her shoulders."

Violet laughed. "These gentlemen don't always think things through, do they?"

"And yet we love them." Julia sighed. She adjusted little baby Philip so he rested against her chest. With one arm beneath him and her other hand against the back of his neck, she rocked him lightly. He was quiet enough for Violet to suspect he'd fallen asleep once more.

"Do all of the Gents participate in the Season each year?" she asked.

"They do, in their varying ways. Digby's participation is exhaustive. Kes's is minimal. He spends a great deal of his time in London amongst the academic set. I know he's hoping to someday gain membership in the Royal Society, and much of his time in Town is dedicated to that pursuit."

How easily Violet could imagine him among a gathering of intellectuals. "Does he allow himself solitude though?"

"He feels an urgency to participate in everything," Julia said. "The Gents have not entirely sorted out why. There's a franticness to it. And fear."

"And grief," Violet added. "I've noticed that myself."

Julia nodded. "You are adept at helping him find the balance he needs. You managed it at the picnic, and you somehow managed it in the carriage when there was no escaping each other. From what Lucas tells me, you defended his need for it the night Philip was born. You are good for him."

"He was so kind to me at the assembly. He has a very tender heart."

"Yes, he does." Julia spoke with the fondness of a sister.

"Do you suppose he and I will ever be able to reclaim the friendship we had?" Violet worried about that more than she'd admitted, even to herself. "I've missed him."

Julia adjusted the blanket around little Philip. "Kes has missed you too. He asks about you. I don't think even he realizes how many times in the days since your return to Irthing Grange he has mentioned his wish that you were still here."

"He has?" Unexpected hope bubbled at the possibility.

"I don't know what, precisely, you'll manage to work out between the two of you," Julia said, "but nothing about this is hopeless. I've told you before that Kes tends to guide his interactions with people by what he thinks they want and need. So long as he believes *you* want distance and indifference between you, that is what he will hold himself to."

"I don't want either of those things," Violet said.

"He doesn't either. I'm certain of it."

As if summoned by the discussion, Kester slipped inside the room in the next instant. Heat splotched Violet's cheeks. Her heart pulsed hard in her neck. How much had he overheard?

"Gladwin said you were visiting," he said to Violet. "While I don't wish to interrupt, I do have something to tell you."

He looked eager to see her. And while that was pleasing, what was shocking was her response to seeing him. A bubble of excitement spread inside. It sent her thoughts into a whirl and left her heart fluttering. She couldn't look away from him standing there, framed in the doorway. She didn't want to.

Had she doubted at all that she wanted him to remain a part of her life, that moment would have proven it to her.

She rose from her seat and moved to where he stood. He smiled at her, and the fluttering of her heart increased. That organ was thoroughly confusing her.

"What was it you wished to tell me?" she asked.

"I received a letter. From the apothecary in Northumberland."

Chapter Thirty-One

Violet excused herself to Julia without a detailed explanation of the importance of a letter from an apothecary, implored Georgie to behave, and walked eagerly with Kester to his library. Once there, he gave her the letter he had received and allowed her to read it.

> *Mr. Barrington,*
>
> *Your notes on Iron Hand are very helpful. That design could be re-created, but my father has seen newer prostheses and thinks we could improve on that metal one. We don't know if the precision you're hoping for can be achieved, but we think it's worth the attempt.*
>
> *I'm enclosing a sketch of what my father has seen so you can have an idea of what's being made now. We are discussing what you are hoping for and learning what we can. If you keep me informed of what you and your inventing partner are discovering, I'll do the same.*
>
> *Clement Miller*

Violet turned to Kester. "There's a sketch of a modern prosthesis?"

Kester nodded and took a paper off the desk, holding it out to her. She eyed it eagerly. It looked less ungainly than the diagram of Iron Hand's prosthesis. She liked that. There were gears and hinges and rods, all protruding from the prosthesis itself. She certainly couldn't wear gloves over something like this. She could only imagine the damage it would do to a silk dress. And yet, even with its imperfections, it was incredibly encouraging.

"Among the things I suggested to him," Kester said, "was sorting a means of placing the mechanisms below the surface of the prosthesis, as well as fingers that move independent of one another and can lock in place in various positions. I also told him we were particularly interested in creating a prosthesis that wasn't so heavy as one made of solid wood. I don't know how many of those things are possible, but he seems to think it's worth attempting."

Violet couldn't take her eyes off the drawing. The prosthesis it portrayed was such a drastic improvement over what she already had. And it wasn't imaginary; it existed already. It existed *now.* Her dreams felt almost within reach.

"You said this apothecary wasn't far away." She looked back at him.

Kester shook his head. "He's actually not terribly far from Brier Hill. I'm certain Julia and Lucas would let me stay there so I could consult with him."

"They've invited me to visit Brier Hill. Doing so would allow me to visit the apothecary as well."

"As this was your project to begin with and as it has the most personal impact on you, it's absolutely necessary that you be an integral part of it. With your permission, I can visit Lucas and Julia at the same time as you, and we can call on Mr. Miller and his father together."

A little bubble of excitement formed inside Violet. "I would like that."

If they both traveled to Brier Hill at the same time, she would see him there. She could spend time with him. The thought sent warmth spreading through her.

"I need to write back to Mr. Miller," Kester said. "But I will draft the letter with you here so you can include your thoughts and questions as well."

He laid a sheet of parchment on the desktop beside a stack already written on.

"How much longer will the Gents be at Livingsley Hall?"

"Only a few more days." Kes took up the paper stack and set it inside the metal lockbox on a shelf behind his desk. "They all mean to return to their family homes or their own estates. Henri will likely either take up residence in his rented London rooms or join one of the other Gents. Julia and Lucas need to travel to Nottinghamshire to introduce Philip to his grandparents and see to it he is christened. We sometimes meet up again in spring before the Season begins, but I don't know if that will happen this year."

She studied him. He so often longed for solitude, yet he didn't seem pleased at the prospect of it. "Will you be traveling after they're gone?"

He left the box lid open and returned to the desk. "I'm not certain what I mean to do with myself."

"You have the possibility of unending space and silence in which to rest from the demands of socializing," she said. "I would have expected you to be more pleased."

He paced a little away, tension entering his posture.

For a moment, she was tempted to change the subject. But the thought of him unhappy weighed heavily on her. Sorting this out would help him. She knew it would. "You told me that you were grateful when I managed to arrange a little quiet for you. You have the ability to claim that for yourself. Why don't you? Why don't you let the Gents know that sometimes you don't want to participate in their unending whirl?"

"It's complicated," he muttered.

"Well, fortunately for you, I am exceptionally clever."

That brought his gaze back to her again. Apparently realizing she was in earnest, he sighed, but not with frustration. It was a sound of exhaustion, of someone reaching the end of his endurance.

She crossed to him and held her hand out. He set his in it, and she led him to the small sofa not far from where they stood and invited him to sit beside her. He did so. For a moment, he didn't speak. She waited and hoped.

"Can you keep a secret?" he asked quietly.

She recognized the very question she had asked him weeks earlier.

"I can." She squeezed his hand that she still held.

"A few years ago, I did grant myself a respite. I didn't attend the Gents' annual gathering because I was weary of people and had experienced a few too many disappointments." His shoulders rose and fell with a deep breath. "Stanley invited me to join them. When I didn't arrive, he wrote again, insisting things weren't the same without me, but I wouldn't budge. I was finding relief and rest, and I wasn't willing to give it up."

"That doesn't seem like a bad thing," she said.

"At that Gents' gathering, Stanley announced to the others that he was going to join a regiment and cross the Atlantic to fight in the war with the colonies. Lucas's brother, James, had already signed up. That was likely what put it in Stanley's mind."

"James's decision was enough to entice Stanley to go?" she asked.

"He was always one for jumping headlong into adventures and excitement. He likely thought this was just another one. Lucas could sometimes turn his thoughts away from the more outrageous schemes but not always. The other Gents were rubbish at it."

She was beginning to piece together the puzzle he was only just revealing. "Were *you* good at convincing him to be sensible?"

Kester nodded silently. Then in a strained voice, he said, "But I wasn't there."

She wrapped her right arm around his left and held it in a gentle embrace. Sensing he needed further support, she leaned her head against his shoulder.

"Lucas wrote to tell me what our friend had decided. The moment his message reached me, I rushed to the port from which Stanley's regiment was meant to sail, hoping I could convince him not to go. Stanley was no soldier. He was not suited to it at all. I knew it was a fool's errand and a greater risk than he likely realized. I made the journey as swiftly as possible."

"But you couldn't convince him to remain?"

"He was already gone." Emotion shook his voice. "I missed him by less than a day. I missed seeing him at the Gents' gathering, the one he had repeatedly implored me to join. I missed the chance to turn him from his foolhardy plans. I missed the chance to say goodbye. He didn't come back alive. I never saw him again."

A rush of understanding spread over her. Here was the reason he was frantic not to miss anything. Here was the reason the Gents saw fear in his eyes whenever he pondered the possibility of crying off their activities and gatherings. He blamed himself for Stanley's death and likely worried something would happen to the rest of them if he wasn't there to try to stop it.

"Have you told any of the others about this?" she asked gently.

"They all grieve him still too. They don't need this added burden."

She'd not known them nearly as long as Kester had, yet she hadn't the least doubt he was wrong on that score. They were burdened by his worries even though they couldn't identify them. They needed to know, and she very much feared he wouldn't tell them. But he had told *her* in confidence.

"Working on a lantern design that I think Stanley would have been pleased with," Kester said, "and doing what I can to contribute to Julia's happiness and doing nothing that would undermine the Gents' closeness doesn't make up for failing him the way I did a decade ago, but it's what I have to offer. It's all I can do to try to make peace with it all. I've needed peace for a very long time."

Before Violet could think of anything to say, Georgie came skipping into the room. She didn't pause but came directly to them. If she noticed their somewhat intimate arrangement, she didn't mention it. "Mr. Barrington, Lady Jonquil says London has sweetshops. Is that true?"

"It is."

"And she said she and Lord Jonquil would take me to one. Do you think they will?"

"I guarantee it," he said. "Lord Jonquil will do so if only to have an excuse to purchase a peppermint for himself. His love of them is rivaled only by Lady Jonquil's love of ginger biscuits."

"Will you take me to a sweetshop when I go to London?" Georgie asked. "After we go to a bookshop?"

"I would like that. I have not had an anise twist in years. To have a sweet *and* a book would be the perfect way to spend a day."

"Will you draw me a map of London so I know where to find the sweetshops and the bookshops?"

"Have you enjoyed your map of lakes and walks?" he asked her.

She nodded. "Violet and I had an adventure yesterday morning using your map."

"I had a good friend who liked nothing better than a grand adventure," Kester said. "I think you would have liked him."

Violet squeezed his arm, recognizing he was speaking of Stanley, a topic that often brought him sorrow.

"What am I supposed to read while I wait to go to London?" Georgie asked.

"Anything in here you would like." He adjusted his spectacles, and Violet's heart fluttered at the endearing mannerism.

Kester rose from the sofa, necessitating that Violet release her embrace of his arm. She missed his touch the moment it was severed. He walked with Georgie over to the filled shelves. With tremendous patience and care, he suggested different books and different topics of study. None of them seemed to appeal to her, but she showed every indication of enjoying their discussion. He smiled at her now and then, his look one of avuncular kindness. Georgie was lighter in his company than she had been at first. She seemed comfortable in this house. How much had changed in the short weeks since they had come to Cumberland.

"Perhaps," Kester suggested after failing to find a book for Georgie, "you would care to write your own."

"I am not a writer," Georgie said.

"If I give you parchment and a quill and ink and you write down a story, then you will be."

Georgie's eyes pulled wide. "Could I?"

"I have every confidence you not only could but would also be remarkably good at it."

Kester looked at Violet as he walked past, accompanying Georgie to his desk. Their eyes met only briefly, but the impact of it was shocking. Her heart thudded against her ribs. Her stomach twisted in hopeful anticipation. Her lungs froze.

Over a single glance.

Chapter Thirty-Two

Violet had come to a swift conclusion as she'd sat in Kester's library, watching him interact with Georgie and replaying in her mind what he'd told her of Stanley: the Gents needed to know this aspect of his grief because they were the ones most likely to be able to help him.

She could not share the details, as that had been told to her in strict secrecy, but the Gents were perfectly aware that Kester had missed that long-ago gathering. They knew Stanley had made his decision to go to war during that time. They knew their beloved Highwayman hadn't returned. If she could turn their thoughts to those things, perhaps they could make the connection themselves.

The rambunctious friends spent most late mornings out on the grounds of Livingsley Hall, enjoying a brisk walk, riding horses, or undertaking hilariously competitive lawn games. That was where a person was most likely to find them.

And so she made certain she was on the grounds the next day as well. When they came within sight, Kester was not with them. Fate meant to be kind. Violet meant to be quick.

Hoping she didn't look too frantic, she moved toward them, keeping her clip swift so as not to waste a moment. They spotted her and offered the expected bows and words of pleasure at crossing paths with her.

"Is Kester not joining you this morning?" she asked.

"He will in a moment," Lucas said. "He had an epiphany about convex glass and wanted to document the discovery while it was fresh in his mind."

This window of opportunity would be a short one.

"You will have to forgive my haste, but there is something I must tell you, and I have to say it before he arrives." She could see they were curious. A glance at Digby told her he meant to begin guessing. She held up her hand to cut off the hypothesizing. "This is more important than I can even say. Please let me get it out while there's time."

Their usual looks of barely suppressed laughter disappeared immediately.

"It has been mentioned by a few of you that Kester prefers quiet and isolation. More than prefers it; he *needs* it. But it's obvious to anyone who spends any time amongst you that he seldom claims it. And Henri"—she looked to that gentleman—"told me you aren't certain the reason Kester requires that of himself."

She glanced in the direction of the house, fearful she would see him approaching. He was not in sight, so she pressed forward. "Years ago, he chose not to attend your annual gathering."

They all nodded.

"It proved to be significant," she said. "Important. Life-altering."

They were studying her. How she wished she could simply tell them.

"I cannot say more than that. I promised him I wouldn't," she said. "But the answer is there. It's all connected. Please, think on it. He needs you to help him finally make his way through this fog. Please."

They exchanged looks of pondering.

"That *was* an important gathering," Aldric said. "It was the last one Stanley attended."

They were sorting it out. She'd brought up difficult topics, asked them to remember moments of grief. It was out of character for her, but it would help Kester. All the cheerfulness in the world would not have brought the healing he needed. The Gents would have to talk of heavy things, would have to tread through the sorrows of the past, but it was the needful thing.

Be sunny or be silent. Being quiet had caused years of heartache. It was time for true compassion, not ignoring difficulties in the name of forced cheerfulness.

"Time's running short," Niles said, motioning subtly toward the house.

Kester was approaching and would be near them in only another moment.

"Can you keep him occupied for a bit?" Aldric asked her. "We don't yet know exactly what you're trying to lead us to, but with a quick moment, we could formulate a strategy for getting him to fill in the gaps."

"You'll be kind?" she pressed. "He's hurting more than you know."

"He's a brother to us, Violet," Lucas said. "We're family."

With that assurance ringing in her ears, she spun away from them and moved swiftly to where Kester was approaching.

"What a pleasure to see you, Violet." He often said that. The sentiment seemed to arise from his very heart, an unconscious display of his feelings. She liked that about him: he was sincere.

"Can I keep you away from your friends for a moment longer?" she asked. "I thought of something I wanted to tell you."

"I will always be pleased to hear anything you have to say."

Heat touched her face at the compliment. "I have been giving some thought to your carriage lantern."

That seemed to surprise him. "You have?"

She nodded. "What if rather than using the mirrors to increase the light, you used them to direct it? A stronger flame, which I know you're hoping for, would produce more light but would be uncomfortable for the coachman if set too close to him and might cause the horses distress if set too near them."

Eagerness entered his eyes with not a single hint of doubt. "The mirrors could allow the lantern to be placed conveniently and safely while still lighting what most needs to be lit." He didn't say it condescendingly but in a tone of one recognizing the truthfulness of something he had not thought of before.

"I haven't the first idea how to increase the strength of the light, unless more candles are used. That, I suppose, is something to take into consideration."

His brow furrowed in thought. She had long adored the way that particular expression made his spectacles slip down his nose. She had the strongest urge to reach over and adjust them. "When Julia has had time to recover from her lying-in, I hope to ask her what she learned from her reading on the matter of fire."

There was something rather lovely about Julia being involved in a project her brother had undertaken in large part out of love for her.

"Directing the light would provide an important improvement over what is available now."

"Enough that you think the Royal Society would be interested?" she asked.

"That, I don't know. Sometimes they're open to new members, and sometimes they're extremely fastidious."

"And in the matter of a certain bespectacled gentleman from Cumberland, they are markedly thickheaded." She made the declaration with more emphasis than she'd intended to, but she meant every word. That a gentleman of his intelligence and goodness, one dedicating his academic prowess to improving people's lives, had not yet found a place among them was a mark firmly against the Royal Society in her evaluation.

He smiled at her. Violet's heart flipped about. It had done that with increasing frequency of late.

"We are proving adept 'inventing partners,' as Mr. Miller so aptly phrased it," Kester said. "I suspect, between the two of us, there is not a single problem in this world we cannot manage to solve."

She knew he was exaggerating a little, but the compliment sent her spirits soaring nonetheless.

"And I hope that—" But he cut himself off. His lips pressed, and his features slipped into forced neutrality. "Forgive me, I am monopolizing your time, and the Gents have been waiting for me to join them."

"Of course," she said. What she wanted to say was, "Finish your sentence. Tell me what you are afraid to say."

But in the next moment, he slipped away and joined the Gents on their jaunt around the grounds. As she watched him leave, the fluttering in her heart was replaced with an ache.

She was regaining his friendship; she hadn't the slightest doubt about that. She would get to see him often as they worked on their inventions and interacted as neighbors. She would get to spend time with him.

As his friend.

She ought to have been pleased, relieved, grateful.

Why, then, did she feel disappointed?

Chapter Thirty-Three

Kes had nearly overstepped himself with Violet again. They'd had a pleasant discussion, a moment of connection, one that had come on the heels of her sitting beside him in the library the day before, leaning against him, her arm folded through his, while he shared a part of his history he usually kept firmly tucked away. He'd been letting himself imagine a future with her again. And that was a foolish thing to do.

He'd caught himself, but only just. He did his best in the few moments between stepping away from Violet and joining the Gents to rein in his thoughts once more.

"Change of plans, Grumpy Uncle," Lucas said, motioning with his thumb away from the lake. "We're aiming for the east lawn."

Kes's first inclination was to object, to insist they stick to their original plan of walking around the lake—he'd come to like it all the more, knowing how much Violet did—but he took his usual tactic and went along with their plans.

"Next time we're gathered here," Aldric said, "we should play a rousing game of cricket on the east lawn. It's perfect for it."

"Do you remember the time at Eton when Stanley challenged Silas Bower and his minions to a not-so-friendly game of cricket?" Lucas asked. "He was so convinced we could best the lot of them that he wagered a month of shining the other team's shoes."

"I had polish under my fingernails for weeks." Digby shuddered. "I have seldom suffered so acutely."

They all laughed. The story was familiar even to those among them who hadn't yet joined the group when the ill-advised wager had been made. Even Kes enjoyed the memory. Stanley had convinced him to do a great many things over the years, adventures and risks and larks of every stamp. Kes's life would have been far less full without his friend. It had been in many ways since Stanley's death.

"What about the time he convinced us to break into Hardfords' London home?" Henri said. "*Quelle folie.*"

"Madness, yes, but also an adventure," Aldric said. "He did manage the thing without getting us into too much trouble."

"We are fortunate *Lady* Hardford discovered us and not *Lord* Hardford." How easily Kes recalled the moment they were found out and the laughter that had replaced their initial panic. "The outcome would have been drastically different."

"Digby smoothed that over for us." Niles slapped the King on the shoulder. "We're fortunate you are very convincing."

"And by 'convincing,' I assume you mean 'handsome.'"

"Not what he said, my friend," Kes tossed back.

Again, laughter rang among them.

"Stanley came up with the most ridiculous adventures," Lucas said. "We all knew we were in over our heads, and he would grin with excitement."

"The Highwayman enjoyed everything he did." Niles shook his head in appreciation. "And everything he did was treated as the greatest lark of all time."

"What do you suppose he would suggest as our next adventure if he were here now?" Digby asked.

If only that were their reality. If only Stanley had remained. If only . . . a lot of things.

"He would already be organizing an effort to meet Finley's coach on whichever road the cad means to depart the county," Lucas said, "and treat the louse to a bit of land piracy."

"And he could even convince Grumpy Uncle to participate." Henri grinned at him. "He was very persuasive."

Kes had already discussed Stanley at some length with Violet the day before. He was not at all ready to do so again. "I do not wish to talk about him."

"You've avoided talking about him for ten years now," Aldric said. "Perhaps it's time we did."

He increased his pace and pushed out ahead of them. "Is this what Violet was talking to you about?"

"Why would Violet be talking to us about Stanley?" Lucas pressed, keeping pace with him quiet easily.

"Because I talked to her about him."

Lucas set his hand on Kes's arm and stopped him. "Why would you talk to *her* about him and not to *us*?" he asked in a tone of hurt.

Kes took a few steps away. "She didn't know him. She's not grieving him like we are. I didn't—" It was too much. He couldn't force the remaining confession to slip from him.

"You've been different since he left." Aldric had caught up to them. "You're somehow more distant and more present. We can't make sense of it."

"Would you rather I be entirely distant?" he muttered.

"No," they all answered.

"What we'd rather," Lucas said, "is that you tell us what weight you're carrying. Even a year on the Continent didn't grant me any insights. We're baffled. We've been baffled for years."

"What is there to be baffled about?" Kes kept walking, not looking at any of them. "I missed a gathering. I regretted it. I haven't missed one since. And that means being present even when I'm a little exhausted from the whirl of it all. It is not such a difficult puzzle."

"Why did you regret missing the gathering?" Henri asked.

"Because I should have been there." He took in a deep breath and slowly released it. "Stanley asked me twice to join in. But I decided instead to spend that time pouting. There is plenty enough in that to regret."

"You were nineteen, and life had bombarded you with difficulties," Lucas said. "We all understood. We missed you, we wished you were there, but we understood. You needed time."

"I needed to be there so I could convince—" He shoved his hands into his pockets.

Aldric stepped in front of him and stopped his forward movement. "Convince *whom*?"

Kes dropped his gaze to his shoes.

True to character, Aldric didn't need an answer. "We tried everything to talk Stanley out of joining the fight in the colonies, but it became apparent rather quickly that he could not be dissuaded."

It wasn't that simple. "I often talked him out of his most ridiculous schemes. I could have then. But I wasn't there."

"It wasn't a lark or a whim," Aldric said firmly. "He didn't go to have an adventure. He went because it was what he was determined to do. It mattered to him."

Kes hadn't heard that before.

"You couldn't have stopped him." Lucas met Kes's eyes. "Though you were better at it than we were, if you had seen and heard him talk of it, you would know how impossible he was to dissuade in this matter." His eyes grew more focused, the look in them more heavy. "Had you been there, Kes, you could not have stopped him."

"But I could have tried." He swallowed down the emotion that rose in his throat. "When I received your missive, I knew it was too late to catch him in Derbyshire, so I went directly to the port where he would be shipping out."

"You did?" Lucas watched him closely.

Kes nodded. "I missed him by less than a day. I wasn't at the house party, the one that *he* had all but begged me to attend. I wasn't there to try to change his mind, and I didn't get to the port in time to talk to him there. Even if I couldn't convince him to stay, I could have at least seen him one last time." The emotion he'd been fighting pooled hot in his eyes. "I never even said goodbye, and it was all my own doing. I could have been there, but I chose not to be. It's my fault."

"He wouldn't have wanted for you to be miserable all these years," Henri said. "He would not wish for you to spend your life suffering and crushed with these regrets."

There was a reason Kes didn't discuss these things. Even these well-meaning reassurances sat like a weight.

"If he were here," Lucas said, "what do you honestly think he would say to you?"

There was an obvious answer to that. "He would call me a hulverhead, probably."

The group smiled at the well-known turn of phrase. They had all been called that by him countless times over the years.

"He would also tell you to live your life," Aldric said. "He would tell you to be happy."

Kes shook his head. "Even if he did, it doesn't change the fact that—that I didn't—"

"He would further tell you," Lucas interrupted, "that the generosity and support you showed Julia when she faced our forced marriage and the loss of so many of her dreams was far more important to him than you being present when he left England. He cared more for her than he did for himself. Her worries would have weighed far more heavily on him than his own."

"I wanted to say goodbye," he said. "I can't simply stop regretting that."

"If you had told any of us about this," Digby said, "we could have informed you that none of us said goodbye to him."

That stopped Kes short. "You knew he was leaving."

"Yes, and we all attempted to bid him farewell, but he refused to allow us to say anything other than to commit to enjoying ourselves until we were all together again. That was the only thing he let us say. No goodbyes. No farewells."

Kes had not expected that. "Do you think he knew he wasn't coming back?"

"No," Aldric said. "I think he thought he would survive. And he nearly did. The Battle of Yorktown came at the very end of that war. The *very* end. He nearly made it."

Kes breathed through the difficult reminder. They'd nearly gotten him back. He'd come so painfully, painfully close to returning to them.

Aldric continued. "I also think he was worried that our concern for him would mean we wouldn't live our lives while he was away. And that wasn't at all what he would have wanted for us."

"You all honored that request," Kes said.

"And it's time you did too." Lucas set his hands on Kes's shoulders. "None of us, and that absolutely includes Stanley, wants you to keep drowning in these regrets. Live your life the way *you* are meant to live it. And when our enthusiastic idiocy gets in the way of that, tell us."

"And," Digby said, "for heaven's sake, don't sever your connection with Violet. Her family moving to Irthing Grange is the best thing that's happened in your life for years."

Words of agreement rippled through the group. They weren't unaware of the disaster he'd made of things, but they were forgetting it rather quickly.

"I gave her my word, and I won't break it. My feelings were not what hers were. And I've sworn not to impose upon her. I will hold myself to that. Knowing friendship is the limit of what I can claim, I don't intend to repeatedly break my own heart hoping for more."

Niles nudged him onward once more.

Aldric spoke on the group's behalf. "You absolutely must keep your promise, but don't give up."

"Hoping for the impossible isn't—"

"On yourself, hulverhead," Lucas said. "Don't give up *on yourself*."

Don't give up on yourself. He felt like he'd been doing exactly that for ten years. But Stanley's last wish for them all was to live their lives, to be happy. It was time Kes allowed himself to do so.

Chapter Thirty-Four

Violet was in the sitting room at Irthing Grange the next day when Kester was announced. All her family were there as well, though her parents sat across the room near the fireplace. He stepped inside, dressed in his usual fashionable soberness, spectacles perched on his nose, a book tucked under one arm. He offered the expected bows and words of greeting and was invited to join them. He moved to where Violet and Georgie were seated on either side of the window seat.

Georgie was "fussing" with Violet's prosthesis. That Violet hadn't even a moment's uncertainty about Kester's response to seeing her without her arm attached was further testament to how much she trusted him.

"A pleasure, ladies," he said. He looked to Georgie. "I had hoped to see you in particular, Miss Georgie. I have found something in one of the books in my library that will be of particular interest to you."

"You have?" She eyed the book under his arm with interest.

He nodded. "It is a book that delineates many of the events of the early sixteenth century. And in the back is an illumination." He motioned to the space between the two of them. "May I?"

Georgie didn't bother discussing the matter with Violet but nodded emphatically.

Kester looked to Violet for confirmation. She gave a quick nod of agreement. He sat and placed the book on his lap, opening it to the back. "This is a facsimile of the Westminster Tournament Roll. And this right here"—he tapped the page—"is John Blanke."

Georgie gasped with excitement. "It's actually him?"

Kester nodded. "The famed trumpeter from Africa, favored by the king and members of the royal court."

With wide eyes, Georgie looked up at their visitor. "May I show the book to my aunt? He is her ancestor, you know."

Kester nodded.

"Be careful with it," Violet added.

Georgie handed the prosthesis to Kester, took up the book, and crossed the room with careful but quick steps to where Violet's mother sat. She began an eager conversation, one Violet could hear only bits and pieces of.

"Thank you for that," Violet said. "And thank you for suggesting that she write her own stories. I fear we will go through a great deal of parchment, but she is the happiest I have seen her in years."

"She has an active mind and such a love of reading and learning and exploring that I couldn't imagine she didn't have ample things in her mind that could be written down."

"Do you still mean to look in the London bookshops for a book about John Blanke?"

"I do, but I'm not certain we will find one. Though he was an important person, I fear not enough is known of him for an entire book to be written exclusively about him. It will be well worth the search though." He held out her prosthesis to her. "I suspect you would like this back."

"I'd rather leave it off."

He studied her a bit. "Is something the matter with it? It's not broken, is it?"

"It's not. But I have a sore on my arm that the cuff is rubbing against painfully. It is a relief to have it off."

"Do you often get sores?" he asked.

"More often than I'd like. All it takes is the tiniest bit of dirt or unaddressed bit of moisture between the cuff and my arm or the straps being buckled unevenly."

"We should mention that to Mr. Miller. He may have some thoughts on the matter."

It would be worth bringing up, though she couldn't imagine raw skin and painful sores could be entirely avoided.

Kester carefully set the wooden arm on the window seat beside him. "Your parents must be eagerly anticipating the possibility of improving your prosthesis."

She lowered her voice, not wishing to be heard over the conversation still happening across the room. "They might be excited if they knew about it."

His brow drew. His scrunched nose shifted his spectacles downward. "You haven't told them?" He matched her lowered volume.

"If we manage the adjustments we're attempting, then I will tell them."

"Why not until then?" he whispered. "Why would you not tell them about something that means so much to you?"

She adjusted the bit of light bandaging she'd tied around the end of her arm. "I don't want them to be disappointed if, in the end, this proves impossible."

"We know it's not entirely impossible. We are hoping for improvements on what already exists, but the most basic of what we want is entirely within reach."

That was true, but it didn't address everything. "There's still the possibility of failure. I'd rather not tell them about this unless I can tell them good news."

His eyes didn't leave her, didn't shift away. She knew the look on his face: he was sorting something out. And that something, she suspected, was herself.

"You are choosing to adhere to the adage that if one cannot manage to be sunny, one has an obligation to be silent?"

"You've heard them say that I am the sunshine in their life and a source of joy and cheer," she said. "Telling them things I'm worried about, things I long for but might never have isn't precisely being a light in the darkness."

"Neither is it being fully honest," he countered. "I suspect they would want you to share this with them."

She knew her role in this family, and she wasn't overly comfortable abandoning it.

Their conversation, though conducted in whispers, was beginning to draw the notice of her parents. Nervousness tiptoed over her, wrapping tightly around her lungs, lodging as a lump in her throat.

"You trusted me," Kester said. "You agreed to share with me the things you worry about and the things that weigh on you. Why not offer that same openness to your parents? Anyone who has watched your family knows how deeply you all love each other."

"And I suspect they like you quite a lot," Violet said. "Your kindness to Georgie alone would endear you. She's going to miss you when you travel. We all will."

He colored a little. "I won't be traveling for some time. I've decided it would do me good to stay in one place for a while. I can work on my carriage lanterns. And I can rest. I haven't allowed myself that in years."

She reached out and squeezed his arm. "Everyone needs to rest from their worries now and then."

He set his hand atop hers. "One way to rest is to share your burdens with people who are willing to help carry them."

"I don't have a great deal of practice with this," she admitted. "It won't come easily."

"I imagine it won't, but one thing I have learned about you these past weeks, Miss Violet Ridley, is that you manage to do difficult things all the time. I believe you are equal to this."

"Do you really?"

He nodded gently.

She took a fortifying breath and rose. Georgie had stationed herself near the fireplace, lying on her belly, the book open on the Axminster carpet, she no doubt studying the depiction of her long-revered ancestor.

Violet took the seat her cousin had abandoned beside Mother and Father.

"How is your arm feeling?" Mother asked. "I wish there were a way to prevent the sores."

"I've given some thought to the difficulties I have with my prosthesis." Violet wished her voice were a little more confident and steady. "It isn't just sores, but—" The words stopped as her courage temporarily ebbed. Kester believed in her; she could do this. "I've long thought it might be nice to have a prosthesis with a moving wrist and fingers. I could hold things and adjust the position so the hand looked more natural. It would certainly be more useful."

Far from shocked, they looked intrigued. She'd expected that. And feared it. If their hopes soared and she and Kester couldn't manage the improvements, disappointment would inevitably follow.

"Mr. Barrington knows an apothecary in Northumberland whose father is a clockmaker. The two of them know about such things." She looked over at Kester, who had crossed the room as well but still stood a few paces away. He nodded subtly. Attention on her parents once more, she continued. "We've been writing to them, discussing possibilities and ideas."

Her parents' eyes darted between the two of them.

"You have?" Father asked. "Why didn't you tell us?"

"There's no guarantee this will be successful. In the end, what is possible might be disappointing."

"Well, of course, there's that possibility, but it's exciting to be pursuing the chance of something more." Father leaned forward in his chair. "And does this apothecary think you could improve upon what you have?"

How tempting it was to simply resort to nothing but sunshine. She meant to trust Kester in this and be fully honest. "We do know some improvements are not only possible but already exist. We're hoping to build upon that to refine the prosthesis even more, but we don't yet know how much can be done."

Mother nodded. "You might not, in the end, be able to implement every improvement you wish for, but every advancement you make would be worth celebrating."

"I don't want you to be disappointed."

"Do you intend to abandon your efforts if you discover some of what you are attempting is impossible?" her father asked.

"Of course not."

"Then why do you think we will be devastated by setbacks? We know how to be hopeful. And we know how to weather storms."

Storms. How often they had used that metaphor. "I am meant to be the sunshine in those storms, not the rain and thunder."

"Rain and thunder are as much a part of life as sunshine," Father said.

"But if a person cannot be sunny, she ought not inflict that on others."

"That blasted vicar," Mother muttered.

"*That blasted vicar*?" Violet repeated.

"I remember the sermon in which he said that, and I remember thinking what a fool he was."

For a moment, Violet did nothing but stare. What had for so long been her guiding principle in life, her mother considered the words of a fool.

"I understand the principle behind it," Mother said. "We have the ability to bring and spread happiness, and when we're able to do so, that is a fine thing. But to insist that a person should contribute nothing, speak nothing, connect to no one in times of sorrow and struggle and worry is not merely foolish; it is dangerous. A burden one is required to carry alone is a burden that will crush a person's soul."

Violet swallowed, unexpected emotion rising at the declaration. She often felt crushed by her unspoken worries. She had seen Kester be crushed by his. But there never seemed to be an escape. Being silent required a person to suffer alone.

"I've heard you use the vicar's words before." Mother reached over and squeezed her hand. "But I didn't realize you'd taken them so much to heart that you weren't even telling us your hopes for fear of causing disappointment."

"We adore that you are a source of cheer in our lives," Father said, shifting enough to reach out and put an arm around her shoulders. "That doesn't mean that your buoyancy is the only part of you that we love. We love all of you, the person you are in your triumphs and in your struggles, in your joys and your sorrows. We want you to be wholly, truly yourself, especially with us. And we need you to trust us enough to believe that you can be."

Without warning, tears began forming in her eyes. "Sometimes I feel very alone," she confessed.

Mother brushed a loose coil of hair away from Violet's face, the gesture a familiar remnant from her childhood. "When you feel that way, darling, talk to us. Talk to your family. To your friends. I imagine Lady Jonquil would be as heartbroken as we are now to realize you've been carrying so many worries alone. You don't need to."

It was so much what she had hoped the Gents would convince Kester of. How had she missed that the same advice ought to be directed at herself?

"It will take time to break the habit," she warned, sniffling and blinking away the moisture still hanging on her lashes.

"We don't expect perfection," Father promised. "We simply want you to try."

From her position near the fire, Georgie said, "We have to at least try to hope."

That brought amusement to everyone's face. Violet had told her cousin precisely that quite often.

"In my view," Mother said, "that is a far better life philosophy than the ridiculous demands of that fool-hearted vicar."

Try to hope.

"Now"—Father squeezed her shoulders—"if you and Mr. Barrington mean to design this miraculous prosthesis, do not let us keep you from it." He nudged her to her feet, though she didn't need a great deal of prodding. She gave both her parents lingering hugs. They each, in turn, told her they loved her. It wasn't rare for them to do so, but she found she particularly needed to hear it in that moment.

She took the few steps to where Kester stood.

"That took a great deal of courage, Violet," he said in a low and friendly voice. "But I never doubted you were equal to it."

"Thank you for believing in me enough to convince me to try."

With a dip of his head, he said, "That is what friends are for."

Friends.

Chapter Thirty-Five

A NOTE ARRIVED AT IRTHING Grange early in the afternoon the day after Kester's visit. Violet hadn't heard anything from the Gents and wasn't certain if they'd found a means of talking with Kester and discovering the burden he carried. She hoped so. Eager for any update, she opened the note.

Dearest Violet,

It is with sorrow that we inform you that The Gents will be making their departures beginning tomorrow. Alas, we recognize your life will be a blank until we meet again.

This absolutely had to have been written by Digby. She glanced at the signature and saw that she was correct. Pleased to her very core, she resumed her reading.

We wish for one last evening of revelry and delight and could not adequately have that without you here among us. Please, deign to join us for dinner and for an evening of what I fear will be absolute boredom. Lord Aldric, you must understand, grows terribly tedious when anticipating a journey. The others are always *tedious. Thus, your presence is needed lest I succumb to the horrors of fatal ennui.*

We wait in anticipation of you.

Yours, etc.,
Digby

How she hoped Digby proved a faithful correspondent. Letters like this one would be welcome for years to come.

She was grateful for the Gents and Julia. And she had every hope that Kester would continue to be part of her life as well.

Again and again, her mind returned to their brief, unexpected kiss. She'd been so confused, so upended. In the time since, that confusion had settled into regret—not regret over being kissed but regret at not having paid even a moment's heed to the whispers of her heart. The hints of tenderness and partiality had been so quiet and subtle that she'd ignored them entirely.

She couldn't do so any longer. But what could be done now? Her chance had fled. Kester showed every indication of being content with mere friendship and an academically focused inventing partnership.

Violet told herself repeatedly as she dressed for the evening and rode in the carriage to Livingsley Hall that having his friendship was far preferable to not having him in her life at all. She silently insisted that she could somehow find a way to be satisfied with so unromantic a connection.

She had not entirely convinced herself by the time she arrived for the evening; she wasn't certain she ever would.

Kes was polite and everything that was appropriate as the evening meal progressed. He was her friend. But no hint of anything beyond.

Julia joined everyone in the drawing room after dinner. She brought little Philip with her, though he was commandeered so immediately that, if Violet had to guess, the new mother would spend little time that night holding her tiny son. Lucas sat beside his wife, his arm around her. They were the perfect picture of contented love.

Violet vividly remembered sitting beside Kester in the library, leaning against him as he shared his burdens and his worries. Of him gently holding her hand as she'd fretted over Julia's early delivery. He had listened and supported her. He had given her the courage to be fully open with her parents about her hopes and her worries. How had she not realized how much he meant to her?

"What is to be our entertainment this evening?" Lucas asked, not moving an inch from his cozy position.

"We have many options," Aldric said. "There are plenty of games we have played already that we might return to."

Digby offered a different idea. "We should choose something new for our final evening."

"New?" Julia said. "Does that mean you intend to be well-behaved for a change?"

They laughed, embracing the jest in good humor.

"What about 'If One Were . . . ?'" Niles suggested.

Eager acceptance rippled through them all.

"I'm not familiar with that game," Violet said. She had learned of more games during the Gents' visit than she had realized even existed.

"It is simple enough," Aldric said. "One at a time, a person is presented with a question about another person in the group. He or she must answer the question to the best of his or her knowledge. If the person is unable to answer or their answer is deemed incorrect, he or she must undertake a forfeit."

Games with forfeits seemed to be a favorite.

"What manner of questions are these?" she asked.

"They always begin, 'If *this person* were . . .'" Henri said. "For example, were it Aldric's turn and he was meant to answer a question about Lucas, I might ask him, 'If Lucas were a book, what would be its title?'"

"And I," Aldric said, "would be charged with answering both correctly and in some way unexpectedly. Accuracy is the goal, but being clever is the added challenge."

She nodded her understanding. It was a simple game, but she suspected it would be an absolute delight.

The questions began simple enough.

Niles was asked where, of all the places in the world, Henri would travel, and of course, he answered, "France."

Lucas was asked which baked good Julia would choose if she were permitted any option. He, of course, answered, "Ginger biscuit." It was not a surprising answer to any of them, but it was the only truly accurate one.

Around and around the room, play went. The questions grew more interesting, as did the answers.

At one point, Digby was asked, "If Henri were to fall desperately in love with a woman, what is the first thing he would do?"

Henri shook his head amusedly even as he reddened.

"Simple enough, my dear fellow," Digby answered in a tone of superiority. "The first thing he would do is make a mull of the entire thing."

They all laughed, including Henri. It was a good-natured game, and Violet couldn't imagine anyone in this group would offer an answer that was hurtful.

Henri raised his hand in an almost papal gesture. "With what mockery ye mock, prepare to be yourself one day mocked."

The Gents all exchanged wide-eyed looks of confusion before bursting into laughter.

With a shrug Violet had seen many Frenchmen employ, Henri said, "I couldn't think of an actual proverb."

"Ask your question," Aldric said to him. "It's your turn."

Henri posed a question to Violet. "If Digby could change one thing about your wardrobe, what would it be?"

In any other group, that might have been a worrisome question, especially with her prosthesis off, as it was, but she knew perfectly well no insults would be offered. "He would insist upon adding a decorative flare to the new prosthesis Kester and I are designing."

That sent the room into a flurry of questions. Kester turned to her, his eyes pulled wide.

"I thought it time to tell them," she said. "I've lived too long in fear of failure or feeling I ought to be a source of only cheerfulness. I want to be myself, fully."

That soft, reassuring smile of his appeared, and for a moment, Violet's heart pounded so hard her mind could hardly think.

"I have decided to talk about the things I need to talk about when I need to talk about them instead of bottling it all up. And when I do tuck my arm a bit away, it will be because I choose to, not because I feel like I'm obligated to."

"I'm glad to hear it," he said.

It took time to get the group focused on the game again, which she didn't mind. They had endless questions about her prosthesis project with Kester. And he kept smiling at her, which was a welcome distraction.

When they did take up the game once more, no one could remember whose turn it was.

They assigned the next question to Lucas. Still sitting with his arm around his wife, he addressed Kester. "If Violet were a flower, which flower would she be?"

Many around the room objected to the question. "A violet," was tossed out as the obvious answer. Aldric insisted Lucas had chosen an easy question and it was unfair, as Kester was the smartest among them.

"I fear he is correct, *mon ami*," Henri said, rocking Philip in his arms. "Violet would be a violet."

"No, she wouldn't be," Kester said, perfectly serious. "She would be lily of the valley. It is soft and comforting. It's beautiful but in a way that enhances the beauty of everything around it. Its presence in a room or a bouquet or a field makes a person want to linger." His voice grew softer as he spoke, and his gaze grew distant. "Its perfume hangs on the air, gentle and welcoming and assuring a person he belongs even when he is all but certain he does not. Lily of the valley symbolizes a return of happiness, and that is who Violet is. When she's gone, everything feels empty. And only when she returns is all as it should be again. Her name may be Violet, but she is lily of the valley, the return of happiness, the promise of every good thing."

The room had gone entirely silent. Violet could hardly breathe, certainly couldn't speak. Her heart bubbled over with the beauty of what he had said. *Lily of the valley.* Tears threatened in her eyes.

With a start, Kester seemed to suddenly remember he had an audience. Discomfort and something akin to panic spread across his face. His eyes darted to each of them, resting last on Violet. He jumped awkwardly to his feet. "Pardon me, I need to—" Whatever excuse he meant to give, he cut himself off and, in a flash, disappeared from the room.

Violet sat frozen to the spot. His were not the words of a man who felt nothing but friendship. A man couldn't say something like that, unrehearsed and utterly sincere, if he had no tender regard for her.

"For heaven's sake, Violet," Lucas said, "go after him."

It was exactly what she needed to snap herself from her shock. She leapt to her feet and rushed out into the corridor. He hadn't gone terribly far, and she was able to catch up to him. "Kester. Please stop."

He halted his forward movement, but he did not turn around to look at her. "I'm sorry. I promised not to make you uncomfortable, and I know I have. I was only meant to suggest a flower, and I—I let my mouth run away with me. I'm sorry."

She slipped past him and turned to face him. "But did you mean it?" she asked. "Did you mean the things you said?"

"Of course I did," he said quietly.

"Why?"

He looked at her, confused. "*Why?*"

"Why would you say those things about . . . a friend?"

He adjusted his spectacles. Swallowed. Shifted his weight from one foot to the other. "I can't explain."

"Why not?" She needed to know. She needed an answer.

He pushed out a breath, then looked back over his shoulder. She glanced that way as well and spotted the Gents in the drawing room door as they hurriedly ducked back inside and out of sight.

He would only grow more distressed with the possibility of an audience looming over them. Violet took hold of his hand and pulled him down the corridor to the tiny room where he'd first learned of her ambitions and her struggles, where their partnership had begun.

She didn't entirely close the door behind them; the room would have been pitch black without light spilling inside from the corridor, not to mention the two of them in so private a situation wouldn't have met with the approval of even the laxest adherents to propriety.

"Why would you say the things you did about me when I'm only your friend?" she asked again.

He shook his head. "I promised you, Violet. I don't break my word."

He'd sworn after that kiss that she would decide how they proceeded, where their connection went. He'd promised not to overstep whatever version of friendship she permitted.

"I wouldn't keep asking, Kester, if I thought your answer would be a breach of that promise."

He rubbed at the spot between his eyes just above his spectacles as he stepped farther into the dim room. She followed after him.

She set her hand lightly on his cheek. "Please tell me, Kester."

He set his hand over hers, wrapping his fingers gently around her hand. He closed his eyes, worry filling the lines of his face. Voice quiet, he said, "I love you, Violet. That didn't change after our kiss. I don't expect it ever will." He turned his head the tiniest bit, enough that his lips brushed against her palm. His eyes remained closed. "I don't want to lose you, but I don't know what you want or how you feel."

She leaned in and lightly kissed his cheek. "I loved you before I even realized I did."

"Truly?"

Violet kept her voice low, though there was no one nearby to overhear. "How could I help but love you? You are compassionate and considerate. You're intelligent and thoughtful. You make me laugh. You give me hope when I'm struggling. I didn't recognize my feelings as quickly as you recognized yours, but I do love you."

Kester slid their clasped hands to his heart, holding them there. His other arm wrapped around her. "I am also quiet and regularly need to be alone. All the things you are anticipating with pleasure in London would exhaust me long before you've had your fill. I might make you miserable, and that is the last thing I want to do."

She lifted her head and met his worried gaze. "I am not Digby."

A hint of laughter entered his expression. "That is fortunate for many reasons."

"I do enjoy balls and gatherings, and I mean to participate in them. But I also take great delight in a quiet evening spent in the company of my family. I enjoy sitting by a fire, reading a book. I gather strength from the sureness of home. Our needs do not conflict as much as you seem to think."

"I don't ever want to be the reason you are unhappy, Violet." He slipped his hand from hers and brushed his fingers along her jaw.

She bent her arms around his neck. "Do you know, Kester Barrington, what would make me excessively happy right now?"

He pulled her ever closer. "I have an inkling."

Their lips met in the dim quiet of the isolated room, warm and tender and filled with promise. The sliver of air between them disappeared as he tightened the embrace.

Violet threaded her fingers into the silkiness of his hair. One of his hands slid up her back even as his lips shifted to her jaw, pressing one kiss after another all the way to her ear.

"I love you, Kester," she whispered. "So much."

He kissed her fully once more. "And I love you, my sweet Violet. My lily of the valley."

Chapter Thirty-Six

Two months later

Kes arrived at Brier Hill more rested and at ease than he had been in years. The Gents had gone to their various destinations, as planned. The Ridleys had called at Livingsley Hall now and then. He saw Violet every day for varying lengths of time. They enjoyed being together. But she never grew frustrated when he needed time to himself. And he reminded her, when she hesitated to share her worries, that being genuine was more important than appearing cheerful, and being seen and understood was far better than being silent.

Neither of them was perfect in these important changes they were making, but there was hope. Every day, things were a little better. Never before had he looked to the future with such enthusiasm.

Violet and her father had made the journey to Brier Hill a week earlier, with Mr. Ridley having already returned home. Kes had waited to join the gathering, not only so he could build his store of energy before expending so much but also to give Violet an opportunity for time alone with Julia.

The Gents now often called Violet Lily, a reference to Kes's accidental confession. It was, by far, the most fortuitous slip of the tongue he'd ever made. He had sworn to pretend he felt only friendship. In an unguarded moment, he had poured out his heart to her. And the result had been nothing short of miraculous.

In the two months since, he had courted her and had come to know her even better. The attachment between them had grown. Love had blossomed further. And he wanted nothing more than to simply see her again. A week apart and he missed her.

Lucas met him on the front drive, sporting his usual mischievous grin. "It's good to see you."

"It's good to be seen."

Lucas's gaze narrowed a little. "Is that because you feel obligated or because you've rested enough that you're ready?"

"The latter," Kes said with sincerity. "Violet was correct on that score. I needed to let myself breathe before I suffocated."

They walked side-by-side toward the house. "We've already been thoroughly lectured by your ladylove and reminded of our obligation to allow you the respites you need."

"She's good for me."

"And you are good for her," Lucas said. "The Violet we first met at Livingsley Hall was cheerful and buoyant, but that wasn't the entirety of her. I feel like we see the whole person now. And the whole person has proven a loving and loyal friend to Julia. Julia has needed that ever since Charlotte died."

"Well, provided Digby's prediction doesn't prove true, perhaps Henri will add to Julia's circle of female friends eventually."

Lucas snorted. "Unlikely. I can't imagine Archbishop ever falling in love with anyone."

Kes chuckled. It wasn't meant to be a negative reflection on Henri's heart or companionableness. He had simply seldom shown himself inclined to such a thing. He'd had his head turned by a few women during their Cambridge years, and a few had caught his eye during their Seasons in Society, but it had been years since he'd shown an inclination toward any lady in particular. He participated in the social world, but he was *never* entangled in it.

They stepped inside the small entryway. It was midmorning—Kester had broken his trip from Livingsley Hall partway so as to arrive at the correct time for undertaking the journey they all meant to embark on that day—and the spill of light through the tall windows illuminated the cozy space. What Brier Hill lacked in impressiveness, it more than made up for with the unmistakable feel of a home where the occupants were loved and cherished.

"How fares little Lord Fallowgill these days?"

"He is perfection itself." Lucas made the declaration with complete sincerity.

"A testament to his mother, no doubt," Kes said dryly.

"A truer statement was seldom uttered."

They laughed again. There had once been so much laughter between them all. Especially when Stanley had still been alive. Kes suspected they would always miss him. There would always be something of a hole in their group without him there. But his influence remained so strong that so long as any of them remained on this earth, Stanley would never be forgotten.

"It is a pity this is the wrong time of year for flowers," Lucas said. "I have quite the variety in my walled garden, including lily of the valley." He made the last observation with a not-so-subtle tone of teasing.

"If you have no objections, I may take a cutting from the rhizomes so I can have the flowers at the Hall."

"And are those the only lilies of the valley you hope will someday be found there?" Lucas kept his gaze anywhere but on Kes.

"My hopes lie far beyond mere flowers."

Lucas slapped a hand on Kes's shoulder. "Glad to hear it, my friend. If she'll have you, you couldn't do better. She is your match in so many ways."

"Violet becoming my neighbor is the best thing that's ever happened to me."

"Just like Digby said." Lucas gave him a very solemn look. "But we would do best not to tell him. The last thing our King needs is added confidence in himself."

Digby wasn't actually conceited, but they did like to play along when he pretended to be.

"As we are meant to set out for this apothecary's shop any moment now," Lucas said, "I had best slip upstairs to see if Julia is ready. Violet has been ready to go all day. In fact, I can't believe she hasn't rushed out here and tackled you already. You're about the only thing she talks of, which, as you can imagine, has been terribly tedious."

Kes smirked unrepentantly. He walked directly to the door of the sitting room, certain that was where the woman he loved with every breath in his body would be.

He wasn't wrong.

He saw her only in profile, but it was enough to do his heart a world of good. She didn't wear gloves, didn't tuck her arm out of notice. She had not forgone her shawl, but that, he felt certain, was on account of the cold winter weather rather than worry over people seeing her prosthesis. She wore a look of contentment, not the overabundance of cheer she had once hidden behind.

"I have missed you, my dear," he said softly.

She turned at the sound of his voice, looking at him directly. The look of absolute joy on her face when she met his eyes sent his heart soaring. She always insisted he take the quiet time he needed, but she never looked anything less than ecstatic to see him again.

He intended to offer a word of greeting or ask her how her journey had been. He fully expected her to do the same. But as she tended to do, she thoroughly and pleasantly surprised him.

She rushed across the room, wrapped her arms around his neck, and kissed him as fervently and lovingly and heart-poundingly as the night of his confession. He held her close, never wanting to let her go, never wanting to stop kissing her.

After a time, she said, "I've missed you too." An answer to the greeting he'd all but forgotten he'd offered.

"It is a shame our friends are so stringently attached to propriety," he said, his forehead pressed to hers. "Having them along on this short jaunt as chaperones will make things decidedly less pleasant than they might have been otherwise."

A smile pulled at the corners of her mouth. He couldn't resist and kissed her again quickly.

"Enough of that, you two," Lucas's voice sounded from the doorway. "It's time we were off. We've a few miles to cover."

Without letting go of Violet, Kes looked to Lucas. "You couldn't have taken your time returning to the ground floor?"

"No self-respecting chaperone ever takes his time." He motioned them out of the room with a twitch of his head. "Let's be off."

Julia appeared in the doorway in the next instant, little Philip in her arms. Her gaze took in the two of them quickly before she laughed lightly. "In case she hasn't made it clear, Violet has missed you, Grumpy Uncle."

Kes looked to Violet once more, warmth filling his heart. "It is good to be together again, isn't it?"

Lucas's voice answered. "It is *nauseating* is what it is."

"Stop that, Lucas," Julia said. "We've an important mission today, and we dare not neglect it."

"I am currently choosing not to neglect something remarkably important." Kester kissed Violet's forehead.

"My apologies, Lucas," Julia said. "I was wrong: they *are* a little nauseating."

Violet laughed almost silently. Her eyes met Kes's, sparkling with happiness. "We should take pity on them."

"And we should be on our way," he acknowledged. "We've miles yet to cover."

"Together."

Chapter Thirty-Seven

Kes had not seen Mr. Miller, the Northumberland apothecary, in a few years. Though he'd been exchanging letters with him of late, he wasn't certain the man would recognize him. He wasn't certain he would recognize Mr. Miller.

Letters had been exchanged, sketches, ideas. Violet and Kes had sent on to him things they had been trying, things that worked, things that hadn't. He, in return, had kept them abreast of what he and his father were attempting. Two weeks earlier, a request had arrived, asking them to make a plaster mold of Violet's left arm at the place where it had been amputated and to send precise measurements of her right arm and hand. They had known what that meant: Mr. Miller and the elder Mr. Miller were ready to make their first prosthesis.

It was that possibility that had brought Violet to visit Julia at last, and Kes to join them. He had no expectations of this prosthesis being the final one or for it to work perfectly, but it was a step in the right direction. It was the first of what he hoped would be years of improvements and adjustments.

Lucas and Julia had laughed their way through the role of chaperone during the two-hour carriage ride, but upon arriving in the small village, they had not so subtly sent Kes and Violet on their way to see to their errands alone. The two couples had arranged to meet at the local inn for a quick repast once they were finished with the apothecary and before returning to Brier Hill.

Kes walked into the apothecary shop arm in arm with Violet. He could see that she was nervous. Many people would likely have told her not to be, to not worry, to be cheerful and hopeful. But she had been told harmful variations of that too often in her life. He meant, if she allowed it, to spend the rest of their lives giving her a safe haven in which to feel what she felt and be who she was. She had given him that gift, and he meant to return the same.

Behind a small table in the middle of the little shop, a man, likely closer to Violet's age than Kes's, looked up at them as they entered, his thick brows pulled low in concentration. Kes felt certain he knew him.

After the length of a breath, recognition dawned on the man's face. "Mr. Barrington." He jumped to his feet as a look of unfettered excitement took hold of every angular feature. He rushed back to the door on the back wall and called out, "Father, they're here!"

Violet looked up at Kes, her own eyes sparkling with excitement. "I think they've enjoyed this."

Kes nodded. "Makes it all the more fun, doesn't it?"

It was her turn to nod, and she did so. "I'm a little nervous though."

"I'm a little nervous myself. This is the start of a new journey."

Mr. Miller returned to where they stood. He reached out a hand and shook Kes's. "A pleasure to see you again after so many years."

"And you," Kes answered. "Miss Ridley, this is Mr. Miller, with whom we've been corresponding."

Mr. Miller shook her hand enthusiastically. "A pleasure. A true pleasure." His attention shifted to her wooden prosthesis. "This is what you have now?"

Violet had told Kes of some of the comments she had endured over the past two years. It would do her good to hear someone who was excited about this difference in her rather than appalled or confused by it. "It is. I've had this one for two years."

Mr. Miller held his hands out. "May I?"

She required but a moment to unbuckle the leather straps. She had worn a dress with wider sleeves to allow her to remove it without unbuttoning the sleeves. She set her prosthesis in his hands, and the man held it as if it were a precious treasure.

He turned it about, studying every plane, every turn, every inch. "This is beautifully made."

"Yes, the carpenter who carved it did an exquisite job."

"What we have to show you today is not so artistic as this one." Mr. Miller eyed her with a look of concern.

But Violet shook her head. "This is likely to be the first of many attempts. Over time, we can combine utility with aesthetics. At the moment, I am anxious to see what our efforts *have* managed."

Mr. Miller appeared immediately relieved. From behind him, a man who was his duplicate, though likely thirty years his senior, emerged with a long, narrow box. He set the box on the table. His gaze dropped to the prosthesis his son still held. "This new one will move more than that."

"Not hard to do," Kes muttered dryly, earning an elbow nudge from Violet.

"I think you should be the first to see it," the older Mr. Miller said to Violet.

She stepped forward, a little hesitantly but clearly eager. No lid was nailed to the top of the box. Little bits of straw poked out, no doubt protecting the contents.

Kes joined her. With her right hand, she peeled back two layers of muslin to reveal an absolute marvel.

"This is not made of wood," she said.

"Not entirely," the older man said. "The fingers are wood, so they could be hinged. The center is a metal rod, thin but strong. The cuff and outer arm-shaped layer is made of leather. We wet-formed the leather so it would stiffen in shape. And we've treated it with beeswax so it won't be ruined by damp."

Violet looked at Kes. "We wouldn't have thought of leather for anything but the cuff."

That was true. Their combined efforts made something better than any of them could have managed on their own.

"Will it be strong enough?" Kes asked.

"Should be," the clockmaker said. "Metal, even no bigger around than a stick, is strong. And the leather layer is thick, stitched with strong wire. I suspect it'll hold up to most uses."

"And if it doesn't," the apothecary said, "well then, we'll know it's not the answer we're looking for."

Violet looked to the younger Mr. Miller. "Will you show me how it works?"

"Gladly."

With eager hands he gave her wooden arm to his father, then pulled the leather one from its box. As they had warned, it was not as aesthetically pleasing as the other, but it looked far more functional.

Carefully, the young apothecary demonstrated the movement of the fingers, which all moved together by the turn of a clockwork key. The short, thin metal rods that controlled the movement lined the back of the hand.

"We've not yet sorted how to tuck the mechanisms below the surface. Carving channels for them proved difficult as the parts move more than we expected," Mr. Miller said.

"What if the hand were hollow?" Kes suggested. "The mechanisms could be placed inside the hand itself."

Mr. Miller and his father looked intrigued. That, no doubt, would be the next thing they'd try.

"It's marvelous," Violet said. "I couldn't wear a glove over it, but having moving fingers would be well worth it."

"You should try it on, love," Kes said quietly. "See how it feels."

The Millers helped her put it in place. It had straps positioned precisely as they were on the one she'd been using. Kes had sent a detailed accounting of where they were and how long they needed to be. It was quickly buckled in place. She looked at it, studying it. She used her right hand to turn the clockwork key. The fingers curled and bent. The movement was not smooth or necessarily natural looking, but there was movement. There was the opportunity for using her hand. Again and again, she bent and unbent the fingers. No one watching her could possibly have doubted that she was deeply pleased.

"Use it for a time," the elder Mr. Miller said. "Make note of what works and what don't, what you'd change and what you'd keep. It may take years yet, but we'll sort this. We'll have you boasting the finest arm an old clockmaker and a young apothecary can create."

"With the help of a learned gentleman and a clever lady," the younger Mr. Miller added.

"This is more than I'd hoped for," she said. "It's wonderful."

"Thank you," Kes said to the men. "Thank you sincerely."

The younger man grinned. "I enjoy my work as an apothecary and don't intend to change trades, but I've found a passion for this. I hope I'm able to do it again, and not only for you. It's the type of problem-solving few people get to undertake. Makes a real difference."

"It most certainly does," Violet said.

Kes settled accounts with the men. They at first refused to accept payment, as they had been grateful to be part of the undertaking, but he knew the materials alone would have set the men back a pretty penny. This was not a large village where an apothecary could make a generous living.

The older prosthesis was carefully set inside the knapsack Kes had brought for this purpose. Violet hardly took her eyes off her new one. It was a marvel.

Kes couldn't have been more grateful. "I'm beginning to suspect the ones who ought to be nominated for membership in the Royal Society are the Millers."

"Never you fret, my dear Kester," she said. "When you present to the Royal Society the improved design for carriage lanterns, they will accept you wholeheartedly or suffer the consequences."

He smiled even as his brow pulled in confusion. "What consequences would those be?"

"I shall seek vengeance against each and every one of them."

They both laughed in unison. They did that a lot. It was a genuine happiness that did them both good.

"Even if I do gain the membership I've long hoped for, it will be unfair. So much of the design has been done by the two of us together. And Julia intends to help us solidify the changes in the candle used. Both of you deserve recognition for that."

"Until women are permitted membership, you shall simply have to be very intelligent on behalf of all of us."

"I promise to do my best."

Their walk had nearly brought them all the way to the door of the inn. He wasn't ready to lose her company to the all-seeing eyes of their chaperones, so he led her into the small yard next to the inn and beneath the canopy of a large, overgrown willow tree. He rested his sack on the ground against the trunk.

He leaned his back against the tree and held his hand out to her. She placed hers in his, and he pulled her gently to him. He wrapped his arms around her. She leaned into his embrace.

"I love you," he said.

"And I love you."

He kissed her forehead, then her temple. "I hate knowing that once we go inside that inn, I have to content myself with merely tucking your arm through mine and speaking little impersonal nothings."

"Lucas and Julia will not tease us too mercilessly if you put your arm around me as we make the journey back to Brier Hill."

He kissed her cheek. "It isn't the same as having time alone though."

"No, it's not." She rested more fully against him. "How long will you be at Brier Hill?"

"A week," he said.

"The estate has a lovely walled garden. I do not think our overly amused chaperones would object to our walking in it most mornings."

"I would like that." He closed his eyes and reveled in the feel of her in his arms.

From the direction of the garden gate, Julia's voice reached them. "Lucas has secured the inn's private dining room for us. If you two do not appear there directly, he will, without question, come in search of you."

Kes shook his head and sighed. "He'll have no qualms about embarrassing the both of us quite thoroughly."

He felt Violet shift in his arms. She pressed the briefest of kisses to his lips, then slipped away. He remained beneath the fall of branches, his eyes still closed. If fate proved kind, someday he would never again have to let her go.

Chapter Thirty-Eight

Sitting beside Kester in a small room of a humble inn on the outskirts of an obscure village, reveling in the warmth of a humble pork and pulse stew and enjoying the company of two of the loveliest people in all the world, Violet didn't have to pretend to be content. She was genuinely joyous.

"This is remarkable." Lucas hadn't stopped admiring Violet's new prosthesis. He'd asked dozens of questions, clearly excited for her.

The rest of the Gents would be the same; she knew they would. They neither ignored her differences nor belittled her for them. She wished only that she'd confided in them sooner.

"I am excited to see what changes and improvements you make to it over the years," Julia said.

"We already have some ideas." Violet smiled at Kester. "Given enough time, I'll have the grandest prosthesis in all the kingdom."

"I'd not want it any other way," Kester said.

"Do you suppose you could hold your spoon in your prosthesis?" Lucas asked, eyes wide with excitement.

She used the winding key to bend the fingers around the handle of her spoon. Between her and Kester's suggestions and the Millers' expertise, they'd managed to create a means of keeping the fingers in their bent position. She could indeed hold utensils in her left hand.

"I don't dare try to eat with it yet," she said. "I'd cover myself in stew, and that would be a terrible waste."

"With practice, I suspect you'll soon be an expert." Julia had a tremendous knack for putting a person at ease without needing to resort to empty platitudes.

"Speaking of experts," Lucas said, "Our Julia has convinced the local chandler that she is one herself."

"An expert?" Kester repeated, curiosity twisting his mouth.

Lucas nodded. "In candles."

"I simply asked him a great many questions," Julia said. "He was impressed that I knew enough to ask what I did. But having received *Kes's* many questions on the topic, I have done a bit of additional studying."

Violet took in a quick breath, both excited and nervous. What if Julia had discovered the carriage lantern could not be done?

"Everything I have learned indicates that the most crucial factor in the brightness and efficiency of a light source is the fuel," Julia said. "The chandler confirmed that."

"That was what we suspected," Kester said.

We. No matter that he'd used that word again and again the past months, Violet suspected she would never grow weary of hearing him say it.

"Oil burns the brightest," Julia said, "but it also creates a tremendous amount of smoke. And the jostling of the carriage is not ideal for oil."

"Then candles are our best approach after all," Violet said.

Kester pushed away his bowl of pork and pulse with a sigh of frustration. "Candles are what have been used, and they aren't bright enough."

"Tallow candles will never be bright enough," Julia said. "Beeswax is better. But the brightest burning fuel is spermaceti wax."

"It's also very expensive," Violet said.

Julia nodded. "For those who have the means, it will provide the most light. But there are ways of making even beeswax candles burn brighter."

Violet set her hand on Kester's, seeing the same hope in his eyes that she felt.

"It is a matter of optimizing the wick width for the size of the candle." Julia smiled, excitement and enthusiasm writ all over her face. "I am working on an equation that could be used to choose the best wick for any size candle."

Lucas grinned with pride. "Have I ever mentioned my wife is a genius?"

Splotches of red touched Julia's cheeks. "The equation isn't even complete. I'll need Kes and Violet to test it and help me refine it."

"We can do that." Again, Kester so naturally included Violet in his plans and his future. *We* was quickly becoming Violet's favorite word.

"Stanley truly began all of this on my account?" A hint of emotion touched Julia's voice.

"For your sake and in honor of Charlotte," Kester said. "He loved you. Both of you."

Lucas put an arm around his wife. "He was the very best of brothers."

"And the very best of friends," Kester added.

"I have enjoyed learning more about him," Violet said. Kester had spoken of him more often of late. And though there was grief in his eyes when he did, the pain wasn't as obviously overwhelming as it had once been. She hoped that meant he was finding some healing.

"I feel like *I* have also come to know him more," Julia said. "He had a great many adventures I knew nothing about."

"Like the time we put a chaise-cart on the roof of the library at Trinity Hall." Lucas didn't look the least bit repentant.

Kester bit back a grin of his own.

"You did what?" Julia didn't seem truly shocked.

Lucas and Kester simply laughed, explaining nothing and offering no apologies. Such joy filled their faces.

Violet leaned against him, still holding his hand. "It is good to see you happy, Kester."

"It is easy to be happy when you are with me." He raised her hand to his lips and pressed the most tender kiss to her fingers.

They spent the remainder of the meal discussing candles and light, mischief and merriment. The conversation more than once turned to little Philip, who was both a delightful and beautiful baby. Violet had never felt so at home with anyone beyond her immediate family. Kester had said being with her made happiness easy to come by. She could, without hesitation, say the same of him.

They made their way from the inn to the waiting carriage. Violet fully intended to spend the two-hour return trip learning all she could about her new prosthetic. She felt certain Kester would prove as curious as she.

Lucas motioned to the carriage lantern. "Someone really ought to think about improving that."

"I know a couple of people who might just be able to manage it," Kester said. He kept Violet's arm through his as they stood beside the carriage. "And I have full faith they'll have something ready to present to the Royal Society in a few more months."

"So do I," Violet said.

He kissed her temple. Her beloved Grumpy Uncle had proven tenderly affectionate, and she couldn't be happier.

"If the two of you keep at that," Lucas said, "I'll sit between you in the carriage. Better yet, I will tie Kes to the roof."

"You wouldn't dare." Violet raised an eyebrow in theatrical warning.

Lucas didn't bother hiding his amusement. He turned to assist Julia into the carriage.

"I do not think he will make good on that threat," Kester said. "I wish, though, he weren't in a position to make it."

"He likes to tease." Violet had come to understand that about Lucas.

Kester, though, did not appear the least inclined to jest in that moment. He slipped her arm from his and turned to face her directly. "What if we could have endless amounts of time all to ourselves? No chaperones, no staid propriety. Just each other, every moment of every day."

She set her hand against his wool outer coat just above his heart. "I would love that."

"I have little to offer beyond an expansive library, a very fine lake, and a Cabin of Cleverness." He brushed the pad of his hand along her cheek. "And I will never be the social butterfly Digby is."

"I am not in love with Digby," Violet said firmly.

Kester slipped his arm around her. "You're in love with me?"

"I've told you that before."

"I know." He pulled her ever closer. "I simply enjoy hearing it."

"I love you, Kester Barrington."

"Enough to marry me?"

She lightly kissed his mouth. "More than enough. *Far* more than enough."

He closed his eyes, then pressed his forehead to hers. "I love you, my darling. I always will."

"I truly am going to have to separate the two of you." Lucas sighed, the sound far more humorous than actually upset.

"You can't," Kester said. "We're going to be married."

Julia insisted on being handed down from the carriage once more, and she and Lucas were beside them in an instant, asking questions, offering congratulations, smiling, and hugging.

"We are going to be remarkably happy, Kester," Violet managed to say in the midst of it all.

He looked at her, his heart firmly in his eyes. "Exceptionally happy."

Chapter Thirty-Nine

February 1787

All of the Gents were once again at Livingsley Hall. They had returned to Cumberland for Kes's wedding.

"Do we now have to start calling Violet Grumpy Aunt?" Digby asked. "Because while it is appropriate in some ways, it is also entirely ill-fitting. And I am nothing if not particular."

"Oh, you are so much more than particular," Aldric said dryly.

Digby assumed the royal demeanor he so often did when responding to teasing criticisms. "As I am the reason Kes will not be arriving at his wedding looking like a costermonger, I expect all of you to be thanking the very heavens for your monarch's particularness."

"I did not look so bad as all that," Kes insisted.

"I beg to differ." Digby's declaration was filled with laughter.

They were a lighthearted and good-natured bunch. Kes had needed that so desperately all those years ago when Stanley had refused to let him pull away. To have them all here on this, the best day of his life, was healing in a way that defied explanation. Years of fear and loneliness eased as he stood among them.

"I do have a concern," Lucas said. "Suppose Kes grows so distracted that rather than fill out the parish register with Violet's actual name, he writes Lily instead and the entire thing is rendered void?"

Snickers sounded in the group.

"Regardless of what name I write, I take pride in the fact that *my* bride will not be arriving dressed in full mourning." He gave Lucas a dry and pointed look.

Far from being saddened by the reminder of the disaster that had been his own wedding day, Lucas burst into laughter. "That remains one of the funniest things I have ever seen in my life."

The other Gents expressed their regret at having missed what was now the stuff of legend.

"Do you know she wore full mourning on the anniversary of our wedding this year?"

"That sounds like Our Julia," Aldric said. "Clever and funny and never misses a chance to get her point across."

"What point would that be?" Lucas asked.

"That you ought not consider yourself to be entirely on firm footing yet," Niles insisted.

Another rolling wave of sincere laughter filled them. How Kes wished they could have been present for Lucas and Julia's wedding. That had been a difficult day for both bride and groom. Having the Gents there would have helped.

While Kes was grateful to have them present for *his* wedding, he hardly needed to be buoyed up. He loved Violet, and he knew without a doubt that she loved him. This was an occasion for celebration. This was the culmination of every dream he hadn't even realized he had.

It was soon time for him to arrive at the chapel for the ceremony. Walking shoulder to shoulder with the Jester, Puppy, the General, Archbishop, and the King, he strode to the local church, through the doors, and directly to his place in the chancel.

The chapel was not full, but it contained every person he most wanted to be there, with the exception of Stanley. The rest of the Gents were there, of course, as were Everett and Bellamy and their families. Violet's family. The Ridleys had expressed their utter delight at Kes and Violet's desire to be wed and had been all that was welcoming and loving in the weeks since. Georgie had taken to calling him "Cousin Kes," which he found he liked very much.

The Dalforths and Overtons were invited to the wedding, having shown themselves excellent and kind neighbors. Both families were in attendance. This would be a happy occasion.

Lucas set a hand on Kes's shoulder. "We're happy for you two. Stanley would be also."

"I intend to live my life and live it happily, just as he would've wanted."

Violet arrived at the back of the chapel mere moments later. She wore her new prosthetic, its fingers curved around the stems of a bouquet made entirely of lily of the valley. It was not the season for them. She must have procured them from a hothouse. Those flowers would always be special to them, a reminder of the moment in which fate had intervened to make certain they did not miss a rare second chance at claiming happiness.

Violet reached the place where he stood. The smile that had first taken his breath away all those months ago spread over her face once more. Her gorgeous eyes twinkled with happiness. Her mesmerizing coils of brilliantly beautiful hair spilled in gorgeous, unpowdered abandon. He had never in all his life known her equal in beauty, goodness, or cleverness.

After a decade of heart-wrenching regret, he had found hope. He had found a future.

He had found love.

Spring came early to Cumberland. Snowdrop flowers peeked out from cold soil, proclaiming the eminent arrival of other blooms. The lake at Livingsley Hall rolled soft and gray beneath the cloudy skies. On its banks, on a bench installed there for specifically this purpose, Kes sat with his wife in his arms. He held her, still hardly believing his good fortune. He kissed her gently. She leaned more cozily against him.

In the distance, Georgie ran about, gleefully enjoying yet another adventure she'd concocted with William, Phoebe, and Charles Dalforth. The Ridleys had found their place in this area of the world. They were a joyous and wonderful addition to the local society.

But for Kes, for the Grumpy Uncle who had lived so long fearing he would never again feel at peace, no member of that family was more beloved than Violet.

He had found more than a partner, more than a friend. He had found the greatest love he could imagine. And they had the rest of their lives to build upon it.

"I love you, my darling lily of the valley, my beloved Violet."

"I love you," she said. "Now and forever after."

About the Author

Sarah M. Eden is a *USA Today* best-selling author of witty and charming historical romances, including 2020's *Foreword Reviews* INDIE Awards Gold winner for romance, *Forget Me Not*, 2019's *Foreword Reviews* INDIE Awards Gold winner for romance, *The Lady and the Highwayman*, and 2020 Holt Medallion finalist, *Healing Hearts*. She is a two-time Best of State Gold Medal winner for fiction and a three-time Whitney Award winner. Combining her obsession with history and her affinity for tender love stories, Sarah loves crafting deep characters and heartfelt romances set against rich historical backdrops. She holds a bachelor's degree in research and happily spends hours perusing the reference shelves of her local library.

www.SarahMEden.com